QUESTIONABLE PRACTICES

EILEEN GUNN

Questionable practices

SMALL BEER PRESS · EASTHAMPTON, MASS.

"Chop Wood, Carry Water," copyright 2013 by Eileen Gunn, appears here for the first time. | "No Place to Raise Kids," copyright 2007 by Eileen Gunn. First published in *Flurb: A Webzine of Astonishing Tales*. | "Up the Fire Road," copyright 2007 by Eileen Gunn. First published in *Eclipse One*, edited by Jonathan Strahan. | "The Trains that Climb the Winter Tree," copyright 2011 by Michael Swanwick and Eileen Gunn. First published on Tor.com. | "Speak, Geek," copyright 2006 by Eileen Gunn. First published in *Nature*. | "Hive Mind Man," copyright 2012 by Rudy Rucker and Eileen Gunn. First published in *Asimov's Science Fiction*. | "Thought Experiment," copyright 2011 by Eileen Gunn. First published in *Eclipse Four*, edited by Jonathan Strahan. | "To the Moon Alice," copyright 2008 by Eileen Gunn. First published in *Lady Churchill's Rosebud Wristlet*. | "Shed That Guilt!" copyright 2008 by Michael Swanwick and Eileen Gunn. First published in *The Magazine of Fantasy and Science Fiction*. | "The Steampunk Quartet," copyright 2010 by Eileen Gunn. First published on Tor.com. | "The Armies of Elfland," copyright 2009 by Eileen Gunn and Michael Swanwick. First published in *Asimov's Science Fiction*. | "Michael Swanwick and Samuel R. Delany at the Joyce Kilmer Service Area," March 2005, copyright 2007 by Eileen Gunn. First published in *Foundation*. | "Zeppelin City," copyright 2009 by Michael Swanwick and Eileen Gunn. First published on Tor.com. | "Phantom Pain," copyright 2013 by Eileen Gunn, appears here for the first time. All stories are used here by permission of the author and any co-authors.

Book design by John D. Berry. The typeface is Dolly Pro.
Cover illustration © Fu Wenchao/Xinhua Press/Corbis.

ISBN (print): 9781618730756
ISBN (ebook): 9781618730763

Small Beer Press
150 Pleasant St., #306
Easthampton, MA 01027
T/F: 413.203.1636
smallbeerpress.com · weightlessbooks.com
Distributed to the trade by Consortium.
Printed on 50# 30% PCR recycled Natures Natural paper by the Maple Press in York, Penn.
First edition: 2013
0 9 8 7 6 5 4 3 2 1

Library of Congress Cataloging-in-Publication Data

Gunn, Eileen, 1945–
[Stories. Selections]
Questionable practices : stories / Eileen Gunn. — First Edition.
     pages cm
Summary: "Stories from Eileen Gunn are always a cause for celebration. Where will she lead us? 'Up the Fire Road' to a slightly alternate world. Into steampunk's heart. Never where we might expect." — Provided by publisher.
ISBN 978-1-61873-075-6 (paperback) — ISBN 978-1-61873-076-3 (ebook)
I. Title.
PS3607.U5477A6 2014
813'.6 — dc23
                    2013047730

CONTENTS

For Michael Swanwick, who doubled my productivity over a decade, and for Marianne Porter, who said "Humor him."

QUESTIONABLE PRACTICES

Up the Fire Road

Andrea

THE MAIN THING TO UNDERSTAND about Christy O'Hare is he hates being bored. Complicated is interesting, simple is dull, so he likes to make things complicated.

Used to be the complications were more under his control. Like one time he went down to Broadway for coffee, but the coffee place was closed. So he hitched a ride downtown, but the driver was headed for Olympia on I-5, so Christy figured he'll go along for the ride and get his coffee at that place in Oly that has the great huevos. He ended up thumbing to San Francisco and coming back a week later with a tattoo and a hundred bucks he didn't have when he left home. I think he was more interested in doing something that would make a good story than he was in gettiing a cup of coffee. But I did wonder where the hell he was.

He's not a bad guy. I don't agree with what my mother said about him being a selfish son-of-a-bitch. But Christy is the star of his own movie, and it's an action flick. If life is dull, just hook up with him for a while. And if life seems slow and meaningless, go somewhere where you depend on him to get you back.

Like the ski trip. It's not that he *wanted* us to get lost on Mt. Baker, where we could have died of exposure, but ordinary cross-country skiing, on groomed trails, with parking lots and everything, is just so crowded and boring. Starting out way too late makes things more interesting. Drinking a pint of Hennessey and smoking a couple joints makes things *much* more interesting and gives the Universe a head start.

That's how we found ourselves, last year, four miles up a fire road as the sun was setting. Early March: warm days, cold nights. Slushy snow, pitted with snowshoe tracks, turning to ice as the temperature dropped. Did we bring climbing skins for our skis? Of course not. Did we bring a headlamp, or even a flashlight? Nope.

"We've got an hour of visibility," I said. "Let's get back."

"It's all downhill. Won't take long. There's a trail that cuts off to the hot-spring loop about half a mile ahead. We can go back that way, and stop by the hot spring." He extended the flask to me. "Here, babe, take a drink of this."

I pushed it away. "It'll be dark by then," I said. "How will we find our way out?"

"The hot spring is just off the main road, the paved one that we drove up. We can walk back down the road to our truck in the dark. No problem."

As it turned out, the hot spring was a lot farther away than that, but it was a natural enough mistake, because we didn't have a map. We didn't have much food, either, just a couple of power bars, and we didn't have a tent or even a tarp, and we didn't have dry clothes. Oh, yeah — we had the cellphone, but its battery needed a charge.

By the time we found the hot spring, it was dark. There was a moon, but it was just a crescent, and it wasn't going to last more than an hour or two before dipping below the trees. I was starting to shiver.

"We got plenty of time," Christy said. "Let's warm up in the hot spring, then we can take our time getting back to the road, 'cause you'll be warmer."

Well, it made a certain amount of sense. Of course, we didn't have any towels or anything, but our clothes were wool, so they'd keep us pretty warm, even though they were wet with sweat from climbing up the fire road. All I had to do was get my body temperature up a bit, and I'd be fine for a couple of hours.

It was slippery and cold getting down to the hot spring. It wasn't anything fancy, like Scenic or Bagby. No decking, no little hand-hewn log seats, just a couple of dug-out pools near a stream, with flat stones at one side, so you don't have to walk in the mud.

We took off our skis, took off our clothes, put our boots back on without tying the laces, and moving gingerly and quickly, in the cold air and the snow, climbed down to the spring, shed our boots, and started to get into the water.

Hotter than a Japanese bath. We dumped some snow in, tested again. Still hot, but tolerable. Soon we were settled in and accustomed to the heat. It sure felt good — I was so tired — but adrenalin kept me alert. We still had a ways to go to get back to the truck.

That's when I saw the old guy, watching us from behind a tree, the moonlight making his outline clear. Creepy, I thought.

I whispered to Christy, "There's somebody watching us. Don't look like you're looking. Over to my left, past the big fir."

Christy liked that, I could tell: it suddenly made things even more interesting. He liked danger. He liked the idea of someone watching us get naked. He sidled around for a better look, and tried not to look like he was looking.

Then he froze. "It's not a guy," he said. "It's a bear."

"What do we do?"

"Stay here and hope it goes away."

"Do bears like hot springs?" I asked.

"Fuck if I know. I don't think so."

I kept my eye on the figure in the forest. It still looked a lot more like a guy than a bear to me. It came closer. It obviously could see us. It waved a mittened hand, and resolved into a guy with a big beard and a fur hat. "How you folks doing tonight," it said.

"Whattaya know," said Christy, "a talking bear."

Christy

I MET ANDREA AT BURNING MAN. She was welding together a giant sheet-metal goddess robot with glowing snakes for hair. She was wearing a skirt made of old silk ties, and nothing else. No shoes, no shirt. Great service, though.

I lost my heart to her. I would do whatever she wanted. It's been that way ever since. She wanted a baby, and now she's got one. Doesn't need me any more. Neither of the women do — her or Mickey. The babies need me, though. I'll stand by my kids, if their mothers will let me.

I'm not going to say that Andrea lies, but what happened on Mt Baker wasn't my fault. I didn't even want to go skiing that day. It was dark and rainy in the morning, and it was a long drive to Mt. Baker. That's why we got there so late: she kept changing her mind about going. And if I hadn't been stoned, I wouldn't have misjudged the distance to the hot spring.

She's always saying that it's my fault when I screw up. Sure, I screw up, but why assign blame like that? Everybody screws up — even Andrea screws up sometimes. That's why I like skiing cross-country: because, when you screw up, you can recover. Usually, anyway.

You can make more mistakes, going cross-country, like finding yourself in the middle of fucking nowhere without a sandwich. But sometimes you get a chance to see stuff that most people, in their safe little lives, never even dream of.

Like the sasquatch. Where would you ever see a sasquatch, if you didn't go cross-country skiing? Or a talking bear, either. Whatever.

I figured it would calm Andrea down if she thought it was

a talking bear, because that's an idea she's familiar with: *ursus fabulans*, the talking bear. We all know the talking bear. Even the Romans knew the talking bear. *Ursus in tabernam introiit et cervesiam imperavit*, as the book says. A bear goes into a bar and orders a beer.

But I knew it was a sasquatch — I'm not an idiot, Mt. Baker is crawling with them — and I wanted, naturally enough, to find out more. Besides, we were sitting there in the hot spring, facing a long, cold, dark walk back down the side of the mountain to the truck. The sasquatch asked us, real friendly, how we were doing. I saw no problem with partaking of his hospitality, you know? Maybe the sasquatch had a nice little cabin somewhere, or a warm cave with a fire already going. Maybe the sasquatch had a treasure and would bestow it upon us if he took a shine to us.

So I said, well, man, my sister's not feeling so good, and we sure could use a place to sleep tonight. You know any place around here, any place warm? Andrea looked at me hard when I called her my sister, but she didn't say anything. She's cool, Andrea. We didn't want to tell the sasquatch our whole story. Everybody needs to keep some truths to themselves. It's the only way.

And the sasquatch invited us back to his place. Polite as can be. Seemed like a good man, this sasquatch.

We leaped out of the hot spring, and got dressed real fast. It was colder now. We were all warmed up, so the hot spring was not a dumb idea, no matter what Andrea thought.

Skiing behind the sasquatch, she gave me a what-the-fuck? look. It was so dark, I couldn't see her face, but Andrea can do the what-the-fuck? look with her entire body.

I gave her a shrug that said *later*. Of course, Andrea was gonna have to rethink what I told her, and she was gonna have to ask why, and she was gonna have to just fuck with me on it, but she knew enough not to do any of those things while we were following a sasquatch through a frigid forest in the middle of the night.

We skied in the dark for maybe a half hour or so: it was slow going. The sasquatch, I noticed, had furry webbed feet that worked like snowshoes. Obviously, sasquatches evolved in the snow, like yeti. That's part of my theory. I'm just learning about this stuff. I found a couple of websites that have been helpful.

So, we were climbing on some kind of a narrow path. Climbing is relatively easy on my mountaineering skis, even without skins, but going down you don't have the control you'd have with steel edges. It was steep and icy. I was hoping we could get out of there in the morning without having to side-step all the way down. When we came to the sasquatch's cave, it didn't look like anything was there at all — just a wall of granite with a row of doug firs in front of it. But somehow there was a gap in the rock, and the sasquatch gestured us in.

Inside, of course, it was bare ground, so we took off the skis and carried them in. No sense leaving them out there, risking that it would snow during the night and cover them up. I've done it, can you tell? Even if you know exactly where you put your skis, it's scary, out in the middle of nowhere, you don't see 'em.

The squatch struck a spark and lit a funny little oil lamp, and me and Andrea looked around inside the cave.

Back from the mouth of the cave, the ground sloped down and the roof was higher than I could see, in the dark. It seemed big inside, even though we couldn't see. I wonder if humans have some kind of sonar, like bats or dolphins.

We followed the wall, and, not far from the entrance, we came to a house made of logs and rocks. We went by several sets of doors and windows, like some old tourist motel, right in the cave.

We went in one of the doors and entered a big room. The

floor was covered with the skins of deer and mountain sheep. No bearskins, I noticed. There was a strong musky smell, like raccoon or bear. Sasquatch, I bet.

There was another lamp, and there were big piles of balsam boughs, which I knew were comfortable to sleep on, and they smelled good. The sasquatch had a pretty nice place. Cold, though.

The sasquatch soon had a little fire going in a firepot, and there must have been a way for the smoke to get out, because the room didn't fill with smoke. There was a pot of water on the fire, and, criminey, the squatch even had a bunch of those heavy, handmade pottery mugs, like the kind you find cheap at the Goodwill. What, did he carry those things all the way into the woods? Sasquatches shop at thrift stores?

Soon we were drinking fir-tip tea, which was good, if somewhat redundant in the mountains.

After a couple cups of tea, Andrea went outside to take a leak, and I got the sasquatch alone. I dug in my pack and pulled out the Hennessey, of which there was still a little left, and offered the sasquatch some. He took a pull, I took a pull, and pretty soon I was breaking out the grass. While I was rolling a couple fat joints, I told the sasquatch that I thought my sister had the hots for him.

He took this a good bit cooler than I might have expected. I mean, Andrea is a good-looking woman. I wondered what sasquatch chicks looked like, that he was so unimpressed. Or maybe there was just no accounting for taste.

I told the sasquatch that when Andrea came back inside, I could set it up for him with her. I told him this all had to be aboveboard. But I could tell, I said, that he was a stable fellow — solid, responsible — and my sister was ready to settle down and have kids. This last part was true, actually: Andrea and I had had The Conversation, though we didn't come to any conclusion, or at least not one that made her shut up about it.

The sasquatch just nodded at what I said, and I took this as agreement. We smoked a joint on it.

Andrea

WHEN I CAME BACK INTO THE ROOM, the old guy was warming up some kind of a soup he's got in a pot near the fire.

"You folks are probably pretty hungry, eh?"

He and Christy had been smoking that homegrown Christy carried with him. Pretty punk stuff.

"Yeah," I said. "We didn't bring much to eat."

"Well, honey, let me tell you." He patted my shoulder, left his hand there just a little too long, y'know? "You and your brother shouldn't go off skiing like this without bringing some emergency rations. You're lucky you ran into me. I'll take care of you."

Yeah, I thought, I'm sure.

But he was nice enough, and the soup was okay, though lord knows what was in it. Roots and stuff. No meat. There was something potato-like, but it wasn't a potato. I didn't ask, because I didn't want to make the old guy feel bad. I've eaten a lot of weird stuff — a little more wouldn't hurt me.

He had these handmade wooden bowls to eat out of. I'd seen bowls like that before. Very rustic, kind of Zen, you know? I took some meditation classes in Berkeley, and the monks, they had bowls kind of like that.

The cave was warming up a bit from the fire, but I wouldn't have called it warm. The old guy noticed I was shivering, and put an arm around me. Christy moved away. Bastard.

"What's your name?" I asked. He said something, but I didn't catch it. It came out kind of funny, like he was clearing his throat at the same time.

"What?" I said.

"Call me Mickey," he said.

"Like the mouse?" I asked.

"Like the mouse," he said.

After supper, I left Christy and the old man talking, and lay down on a pile of balsam branches. I was tired, and it was soft and kind of cozy.

In the middle of the night, I heard a noise in my sleep, and I opened my eyes. Was it a noise I dreamed, or a noise in the real world? It took me a while to wake up. The oil lamps were out, but the fire was still burning, and by its dim light, I could see the old man moving across the room. He was wearing some kind of a tall hat. Other people came up behind him. It was very dark and shadowy, and completely silent. I wondered a bit if I was dreaming, but it didn't seem to be a dream.

Where was Christy? He wasn't next to me. One of those people looked like him.

I got up from the pile of branches and slipped my boots back on. I stood there in the dark, very quietly, thinking they couldn't see me.

The old man came closer to me, and the group moved with him. Yes, that was Christy there, in the tall hat.

The people moved so strangely, like they weren't used to walking upright, and the cave was so dim, lit with a faint orange glow that seemed to come from within the people themselves, that I thought again that it was a dream. They were carrying ropes of twisty brown vines with yellow and orange berries on them, like swags of tinsel from a Christmas tree, and they encircled me, looping strands of vines over my head. It wasn't scary, though, it was like an interesting slow-motion dream. I felt that I could duck out of the vines and run away if I wanted, or wake up from it, but I didn't want to. The berries seemed to give off a dim light, and I was able to see better, like my eyes were getting used to the dark.

The people were all dressed in rags that looked like dead oak leaves. Their garments fluttered, although there was no move-ment of the air. I tried to talk to them, but they couldn't seem to understand what I was saying. I'm not sure there was any sound coming out of my mouth. The visitors looped the vines around me and Christy and the old man and pulled them tight, bring-ing us closer and closer, until we were bound together as if we were sticks in a ball of twine.

Then, suddenly, as if a bubble had popped, the room was dark again. The visitors disappeared, and then the orange ber-ries went out quietly, one by one, and the vines bound us less and less until they were gone. We sank onto the balsam boughs, Christy on one side of me, and Mickey on the other.

Christy fell asleep right away. I was feeling dizzy, but I wasn't falling asleep. It was like being stoned, maybe because I'd been asleep already. Mickey was staring at me intently. He didn't seem so much like an old man, just like another human being who was concerned about me.

"I'm okay," I said. "I'm just a bit out of breath."

He ran this hand down the center of my back to just below my waist, and pulled me towards him. He kissed me very lightly on the lips, and I could feel my whole body respond to those two points of contact, his hand and his lips. Now he didn't seem like an old man at all.

Christy

I CAN TELL YOU that nobody was more surprised than I was to find out that the squatch was a girl. How could I have thought the squatch was a bear or an old guy? It must have been some trick of the light. But she had looked like a guy — how was I to know?

And of course, when I found myself in bed with this beauti-ful girl, what could I do? I was putty in her hands, just like with Andrea. Obviously she had targeted me right from the beginning, there at the pool. She didn't say anything about that, but she didn't have to. I could tell.

So Mickey was there, she was willing, and I was certainly able. That was just how it goes sometimes: the right moment, the right two people. Andrea was asleep next to us, but I knew that this was okay, that she wouldn't wake up. I mean, she was out cold.

All I can say is we had a blast. Mickey was hot, she was juicy, she was gorgeous, and boy did she give good head.

Afterward, when all the other people appeared, it was strange but familiar to get up and join them. Mickey gave me a tall hat. It was a sort of a wedding, I think, but I was not a one-hundred-percent cooperative bridegroom. I just walked around in a fog, and then Andrea woke up and she walked around, too, with me and with Mickey, and I thought that made everything okay. The three of us being together like that, I mean Andrea must have known, when she woke up and saw us. But I thought, what would Andrea do, now that Mickey and I had this thing going?

The other people, they had ropes of bittersweet, which I thought was odd. I'd never seen real bittersweet in the Northwest. They have something else here that they call bittersweet, the stuff with the little purple flowers and the red fruit, but I call it nightshade. Where I grew up, the bittersweet has orange berries with little yellow shells that cover them. Beautiful, but it strangles everything that comes near it. My mom used to have me busting my butt out there in the back field, cutting bittersweet away from the trees, because it would just take over, climb all the trees and overwhelm them. It was real pretty in the wintertime, though, with the yellow and orange berries sticking up in the snow. So I loved seeing those people with the bittersweet vines, even though I knew that if it took hold, they'd never get rid of it.

Andrea was dancing faster and faster, sort of pulling us along in this frenzy. The visitors roped her in with the bittersweet, her and me and Mickey, all together, until we fell on the bed of balsam branches, all hot and sweaty, and I had a brief thought that maybe we could get a threesome going, and I was getting a hard-on, and then I was coming and falling into a deep sleep at the same time. You know, a lot of that night is just a blur to me. That was some weed, I'll tell you. I don't remember any more.

The next morning, the three of us were like old married people, chewing on roots around the fire, eating some kind of a porridge of seeds. Andrea and Mickey, they seemed pretty friendly, in spite of what went on last night. So things were okay in that area. I didn't notice the musky smell any more. Probably that was what I smelled like myself at this point.

There was a thing about caves that I actually hadn't thought through: they're dark. If you stay in your cave, the sun might as well never have come up. I needed to get out of the dark, get outside, take a dump, and prepare for a long ski out, maybe through the woods, the way we'd come up. I hoped there was a forest road nearby, but my guess was the sasquatch was a deep-woods guy, as far from civilization as he could get.

And we needed to get going pretty soon too.

So I put on my parka, and went out to the mouth of the cave, and you know what? It was raining, raining hard. Water was flowing in the snow, down the slots of our tracks, down the slope of the mountain, down through the trees, down to the hot spring, down to the road, which was, by my guess, a couple thousand feet below us. Staying over had not been a very good idea, if getting home soon was our goal.

But I'll tell you what I do when something doesn't work out: I go with the flow. I let life keep happening. I keep an eye out for opportunity.

And, to my mind, the opportunity at this point was to find out about the treasure. Easiest thing would be to get the info directly from Mickey, not poke around in acres of rock. Might involve smoking a few more joints, a bit more bonding. I could handle that. Andrea would find something to keep her busy.

Andrea

MICKEY WASN'T BAD IN BED. He was younger than I had thought, and he gave good head. He was a lot gentler than Christy, too. Christy likes it kind of rough and fast. Not that there was anything wrong with that, but Mickey was a gentleman, and quite attractive in a way. Kind of hairy, though. Some guys are just, like, bears if they don't wax it all off, but I'd never slept with a guy who was as hairy as Mickey.

So he was talking afterward, real quiet, the way some guys do, just trying to find out a little about you, and maybe trying to impress you a bit with who they are. He mentioned this workshop that he had. To hear him tell it, he could make anything he wanted, which I guess explains about the bowls and the cups. Well, what he said was "it" could make anything he needed, but he was a little vague about what "it" was. Didn't trust me, I guess. But he said he'd bring me something nice, something that was useful. I wondered what he meant, because if he could have anything he needed, why would he be living in a cave?

Maybe "it" was the secret treasure that Christy told me about. I asked if it could make money. But Mickey said he didn't need money. I guess that made sense to me: having what you need is not the same thing as having money. Because the only thing that you *need* about money is the ability to turn it into something else.

So the next day, Mickey gave me a silk undershirt. It was warm and light, and I could wear it without Christy wondering what it was and where it came from. It was kind of a weird color, not olive-green, not an earth-tone, but something that could be described as either of those things. Mickey said it was a wedding present, that we were now, the three of us, bound to one another.

I noticed that Christy had a new wool hat, because he'd lost his old one when we skied up to the cave. I wondered if Mickey had given it to him, also as a wedding present. I bet that was true. I wondered what else it could make.

In the days after our first night together, I didn't see any of the other people who were there that night. It was like there wasn't anybody in the cave but the three of us. I figured there were other caves with the other people in them, or maybe they lived further back in our cave. I asked Mickey where his neighbors went, they seemed so nice. He said something about they were "respecting our privacy." Okay, okay. If he didn't want to give me a straight answer, he didn't have to.

So I thought I'd take a look further back in the cave, and just see if there was any sign of people living back there, plus maybe that was where the warehouse was. Maybe they were all together in a workshop there, making pottery and knitting hats and tie-dying shirts, like some ancient hippie cult. I mean, anything seemed possible.

I got one of the oil lamps, which are pretty bright, and I walked back in the cave, which got narrower as I went back. It wasn't scary, as it would have been when we first came to the cave. It was a bit damp, sure, but it wasn't dripping, and there didn't seem to be any animals or big spiders moving around. When I got way to the back, the cave was much more like a tunnel than the big room it seemed like out near the front.

On one of the walls, I noticed some painting, right on the rock. A large group of dancing figures, one with a tall hat, just like the one Mickey had worn at our wedding. They were carrying garlands of red-orange berries with yellow casings. Bittersweet.

The figures had recognizable faces. There was Mickey, there

was Christy, there was me. And there was my mother. Had my mother been there at the wedding? I didn't remember her being there, for sure, and it seemed so unlikely that she would have just appeared there in the woods and gone away without taking me back with her.

Had Mickey come back here and painted this scene? I was touched, really. It was sweet, in a mystical sort of way. I stood there looking at the drawings for a little while, and my oil lamp started guttering. The figures had looked so lifelike, and now they started to move. My mother turned to look at me, and she seemed to be speaking. What was she saying? The oil lamp guttered more, and went out.

I stood there in the dark, not knowing which way to move, and for the first time I was afraid. I heard my mother's voice. "Calm down, Andrea," she said. "You never get anywhere by panicking." I waited for a minute, and took a few deep breaths. The darkness did not seem so deep. Was my mother there with me or not?

As I stood debating the question, it became clear that there was a dull light coming from a part of the darkness, and I thought that maybe that was the direction from which I'd come. "Go ahead," said my mother's voice. "Trust yourself." Well, that certainly sounded like my mother. All that new-age crap. I walked towards the dim light, and as I walked the light got stronger. Soon I was back at the front of the cave again.

Christy and Mickey weren't anywhere to be seen. I looked out the front of the cave, and it was fucking pouring down rain. Where had they gone? Mickey's little house was empty. I yelled out a bit, calling Christy's name. Everything seemed so much like a dream. Was I on some kind of strange drug? Was I in the woods at all? Was I at my mom's house, and having some kind of a psychotic episode? I thought I was past that kind of thing, really.

The fire was still going, and I lit a couple of the oil lamps from it. Just about the time I was starting to get worried, Christy and Mickey came out of the back of the cave. Christy had an oil lamp. I wondered where they had been, since I hadn't seen any light back there at all. They looked funny, but I couldn't put my finger on why. Christy had his hand on Mickey's shoulder, but he moved it when he saw me.

"Andrea! There you are!" he said, as though he's been looking for me. I know that lying tone.

"Where'd you go? I was worried," I said.

"Everything's fine. Just go with the flow, babe. Just go with the flow."

That's good advice if you've got a flow to go with. Christy did, Christy always did, but he wasn't going to tell me about it.

Mickey had started poking at the fire, stirring it up, and was putting the big pot on the hook over it, and tossing stuff in the pot. I thought maybe I could help with that, and pretty soon we were working together on chopping up stuff and it was starting to smell pretty good. Christy didn't make himself useful, but then he never does, you know?

I asked Mickey about the paintings I'd seen in the back of the cave. He said maybe we should go back there while the stew was cooking, and he squeezed my shoulder. Christy was nodding off anyway, so we slipped away easily, grabbing a lamp on the way out.

Walking towards the back of the cave, I noticed more pictures and some strange writing, like lines and circles. I asked Mickey what it meant.

"Instructions and rules, mostly. Stuff you need to know to raise your kids right."

"Do you have kids?"

"Mmmmph." It was a yes, I thought.

"Where are they? Are they grown up?"

He made some more noises. "Old enough. Scattered."

Poor guy, I thought. Getting old up here in the mountains, and his kids off somewhere, probably don't visit. I wonder if they even know he's living in a cave now.

"That was nice, last night," I said. "I was wondering about the pictures in the cave of us dancing." Mickey didn't say anything, he just kept leading me deeper into the cave. "Haven't we already gone past the painting I was talking about?"

"It's a circular path," said Mickey. "We'll come by it again." We walked, and it did seems as though we were going uphill and around a curve.

This isn't what I thought it was like, but I have to agree that it did look as though the picture was coming up again.

"There!" I said, "There's the picture." We stopped, because I made us stop. Mickey would have continued on by.

"See that?" He nodded. "That's us there, isn't it?" He nodded again. "And there, towards the back, that's my mother." He nodded again.

"Okay," I said. "How did my mother get there?"

"Your mother is a very strong soul," said Mickey. "Whatever has been done to her, she has fought back, and has entered the realm from which there is movement back and forth."

" I don't understand," I said. "Do you know my mother?"

Mickey kissed me. "And you are also a very strong soul. I am sure I am seeing your mother in you."

"Was she here? Do you know my mother? What is she doing in the cave?"

"We need to keep walking, just past here," said Mickey. He moved a curtain aside, as we passed, and there was a small room cut into the rock. We stopped and went inside, and he was so nice and gentle, and he has a deliciously masculine scent.

———

Christy

SO WE FIGURED to stay for a few days. Seemed like the easiest thing to do. A lot pleasanter than walking down the mountain in the mud.

Mickey was totally great, and Andrea seemed to be okay with what was going down, whatever she thought. She never said a word to me about it.

Mickey and I had a lot of chances to get together, and we took advantage of them. She was a total delight. Not to say that Andrea wasn't neat, but it's the unexpected treat that is sweetest, isn't it? Even Andrea would understand that.

Andrea and Mickey seem to be becoming friends too, which is more than I could have hoped for. They went off for long walks into the cave together, and they always came back hand-in-hand and smiling. I wondered sometimes if they were talking about me, but Andrea had no idea, and Mickey seemed to live on another planet when it came to fucking.

The few days became a week, and the rain continued. It was a lot of work, just to get water and roots and dry wood for fuel. I always liked to camp out, but then I had those packets of freeze-dried shit. The week became several, and then a month. But I will never complain about rainy weather again. It was the happiest time of my life, at least to date: two women, both of them great in bed, and each of them devoted to me.

Though, clearly, Mickey was a lot more devoted than Andrea. This is completely understandable, and I don't fault Andrea for it in the least. She was much more the modern woman, with her complaints, and, let's face it, her neurotic shit. There are consequences for that, is all. I totally support her in her struggle for getting a handle on what goes on between men and women, I just think she's taking her own sweet time at it.

I asked Mickey a few times about the people who were there that first night. Who were they? Where are they? How come they don't come around at all, and she said they were giving us the time we needed to create our family, our oneness. And this made sense, though I did feel I was getting the shut-up explanation. I mean, it's no skin off my ass if her friends don't want to come around and see us. Really. What do I care?

But they never did come around during the daytime. Or even at night, except that once. And we were there for, well, it was nearly six weeks, I think. We stayed — and I would have stayed longer, let me be clear about it — until Andrea started throwing up and said she thought she was pregnant.

I tried to convince her that this was no problem. Lots of women give birth at home, away from hospitals, but she wasn't hearing any of this. She said she had to go home, she had to get hold of her mother, and she had to have some answers. Naturally, I thought the answers thing meant she'd finally decided that it wasn't okay about me and Mickey, but that wasn't what Andrea meant at all.

Turns out she'd been stewing on this wonky idea that her mother was some kind of alien or something, and that she was in like psychic communication with her. Fuck. Andrea's mother is the least-psychic middle-aged woman I have ever met. She's all business, she's an accountant or something, and she always treats me as though I had a communicable disease, which I'm quite sure I don't have, and if I did, she'd be the last person I'd give it to.

When Andrea told me she was pregnant and wanted to go home, I confess I had to think about it for a little. Not that I wouldn't have taken her home, but I needed to think about what I would say to Mickey, and whether I would want to come back to the cave after taking Andrea home. On the other hand, Andrea and her child were my responsibility too, and it's funny how, well, connected I felt to her, knowing it was my kid she was pregnant with.

When I talked to Mickey, it turned out she was very cool with it and didn't seem surprised or hurt. Kind of the ideal woman.

And then she told me that she might be pregnant too. As you might imagine, this was both a pleasure and a shock. Two babies? I was always aware that unprotected sex could create a baby: I was completely with that program. But I confess I hadn't considered the idea that unprotected sex could create two babies in a month.

Okay, okay, it was dumb of me. I hadn't thought it through, okay? But I can tell you I was pretty proud of myself. Or at least that was my first reaction. And then I thought, well, I am going to have to get a job.

But the women, Andrea and Mickey, were so much more practical. With them, it was always, what am I going to do now? Andrea was for going home to her mother, and Mickey was for staying there in the cave and giving birth all alone by herself.

This was a little too close to the mama-bear-baby-bear thing for me, but Mickey seemed so at home with the idea, it seemed to make sense to me as a solution. Only it wasn't one, was it?

So when Andrea told me that she wanted to go back to the city, I figured I'd take her there and then come back to be with Mickey. After all, Andrea has her mother, right? And Mickey hasn't got anybody, since her friends — her supposed friends, the useless twats — never come around.

I tell this to Mickey, figuring it'll make her feel better. Instead, she goes all weird on me. Like, we've never fought. We've never even disagreed. But all of a sudden, she's like, "How could you?" As if I'm some monster because I want to stay with her.

"Andrea will need you," she says. "How could you leave her at a time like this?"

"Her mother will take care of her," I say, wondering what the big deal is. "Her mother will, in fact, take much better care of her than I could."

"That old bat?" says Mickey. "She can scarcely feed herself. She can barely walk and chew gum at the same time. Look what happened to Andrea, under her care."

"What? What happened to Andrea?"

"She was running wild, and Lord knows what all. She got involved with *you*."

My feelings were hurt, but I wasn't inclined to let her know that. "So did you."

"That's different. I can take care of myself. I know what I want and how to get it. But Andrea just sleepwalks though life, accepting whatever is handed to her, not taking charge. Somebody needs to take charge."

"Excuse me for not grasping your point here, but what's your point? If I'm such a dolt, how come you want me to take care of Andrea and the baby?"

"That's a very good question, Christy. But I'm not going to answer it just now. You just get her out of here and get her back to Seattle safely. Can you do that?"

Yeah, I could do that, and I did. But the price of that is I was shut out of Mickey's life. She made it clear she wanted me out, and I didn't need to come back.

Andrea

AS WE LEFT, I was not sure whether I was going home or leaving it, going out into a strange and dangerous world. I wasn't anxious to go back to the city with Christy. Would he and I stay together? I didn't want to be with him, but I had to worry about having a baby by myself and taking care of it.

I understood Christy better than I ever had before, but I didn't like what I understood. Never had, I guess, but when it was just me, it didn't seem so important, as long as life was interesting. Maybe I hate being bored almost as much as Christy.

We slogged down the side of the mountain, carrying our

skis. It was a pleasant-enough spring day, a little overcast. The snow was long gone, and the trees were starting to bud green. There was skunk cabbage poking up in the wet places, and some little white flowers here and there. What were they? I couldn't remember. As we walked, everything that had happened in the past six weeks seemed like an extended dream.

It was a hassle getting down to the car, because the fire road in some places was pretty soggy. When we got down to the main road and looked for our car, of course it was gone. "Forest Service towed it, babe," said Christy. Well, duh. We started walking, and after a few miles we got a lift from a guy in a pickup truck.

"Mud skiing?" the guy says when he stops, nodding at our skis. A humorist.

Christy says, "We been up the mountain for a while."

"Whoa," said the guy. "Are you those two skiers vanished a month ago? You're alive?"

"Six weeks ago," said Christy, "but who's counting? I think we're alive."

"Rescue copters were over here for three days, combing the area. How do you feel? Need water? Something to eat? You want me to drive you to a hospital?"

"I just want to get my car back, man. I need to get my girlfriend here to her mom's house. She's pregnant. My girlfriend, I mean."

"I think I better take you to the sheriff's office. They'll know what to do. Where you been, anyway?"

"Ripvanwinkleville," said Christy.

Great. The sheriff's office. I hope Christy's not packing out any of that homegrown.

Christy

WHEN WE GOT BACK, I figured I had to do something fast to support me and Andrea and the baby. I mean, Andrea wasn't going to be able to bring in much from waitressing after a few months.

I figured there should be a book in there somewhere, if I could just find somebody to write it. Any real writer would jump at the chance. So I got hold of this guy I knew at *The Stranger*. We'd talked about doing this Hunter Thompson thing once, over a pitcher or two of margaritas, but nothing ever came of it. He wasn't against the idea, but he said it would be easier to sell the book if it was a news story first. He said if the story had legs, it would walk, and then he'd write the book. First he had to finish a book on hiking in Peru, anyway. But he thought his friend Darla could help with the news story.

Darla was kind of a mistake — all she knew was the confession market. So the story broke in *News of the World*, and everybody thought it was a big joke. I guess I can't blame them. That headline wouldn't have been my first choice: "He fathered a bigfoot baby… and became a deadbeat dad."

I got phone calls and email from all my old buddies, who basically figured I'd pulled off a scam of some kind. I mean, it's nice to be congratulated, but if it's your life and not a scam, it's a little embarrassing.

It wasn't my idea to contact Maury. That was Darla, came up with that. I had had my sights on Oprah, actually. A lovely woman, a bit matronly, but clearly someone who could converse on a higher plane, who would not judge me because I had left my little one behind with a loving parent. I could hear her: she would extend her generous hand to me, and she would say, "You sharing your story here with us today has brought us all a bit closer to an understanding of our relationship to the wilderness." That's how I wanted to tell my story.

But Darla couldn't get the Oprah people to even return her calls, so she went on this website and sent my story to the Maury show. So we don't hear from them, and we don't hear from them, and we don't hear from them. They are really into deadbeat dads there, which isn't my story, in my opinion. But like Darla said, we didn't have time to wait for them to do a show on bigfoot babies. I had to fit into the story they were doing.

So, anyway, I went to the show, and they had a woman up there and three deadbeat dads. Maury talked for a while, and the woman cried, and then the deadbeat dads talked. And then I interrupted, and I took the dads to task for not taking better care of their kids. I really pitched into them. I was like, I'd give anything to get back to my kid and take care of him or her. And this was true, or it seems true when I think about it. Anyway, I did my stuff, and pretty soon I was sitting up there with the deadbeat dads, and we were all crying and Maury was comforting us.

The part I didn't understand was that not only did Mickey not want to spend any time with me, but neither did Andrea. She was into the whole idea of having a baby, but not into the idea of me any more.

So then, Maury kind of jumped all over me, y'know? He asked how come if I was such a good dad I wasn't supporting my kid either?

Even the deadbeat dads joined in. I think this is the result of all those therapy programs at prisons. We've raised a whole generation of ex-cons who are in touch with their sensitive sides.

It was rough — Oprah, like I said, would have been a much better choice — but I stood up for myself, and Maury even said I was making a good case for parental responsibility in the abstract, if not in actuality. Eventually, we all hugged, and I got out of there alive.

The Maury people liked how I handled it, and they did a follow-up show a few weeks later, where they had me working with this psychic who said she could lead me to the cave again, but she couldn't. We got a couple of TV shows out of it, including one where people who've been cheated by psychics confront the cheats. And then I met this guy that wanted to do a film script. When he finished it, he said, he was hoping they could get Ben Stiller or Luke Wilson to play me. I always liked Owen Wilson better than Luke, but apparently he wasn't available or something.

Andrea

WELL, IT'S LIKE I THOUGHT. Christy always lands on his feet.

We had a hard time getting along after we got back to Seattle. Before, we had mostly the same opinions about things, but now, it seemed like whatever he wanted to do was totally screwed. I don't know why, but I just didn't want to go along with his schemes. Me being pregnant made a difference, for sure. Christy was completely sure it's his baby, but how could he be so sure of that? I didn't rub his nose in it, but I think he knew there was something going on between me and Mickey. He would believe what he wanted to believe, just like he would tell the stories that get him the biggest reaction from other people, when you got right down to it, whether he believed them or not.

He wasn't a bad dad, though. He's very into the baby, and he doesn't seem to care whose it is. When I was pregnant, he was always bugging me to eat right, and exercise, and all this stuff. And once little Baker arrived, Christy was all over me with baby-care advice from the shopping channel.

But, give me a break, I knew how to take care of a baby. I used to be a babysitter. It's no big deal. Just keep them breathing and don't drop them.

And of course my mother was delighted. She certainly didn't think it was Christy's baby. When Baker was born, she took one look at him, and she said, "We've got to talk." And of course, when we sat down to talk, which was, with one thing and another, a month later, she wormed the whole story out of me, just as you have.

"I knew it," she said. "I knew it. I had a dream."

The thing that I wondered about was the story that Christy told — about him and the bigfoot baby. I mean, I'm the one that should have been on Oprah or something, technically. Mickey threw us out of the cave, after all — so didn't that make *him* the deadbeat dad? I mean, really, if Mickey is Baker's dad?

It's kind of soon to tell, but there's something about Baker that is *so* not like Christy.

So I watched the Maury show. It's not something I'd ordinarily do, but I had to watch it, when he said he'd be on it.

It was a show on deadbeat dads, and while "deadbeat" probably does describe Christy pretty well, I didn't figure that he was completely aware of that. So I thought there would be some acknowledgment by Christy of just where he went wrong, you know?

So I tuned in, and it wasn't like Christy was actually on the show: Christy was in the audience. Why did I believe him, I thought. Had again.

And then, when he spoke up from the audience, and accused those young guest guys, I thought, what?! He wasn't telling this straight. What was going on? And then I realized that he was talking about Mickey.

He even mentioned his name: he even called him Mickey. But he was talking about him like he was a girl. This I didn't understand. Christy embroiders, you know, but he doesn't usually tell bald-faced lies. It's too easy to get caught, for one thing, telling bald-faced lies. Christy is smarter than that.

And he was crying like she broke his heart and stole his baby. Mickey? Hey! It's my heart that was broken. I'm the one who got seduced and abandoned. Mickey's the deadbeat dad, not you, I thought. And I've got the baby.

So after the show, I went to the Maury people. I told them Christy was taking advantage of them. They weren't interested in that story. And why should they be? They had a good story already in Christy. But I said, you're on a roll here. If they kept it going, maybe they could bring Mickey in too.

They liked that idea. "Do you know where she is?" the guy asked.

"He's a he!" I said. "Mickey is a he. I ought to know. He got me pregnant. I don't know why Christy is pretending he's a girl. This is my story, and he swiped it!"

I would have thought they'd be surprised by this, but it turned out they're used to this kind of a story. If it's a love triangle, they can keep bringing people back until the cows come home. If it's got a bi angle, they love that too.

So I met with them again, with a story doctor. Very professional, very slick. They do this hundreds of times a season. Kind of creepy, actually.

I had little Baker with me, 'cause I was nursing him, and they glommed onto him. "So this is Bigfoot's baby?" they asked. For Pete's sake, he's just a baby, I said. Leave him out of this.

So the deal was, they were not going to tell Christy that I was going to be on the show, or Mickey, if they could find him. They kept calling Mickey "she."

Christy

WHAT DID I LOOK LIKE, I wondered. Wardrobe had tried to spiff me up a bit, with a haircut and some clothes that weren't too bad. They even shaved me, sort of, with a razor that left me with a nice even stubble.

I wasn't expecting Andrea. They had made her up to look very wholesome and earth-mother-y, with a peasant skirt and embroidered blouse, like some sort of old-country woman headed for the market. Her hair was wound into a braid, and the braid was curled into a large round bun at the back. I felt like I'd been set up. Where was the hot babe with the welding gun who had won my heart at Burning Man? This was a mom!

They brought us out like the contestants in some old game show, sitting on chairs in front of the audience.

Then Maury came out and he introduced us, and he started asking us questions about where we live and how we met. Pretty soon we started talking, and I didn't think it would amount to all that, or that we could talk about it in public.

Then they started showing the videos of the kid. I mean, babies are babies, and we're hardwired to find them cute. But gee whiz, the audience went a little wild at the baby video. I admit, Baker is a cute kid. I looked a lot like that when I was a toddler. I can show you the photos.

And then they said they had photos of the other baby, but they ran videos of some bear cub instead. The audience was confused, but game. It was a tease, I thought. They don't have any photos, because they've never been able to find Mickey, because I've never been able to find Mickey. Cute little cub, though.

And then they brought out Andrea's mother.

Andrea

SO MY MOTHER WAS on the show, which I wouldn't have agreed to if anybody had asked me. And she and Maury, I swear, they tag-teamed me, and pretty soon I was telling the unexpurgated version.

I said, which I had never said out loud to anyone, even Christy, that I didn't think the baby is Christy's. My mom said, basically, that she certainly hoped not, and that Christy was an aimless good-for-nothing.

Christy acted like he was outraged, and he threw himself off the chair and onto the floor and kicked his heels a lot and yelled. Since he knows perfectly well how my mother feels about him, I felt this was a little stagy, but I think it's something that men have to do on the Maury show.

I said that I was just a bit annoyed that my own mother would rather see me with a fatherless kid from some hookup with a grizzly half way up a volcano than for me to have a baby with Christy.

But my mom just looked at me and said, "That's the way it is."

Maury was still in control, though, whatever my mother thought, and he started talking to my mom about her entirely misspent youth. And she told this perfect stranger — she doesn't even watch his show — stuff she had never told me in my entire life. My mother told Maury that she used to hike on Mt. Baker, and that she, in fact, had had her own fling with the sasquatches, way back before I was born.

She made it sound like a picnic of some kind. No long weeks in a cave. It was summer, and the weather was warm and sunny. It was like some fantasy romance. The love sasquatches. I don't know why I got so angry about that.

But I was pretty incensed by it all. My mom had always been so tight with the details about my dad that I assumed he was some kind of criminal. And now I find out he's a sasquatch, and on network television. If I were a typical Maury guest, I'd be jumping up and down and crying.

But I know that doesn't work with my mom. So I just ask her: was Mickey my father?

She said, "Honey, I don't know. It was a long time ago. Life was different then, before I took the accounting course. I didn't always keep track of stuff."

There was a lot of yelling from the audience, some of them laughing and some of them scolding her.

And then they brought out Mickey.

Christy

I DON'T KNOW how they do this stuff. I certainly didn't have anything to do with it. They didn't ask me for any advice or help.

But somehow they found Mickey, or maybe Mickey just decided to allow herself to be found.

Either way, she walked out onto the stage at the Maury show and paused. She looked great. Elegant, all spiffed up in some kind of classy New York clothes. She looked like Candice Bergen, maybe, or that woman who lives in Connecticut and does the magazine — Martha Stewart. Older, you know, and maybe a little authoritative, but still pretty great-looking. I guess I hadn't thought about it, but maybe Mickey does that craft stuff too, like Martha — that's how she gets all those hats and bowls and coffee cups and stuff.

They told me later that, to the studio audience, Mickey looked like a sasquatch. Some people screamed, other people laughed. But I wasn't paying a lot of attention to the audience reaction at the time.

Of course, I wanted to run to Mickey, but Maury gestured to me and Andrea to stay in our seats. He went over to her, rather cautiously, I thought, and guided her to a seat next to Andrea's mother, who looked at Mickey speculatively.

Andrea looked at Mickey too. Tears welled up in her eyes, and she said to me and the studio audience, "He's lost weight."

I swear I thought at the time, she's not even seeing the same person I'm seeing. I said, "Looks to me like she gained about ten pounds, but I figure, she had a baby, she's going to gain a little weight."

Andrea looked at me intently for the first time, like she was actually listening to me. "What are you talking about?"

I said, "Well, you gained weight."

Andrea gave me the evil eye. I said, "I'm talking about Mickey, that's who. She had the baby, and she's still carrying a few extra pounds. But it's nothing to me. She looks great. You look great. Jeez."

Then Andrea said to me, right on camera in front of the TV

audience, "Mickey is a man, you idiot."

I was surprised, but I was not going to put up with being treated that way. Idiot. Huh. I said, "I understand how you could have thought that, but the fact is that she's a girl. I found out for myself in the traditional manner."

Of course by now, there were more people in the audience screaming and laughing. I've done some street theater, and this happens — people act out, and certainly on the Maury show the audience is encouraged to act out. I've found that the best way to deal with it is to ignore it.

And then Maury turned to me and Andrea, and he looked sort of sad. "Christy and Andrea," he said, "Is this your friend Mickey?" We each nodded. "And you each say you've slept with Mickey?" We each nodded. Andrea's mother just shrugged, and then she nodded too.

"Well, you've shown us here today that not everyone is seduced by Hollywood's ideal of beauty..." I was about to object to that statement, when I saw Mickey sort of focus on Maury. He did kind of a double-take, then said, "...though of course you... you would carry it to a... new standard." He shook his head a little, like there was something wrong with his eyes.

Then Maury pulled himself together and held up a manila envelope. "I've got the tests right here," he said. The Maury Show is very supportive with the paternity-test thing, and I was looking forward to the results. Maury tore the envelope open and pulled out the lab report.

At that point, Mickey stood up and said, "I don't think we need to hear this." She gestured with one hand, and an opening appeared in the floor of the stage right in front of us. It looked like it led into a cave, and it sure was dark down there.

Then people started coming out of it, people with tall hats and clothing that looked like it was made from dead oak leaves. They were carrying bittersweet vines and two babies, neither of whom looked to me like a bear cub, though I've been told that, to the audience, they both looked like bear cubs.

The people in hats danced with Mickey and Maury and Andrea's mother, and they handed the babies about while they danced. Maury danced, but Andrea and I did not dance. We watched, slightly paralyzed, while Mickey and Andrea's mother entangled themselves in the bittersweet, and then entangled Maury. Then they all danced down into the trapdoor with the babies, even Maury.

But Maury looked a little worried, just a tiny bit. As he descended down into the floor, he looked right at the camera-man and said, "Keep it rolling, Anthony." He disappeared into the cave, wrapped in bittersweet. Maury was a pro, I thought, and I respected that.

Andrea and I were left sitting on the sound stage, looking at the audience. I'm sure you've seen the clip on YouTube.

Chop Wood, Carry Water

THEY SAY YOU CAN'T REMEMBER before you were born, but *I* remember. I was cold, cold and damp and clammy. I wanted nothing. I did not know hunger, thirst, or desire. I lived in the dark, and I didn't have a thought in my head. I was free.

Then, of course, things changed. I awoke from a dreamless sleep to the dreadful noise of three black-clad men bowing and chanting psalms, to the stench of burning metal and baking clay, and to a pall of steam hanging over it all on the muddy bank of the Vltava. I was torn from my bed. I was granted this half-life and became subject to the will of the Rabbi.

The Rabbi was not a bad man: things could have been much worse. He was a compassionate and contemplative human being, interested in dispelling those mysteries that are man's to dispel. Moral issues were important to him, and he seemed to consider worthy even the life in golems.

But I lost, in that instant of formation, my merciful shapelessness, my oneness with the universe. Yet I did not gain the one thing that would have, I am told, been recompense for those losses.

I must tell you now that, in my opinion, souls are overrated. Compared to the deep, volitionless comfort that comes from being truly a part of the earth, humans and their souls never know a day of rest. They hunger, they thirst, they long for one another in ways that I am not equipped to understand. They lack deep peace, and a soul seems poor compensation for this absence.

Every day, the Rabbi would ask me to do certain simple tasks, and each day, I would do them to the best of my ability. I would chop wood and carry water. As the Rabbi told me, these tasks were much revered by religious people, even in other lands, and I should not feel ashamed to do them. Indeed, I was pleased to have simple tasks, and could do them without stopping, until the Rabbi told me to do something else.

I knew that I could also be called upon, at any moment, to defend the community against outsiders who would wish to harm it. Thus far, I had done that only one time and in a minor way, and after that the outsiders had left us alone. The Rabbi wondered whether they were in fear of me, or whether they were simply planning something extraordinary. This uncertainty gave a special urgency to my distress on the day my strength disappeared.

My first task on the day in question was to serve the dead. Very near to where the Rabbi lives, there was — there still is — a small cemetery, the only cemetery, aside from the one where the plague victims were placed, in which Jews were allowed to be buried. It was not so much a problem as it might seem that the cemetery was overcrowded: the bones were stacked many layers deep: graves were piled upon graves, gravestones upon gravestones, jutting out like loose teeth. The effect was one of deathly chaos.

The Rabbi was in charge of the cemetery, and it had been one of my tasks since my creation to carry new gravestones to the graves. My strength enabled me to pick up a stack of stones, five or six at a time, and place them at the gravesites. And yet, this time, when I approached them, I found I did not have the strength to pick them up. I took them one by one from the stonecutter's room to the edge of the graveyard, but still I could not carry them out to the graves. I simply didn't have enough strength.

Since my strength was the only purpose of my vitality — I have no soul, after all, and thus have no reason for my existence except to serve — I thought that its failure in this instance might be cause for concern by the Rabbi. It might cause him to unmake me, and I could go without protest back to my ideal existence as a cold and unthinking component of the living planet upon which the warmer, more volatile beings scurry about.

Right now, the scent of those small white flowers outside by the iron gate is driving me a little crazy. Their perfume fills this storeroom. There is nothing I want to do with these flowers. I cannot eat them, and indeed, have no desire to do so. I cannot impregnate them, I cannot hold a conversation with them, and I could not even were I able to fuck and talk. They no doubt have their own vegetable goals and interests, but such things have nothing to do with me. So why are they trying so hard to hold my attention?

To continue: my first thought was that I must find the Rabbi and indicate to him that I was useless for the purpose of carrying gravestones. I hoped that he would see that this meant my usefulness was finished, and I must be returned to the soil.

The Rabbi, I feared, was entranced by the implications of my existence, and would be reluctant to bring it to an end. He breathed life into me, just as, as he saw it, his maker breathed life into him. In the view of his people, and perhaps in his own eyes, this made the Rabbi more like his maker than he was like other men. This, he said, was the sin of Lucifer, and he feared it. He thought too much, the Rabbi. And yet, that was one of his most worthy traits.

It is not clear to me whether I am a man or something less than a man. It is not even clear to me whether I am a Jew. Although I am dependent on the Shem — the sacred name, which the Rabbi places in my mouth to animate me — I am not otherwise a religious person, and I do not lay Tefillin or study Torah. But I think that it is not necessary for me to be religious in order for me to be a Jew, nor, if I were not, would it make me a Jew to be religious.

The scholars debated whether I could be called upon to make a minyan, and have not, even now, made a clear decision, so I was never asked to perform this mitzvah, this duty. But the Rabbi allowed me to rest on the Sabbath, as a Jew would. It is not clear to me, though, whether he thought I was a Jew, as he had me rest by removing the Shem from my mouth, as if I would not otherwise refrain from labor. This took the power to do so or not away from me, as if I were again a piece of clay. I asked him about this, and he said, "Animals have the same rights as humans do. Even animals rest on the Sabbath. You who have something of the animal and something of the man, as well as something of the earth, should rest as well."

In truth, I don't know whether, without his intervention, I would refrain from labor, or work as dutifully as usual. My nature is mixed, as he says.

And yet I must be a Jew, mustn't I, if the Holy Name has power over me? Without it, I lose life, although I retain the form of life, a form very similar, but not identical, to that of a man. Women, it is clear, do not consider me a man, and yet they are fearful of me in a way that they are also fearful of large, bad men, not in ways that they are fearful of beasts. This is puzzling to me. If I am not a man, I cannot be a bad man. My fault here, I think, is that I am large.

Perhaps it is because of my mixed nature that I have not accepted the yoke of mitzvot, of the necessity of taking one's duties as a human seriously. In any case, I do not fully understand what those duties are, so that even should I want to fulfill them, I have not the means. I am not religious, and I shall not pray for the means. Would a rock pray to be human? Would it be right to grant such a wish? Personally, as a rock, I have no ambitions to be human, and I find it makes my head hurt to think about this.

Through the window of this storehouse, high in the Altneu-shul, I can see a being on the branch of a tree near by, watching me. Sitting on a branch it looks very much like a tiny bird, but when it rises into the air, it does not move like a bird. It is trying to get my attention, with its abrupt movements and its twitter-ing. It is filled with life, but I don't understand what it is trying to tell me. Why are the birds and the flowers so concerned with communicating with me?

I need no messages from birds and flowers. They have noth-ing to tell me. I served the Rabbi, and the Rabbi served G-d. What I know, I know from my closeness to the Rabbi, just as what he knew came from G-d.

That day, before I discovered my weakness with respect to the gravestones, I met the daughter of the ratcatcher. However, it may not be quite correct to say that I met her, since no introduc-tions were made, nor were names exchanged. The ratcatcher's daughter had come to the cemetery to visit the grave of her mother, and she had left a few pennies on the grave. I saw this, and I thought she had forgotten them, and brought them to her as she was leaving. She was afraid when she saw me approach her, and would have run away, but I held the coins out to her. She saw what I offered, and recognized them as her own, but it did not make her less fearful of me. Unlike the flowers and birds here, she was not at all interested in communicating with me. I put the money down on the ground in front of her, and stepped back.

She looked at me warily. She was a dark-haired woman, thick-waisted and sturdy, and courageous, I think.

I did not try to talk, for if I did so the Shem would fall from my mouth, and my sounds were worth nothing at any rate. But

I think she understood my gestures.

"You can have the money, Yossele," she said. I remember even now the sadness of her expression. "Or you can leave it for some other unfortunate. I left it there so that whoever needed it could take it in my mother's name. People should not have to ask for alms."

An unfortunate, I thought. Am I an unfortunate? At the same time, I was thinking: Yossele. She knows my name. How wonderful that I have a name and she knows it.

I thought, was I fortunate before I had a name, before I was given a sort of life? If so, how would I become fortunate again? Was I unfortunate because, even though I had a name, I had no soul and therefore could never know the ecstasy that I had seen on the faces of the men when they danced? Or was I unfortunate in that I could not talk or procreate, and thus could not participate fully in the life of the community that I defended?

At the same time, I thought: Yossele. She knows my name.

And I thought: she thinks I am a monster. She is afraid of me even though she knows I am the protector of the Jewish Town. How sad that is. Is that why I am an unfortunate?

At any rate, I took up the pennies again, since she had said I could have them. Perhaps I *am* an unfortunate, and they would therefore be of some assistance to me. I had no place to put them for safekeeping — a golem has no use of pockets — so I put them in my mouth, with the Shem. The Rabbi could keep them safe for me when he took the Shem out of my mouth for the Sabbath.

It was after this this, upon returning to work, I discovered that I was unable to lift the stack of gravestones, or to carry even a single stone to a gravesite.

Because I did not talk, they thought that I did not have much of an intellect. I suppose this is to be expected. How would they know? Men, in those times, depended so much on words, on talking and writing. Perhaps I could write, but no one has ever given me access to writing tools and told me to write. I would never write on my own. I can imagine it, but I cannot do it.

Talking was a special case, indeed. Perhaps I could have spoken up, but no one seemed to want that. Most people felt no need to know what I thought, and even the Rabbi did well simply on intuition. No one really understood that I could talk, and that was fine with me.

In part, their mistake came from the fact that men think intelligence depends on the soul, which is demonstrably not true, at least in my case. Some say that it is the physical brain in which intelligence is seated, but I am made of clay, all the way through. However, it is possible that my intelligence is derived from that of the Rabbi. If so, he lives on somehow in me even now, although he has been gone nearly four hundred years.

In those years, I was not sure what the soul did or if I had one, but I knew, even back then, that I had intelligence, contrary to what the Rabbi and his students thought.

The problem was, of course, that an intellect must be fed in order to grow. But, you know, they set me to work day and night, six days a week, and they did not stay up all night to watch me. No, they were too busy, eating and drinking well, dancing in worship of G-d, and calling forth cries of pleasure in their wives. So I had time, late at night, to sneak into the Klausshul, where the Rabbi studied and taught, and I gave myself an education by carrying books around. I understood that the Rabbi and his students read the books and debated what was in them, but I was able to understand their contents just by lifting them and moving them from shelf to shelf.

Not that I apprehended the books' arguments immediately. I became gradually aware, over a few weeks' time, of ideas and images, of knowing the answers to questions I had not been asked.

Not that anybody ever asked me any questions, of course — why would they ask the golem? But I always was aware of questions in the air, of hesitancies, of questions suppressed. And I knew the answers to many of them. Not that I would answer. Who would believe the golem, if it offered information or advice?

When I first started acquiring knowledge from books, I was astounded and horrified. Astounded at the transcendent heights of human knowledge, and horrified at the depths to which mankind can sink.

I have read the entire breadth and depth of human learning, as it is stored in the shul's books, and now I understand why the good Rabbi called me forth to protect the ghetto. The world is a fearful place. It has not gotten better as the centuries have run, nor do I see any indication that it will get better in the future.

The more I read, it seemed, the more I understood about the past. And the more I understood of the past, the more I could intuit of the future.

It is just as well that the Rabbi did not know what was in store. Knowledge of what has come in the past four centuries would not have been of any help to him, nor would it reinforce his belief in a G-d of the Jews. I assure you, it has done nothing for mine.

Not that I am saying that G-d, as the Rabbi understood him, exists. I know that the Rabbi sought to understand G-d, not just find a reflection of himself. But I saw no evidence that the rabbi — or any other human being — was even on the right track.

If there is a G-d, it doesn't seem that it is a player in human affairs. I heard people speaking all the time of events that they called blessed, as if the G-d were enthusiastically endorsing their lives. And yet blessings did not go consistently to the good, nor did misfortune visit only the bad.

The future, as I saw it then, was not all dismal: there clearly were some joys ahead for the Rabbi and his family.

The Rabbi had a daughter of many accomplishments, named Feigeleh, who had at that time given birth to a girl child. The Rabbi's granddaughter, whose name was Eva, still had the big grey eyes of an infant, and yet I knew that this being had a love of knowledge, and an ability to absorb it that transcended my own. It came to me, as if I saw this with my eyes, that she would be a respected rabbinical scholar herself, she would have children who would also become rabbis, and she would die in vigorous old age, while journeying to Jerusalem. This was a wonderful thing for me to know, and I longed to tell the rabbi, but of course I had no way to communicate it. I was less effective than a flower or a bird.

And I ask myself now if it would it have been good for the Rabbi to know of the full life awaiting his granddaughter if he also had to know the horrors awaiting some of his other descendants? It may be a blessing to them, that humans cannot see into the future.

I think that Praha is a beautiful city, though I have never seen any other with which to compare it, nor even seen all of Praha itself. Maybe all cities are filled with such delights as the clockwork in the town square that displays the state of the universe, all day and every day, for the benefit of the townspeople.

Working for the Rabbi, I had sympathy for the clock, which performed rain or shine, and was never rewarded except with a nod when someone passed it by. It gave pleasure to others, but received no pleasure from anyone. In that way, I felt, it was superior to myself, for although I offered security and performed many tasks, I never offered anyone pleasure.

Perhaps if I offered pleasure, I thought, I would fulfill my purpose and be allowed to return to the earth. Although, even as I thought that, I realized that both the clockwork and its creatures — the gothic figures that guarded its perimeter — were taken, like myself, from the earth, but were unlikely to be allowed to return to it. So it made no sense for me to have such an expectation. But it was an idea, it gave me something to try. My options were so few.

However, I was not sure how to go about even trying to give pleasure. I tried to observe the people around me offering joy to one another. I saw the Rabbi doing small favors for his wife, and that she was made happy by them. I saw her cooking special things for her husband and children, and that all, even herself, were made happy by the acts and the foods. I heard the noises that the Rabbi and his wife made at night, while I was cease-lessly stacking stones and chopping wood, and I understood that these noises meant they were offering pleasure to one another.

I tried to do small favors for the Rabbi, but he did not seem pleasured by the things I did under my own volition. The more I did by myself, in fact, the more he wrinkled his brow. G-d him-self, if the stories are true, does not like to see too much initia-tive from his creations.

I could learn to cook, I supposed, but as I didn't eat, I had no way of knowing whether things I cooked would be pleasing. As for my making the Rabbi or his wife give forth sounds of plea-sure in the night, perhaps the less said about that the better. I didn't know much, but I did have a sense of my own limitations.

But here I am getting away from the thread of my story: the loss of my strength. The Rabbi had been told that some of the townspeople were preparing an attack on the Jewish Town. This was why he created me, to defend against such an attack, and I was very interested and needful to learn more of what defend-ing my people entailed. If I had had my strength, I could have picked the attackers up like rats, tossed them in a sack, and thrown it in the river. Or perhaps I could have kept them, bred them, and turned them loose, as it was sometimes said the rat-catcher did, though I have no idea to what purpose.

Praha was then a relatively comfortable place for Jews to live, and had been so even before the Rabbi arrived. The Emperor Rudolph and his father before him understood that gentiles and Jews could do business together without undue conflict, and each could become more prosperous in the bargain. But there were some who saw prosperity among the Jews as something taken from the gentiles. In earlier times the synagogue had more than once been painted with blood, the blood of real people, and the Jewish Town had been burned. Jews were beaten and killed, and plots were hatched to create fear and hatred of the Jews among the other citizens of Praha. This seemed to be a way that the unstable among the goyim sought control over their small area of the universe.

I wondered what happened to the unstable Jews? Why did they not do the same thing? Also, I wondered, why did these goyim not have their own golem, who would fight for them as I would fight for the Jews? Then they would not have to savage other human beings, and the two communities could just put their two golems to battle.

But on the day of which I am speaking, I worried, though there was no danger evident, that if I could not even hoist an armload of gravestones, I would be of no use against an attack by the goyim. I would be unable to pick them up like rats. And, in my silence, of course, I could not talk them out of their insanity, as someone might do who was not reliant on physical force.

The only sensible thing to do, I thought, was to understand the scope of the problem and lay it before the Rabbi. I would test my strength by trying my simplest accustomed tasks, chopping wood and carrying water. I left the cemetery, and headed for Široká Street, where the Rabbi's house was.

I approached the house from the back, to go in by the tool

room door. There was no one in the yard. Usually the place was buzzing with servants and children. I entered the house, walking past the oiled sharpened axes and into the big family room. There was no one inside. There was no fire, there were no lights.

I walked out the front door and out the gate. It was dark, and the streets were empty. There weren't even any stray dogs searching the gutters. The other houses of the Jewish Town were quiet; the lights were dim, the windows were shuttered. Did nobody know that Rabbi Loew's house was empty? What was going on? I heard a sound from the alleyway and turned in that direction. It was no threat to me, of course. I am afraid of no one, and, really, if I were, the idea of death by someone's hand would arouse in me only enthusiasm.

It was the ratcatcher. He was moving very slowly, limping as though his leg were damaged, and making very low noises to himself. He looked up as I approached.

"Yossele," he said, although the sound of my name was not so attractive as when it had issued from his daughter's mouth. I wondered why that would be. He is very similar to his daughter, in coloring and facial structure. And yet they have such a different effect upon me. The ratcatcher's voice tears at me, like the voices of many trapped rats. His daughter's voice is as light and sweet as the piping of a happy rat, free to do as she wishes in a fruitful midden, unmolested by humans.

"Yossele," said the ratcatcher, "help me home." I looked at him closely, and saw that his clothing was torn and bloody. He was not a neat or clean man, but his clothing was not usually in such disarray. I picked him up.

"Yossele," he said, "they set upon me, and beat me, and ran off. And then the emperor's men came and took the Rabbi, and all his family." I almost put him down, I was so surprised. But I kept walking, and waited for him to tell me more.

"The Emperor, Yossele," he said. "The Emperor! What can be done? The Emperor, I thought, knew the Rabbi and valued his wisdom. But he has turned out to be as treacherous as other gentiles. What will we do, Yossele? What will we do? What can you do for us?"

What *can* I do? I thought. I no longer had the strength to do anything extraordinary. It seemed to me that the only thing to do was to go find the Rabbi, wherever he was, and do what he told me. That was my one skill.

Although now it taxed my strength to do so, I carried him to his small, filthy doorway, so like a rathole that men and women customarily walked out into the street as they passed it by. But there were no people walking in the street that night.

I put the ratcatcher down carefully at his door. It was, so far as I could see, the poorest, ugliest, most beaten-down door in all of Praha. There was, of course, nothing I could tell him, nothing I could say. I don't have an expressive face, I suppose because it is molded of clay. People do not generally have any idea what I am thinking, however much they offer suggestions.

The ratcatcher stumbled. I was uncertain whether he could even summon the strength to raise his own household, so I knocked at the door for him. It was answered quickly by his daughter. She saw me first, and was unafraid. I was impressed by that. Then she saw her father, and was much shocked. She gave me a fierce look. I bent down and picked her father up gently, and she allowed me to carry him into the house. I put him down on a pallet near the wood stove, from which a mild heat radiated.

I enjoy the cold and damp, and I do not ordinarily seek the presence of heat, which dries me out uncomfortably, and makes my skin crack. But this room, with its tiny fire, was perfectly tolerable to me. I wondered how comfortable it could have been for the ratcatcher's daughter. Could it be that she also was a golem?

I looked at her, as she moved quickly about the tiny, dark, cold room. She brought a thin blanket for her father, and stuffed sticks into the stove. It heated up, but those sticks would not last long. Even if she was a golem, it was obvious that her father was not.

What would the Rabbi do? I wondered. Would he just give the ratcatcher fuel? If he did that for every poor Jew, I figured, then he would shortly have nothing. But the Rabbi did not have nothing.

So what did he do? I thought about this. I had seen what happened. The Rabbi would go to a rich man, either a Jew or a gentile, and he would ask him for charity for a poor Jew. The rich man would say yes, or he would say no. If he said yes, the poor man would benefit. If he said no, the Rabbi would simply go to the next person on his list.

I did not have a list. I am not the Rabbi. But I knew where there was wood that was not being used. The Rabbi was for my purpose a rich man. If he was imprisoned or dead, he would not mind that his wood was warming someone else. In case he was on his way home, I would leave enough for tonight, and tomorrow I would chop more.

I nodded at the ratcatcher's daughter. Perhaps she understood me, perhaps not. I went quickly back to the Rabbi's woodpile, and picked up as large a stack as I could carry. My strength was so limited now that I was ashamed that people might see me struggling with such a small load. But it was dark, and no one was watching. I shouldered on, and brought the small armload of wood to the door of the ratcatcher and his daughter. Then I went back for a second and a third load. I also brought her several buckets of water. Even without superhuman strength, I could perform these simple acts, as any human might.

She welcomed me in and told me to put the wood inside, as though it was a precious substance, something that might be stolen. Since I had, in fact, stolen the Rabbi's wood, perhaps this was true.

"Yossele," she said, "we can never thank you enough."

That is right, I thought, no one can ever thank someone enough. There is always room for more thanks. I nodded and left.

Now that the ratcatcher was taken care of, I needed to find Rabbi Loew. How would I do that, I wondered, especially how would I do it in the dark of the night?

The first place to look, based on what the ratcatcher had said, would be the castle. It is not so far from the Jewish Town, and I walked easily through the dark streets to the Vltava, across the bridge, and up the hill to the castle. There were people in the streets, angry, drunken, violent people. But they did not attack me, and they were not at present attacking others. I let them be.

The castle was guarded, of course, and I could not think how I might approach the Emperor. But I would deal with that problem when it presented itself. First, I needed to find the way in.

I had never been to the castle: I was the defender of the Jewish Town, and there, for the most part, I stayed. I walked around its base, looking up at its forbidding walls. Even in the middle of the night, there would be a way in. Eventually, I found myself at a highly fortified gate. I walked forward and presented myself to the guard. They were startled by my appearing there, but they clearly recognized me. I was the only golem in Praha, after all.

I opened my arms, to indicate that I intended no harm. The guards jumped back, their weapons at ready. I stayed still, my arms held apart and slightly raised. The guards were puzzled, and I could not blame them. We might have stood there like that until dawn, had the commotion not caught the eye of an officer, who intervened.

"If it wanted to destroy us, it would done so already," he said to the guards. "But do not let it advance." As if, had I my strength, they could have stopped me, had I wanted to move forward.

I nodded to the guard and the officer, and I waited. I was, of course, aware that even a quiet golem was not inconspicuous, and I was hoping one of the Emperor's retainers would notice me. It was in the dark of the night, however, and I was sure I would be standing there for some time.

As I stood awaiting the next thing that would happen to me, I noticed a small brown bird on a branch. What, I thought, was that bird doing there, in the cold and the dark?

Then it started singing. It sang a lovely, long, complex song that filled the air like perfume. The bird sang and sang.

The windows of the castle were not open, but as I watched, they opened. It was a cold night in the middle of winter, when the windows were usually kept sealed. But the song of that bird was never heard in winter, although it was common and beloved in the summer months.

The bird sang loudly and persistently. The time was late, but people in the castle not only opened their windows, they came out on their balconies, wrapped in fur, to hear this remarkably unseasonal bird.

Among these people was the Emperor, who looked out to see the bird, and saw the golem, myself, waiting there by the guard station.

The Emperor sent a page to order that I, the Praha golem, be brought to his offices in the middle of the night.

A contingent of officers led me through the dark, silent streets of the castle. It was like a little town there, like Jewish Town maybe, except there were no hovels, no hunger, no cold, even in the winter.

I have heard the Rabbi say that there is sadness in castles, just as joy is available to people at the extreme of poverty, but I saw neither sadness or joy that evening. I walked, led by the guards, down a quiet alley, to a rather plain building. It looked efficient, a place in which work was done.

I had never thought of the Emperor as someone who worked, but I confess I hadn't given it much thought at all. The headman of the guard knocked at the door, and words were exchanged, from inside to out. The door opened, and I was led inside, down a dark corridor, and into a large room filled with retorts and alembics.

At the far end of the room was a small man, dressed warmly, but not overdressed. I noticed that he was attended by a team of people, and on looking closely, I saw that the Rabbi was among them, and his wife and family were off to the side.

"Ah," said the small man. "This is your golem, at last."

The Rabbi nodded. He had his usual gravitas, but he did not look at ease.

"Tell me how you work it, and why you have commanded it to come here."

"Your Excellency, I did not command it," said the Rabbi, "nor do I work it, in the sense that you mean. It works itself. It requires merely a few words from myself to set it to a task, and then it will pursue that task with a will of its own."

"Set it a task," said the emperor. "I want to see it work. Set it some task that is impossible for a human being."

"Your excellency," said the Rabbi, "it does not necessarily do things that are impossible, but it has the strength of ten men. So if you have some lifting or some tearing down, those would be an ideal way for me to show you the golem's strength."

"Very well," said the Emperor, "have it move the gate for me. I have been planning to extend the yard here and have more protected space for men and horses. Tell your golem to take apart the stones of the gate and rebuild it on the other side of the guard building."

I was taken aback by this, as I am sure you can imagine.

I knew I no longer had that strength, and I feared that, even though the Emperor meant us no harm, as soon as the less stable gentiles found out about my weakness they would come to the Jewish Town and they would set fire to our synagogues. They would bash the heads of Jewish babies against the stone steps. They would kill young women and men, and leave the old for the dogs.

The Rabbi immediately noticed my distress. He showed no alarm, but in a calm, even voice said, "My Emperor, the golem is an automaton and a creature of chaos. He has no thought or will of his own. I must tell him, very carefully, to do exactly what you want done and in the order you want it done. Otherwise, instead of accomplishing your task, he will simply create chaos."

"Is that so?" said the Emperor. "I will keep that in mind in building my homunculus. For now, for the demonstration, just have him move the slabs of stone to the site of the new gate, over there."

"Yosef, do this," said the Rabbi to me quietly. I tried to speak to him with my eyes, but, as I have said, I do not have an expressive face. There was no way that I would have the strength to do that, and yet I could not disobey the Rabbi. My body moved and tried to act. Again the Rabbi noticed my struggle. There is nothing that escapes his benevolent attention.

"My Emperor," said the Rabbi, "it was kind indeed of you to bring us here under your protection, but tomorrow our Sabbath begins. Please allow us to return home and prepare to honor that day, on which even the golem does not work. We now have our golem to protect us if necessary, and as soon as the Sabbath is over, the golem will move the stones. He can work all night. Later, when it is time to put them in position, the golem and I will return and he will do that under my instruction and the supervision of your architects."

"Very well," said the Emperor. "We here are very close to

creating a homunculus, using alchemical means rather than your Kabbalah. Seeing your golem at work would be instructive: we must find a way to keep the chaos at bay.

"Come back after your Sabbath and my own, in three days. Then we will see what your golem can do."

The Emperor offered his guards, but the Rabbi declined in a courteous fashion. I was to be his guard, and I think he would have said the same even had he known the full extent to which I was disabled. Our small party walked out of the Emperor's workhouse, across the tiny townlet, and out the big gate that he wanted me to move. My height alone, I felt, was sufficient to discourage the sort of cowardly attackers who would lie in wait in the dead of night, and the Rabbi, I was sure, was doing this to make the point that he feared nothing, and that I was sufficiently strong to defend him and his family and, by extension, the entire Jewish community.

When we got back to his house, inside, in privacy by the fire and near my pallet, I demonstrated for the Rabbi that I could lift small objects, of the sort that the average human might lift, but I could not budge objects of the weight and heft that I had previously handled. The Rabbi was clearly puzzled, but he told me to rest, and the next day we would figure things out. By now it was the small hours of the morning, and we all went to bed, me on my pallet away from the fire, and the Rabbi and his wife in their comfortable room in which only they slept, their bed close to the warm wall of the chimney.

The next day there was much to do to prepare for the Sabbath, which started at sundown. Wood needed chopping, water need hauling, food for the Sabbath meals had to be prepared, as well as that day's food. My labors were limited in preparation for the Sabbath, as my role was less one of serving household needs than it was of serving the community. The Rabbi had a few comforts, however, that he allowed me to provide: the water and wood for his bath and the occasional draft of water from a country well. I believe that his thinking was that, to some extent, the community's well-being depended on his own well-being, and my serving him in those ways aided the entire community. The Rabbi was a reasonable man, and not an ascetic.

At any rate, only the Rabbi and perhaps his wife, from whom he had no secrets, were privy to the information that I was lacking my usual strength, and I was able to accomplish my tasks without drawing others' attention.

Just before the beginning of the Sabbath, the Rabbi commanded me to open my mouth for the removal of the Shem, so that I might rest. It was then he found the coins that the rat-catcher's daughter had given me. He nodded and said, very solemnly, "Yosef, I think I have discovered the source of the problem. You will need to resolve this, but like all of us, you shall rest on the Sabbath. " He removed them, then removed the Shem, and I fell into a deep and dreamless sleep, a brief return to the great silence of the earth.

On the first day of the week, I was awoken after sunset by the Rabbi putting the Shem into my mouth, just as it happened every week. He sat by me on my pallet. "Yosef," he said, "I have given your situation much thought, and I believe I know what you should do."

I had hoped he would figure it out, and I indicated my thanks to him.

"You should not be so quick to thank me," he said. "There is little I can do for you. You must accomplish this yourself."

I looked at him in doubt and worry, and he read, as so often he does, the voice of my stance.

"Yossele, you can do this. G-d does not require of us what we cannot do."

That's all well and good, I thought, but I am not human. G-d did not create me, the Rabbi created me. G-d's own creations are more capable (meaning no offense to the Rabbi), so His expectations may be elevated well beyond my abilities.

The Rabbi ignored my reservations, although I know that he saw them.

"Listen to me," he said. "You put this money in your mouth with the Holy Name. I do not know where you got the money, but now it seems to me that its appropriate use is charity." The Rabbi sighed. "Do you understand? You must give this money to someone less fortunate than yourself."

Well, of course I understood that. It's the principle activity of the Rabbi's life, as I have observed it, aside from his studying the Torah.

I nodded, and he told me to go and fulfill my obligation. "Do this before you come home," he said.

I lumbered out of the family compound, but not with my usual calm confidence that I could accomplish my assignments. Where would I find these unfortunates, and how would I tell whether they were even less fortunate than myself?

The emperor, I decided, did not qualify as an unfortunate. He was busy, he was unhappy, he had many demands on his time, but he had many advantages that others did not, and as human lives go, he was fortunate indeed.

What about the ratcatcher, I thought? He had a miserable job and was derided by many, sometimes even set upon. He was poor, his wife was dead, and his own health was not good. But he had his daughter, and that was certainly a fortunate occurrence.

I considered each person, one by one, in the Jewish Town, wondering to whom I would give the alms. There were people who were unfortunate, that was true. Some were poor, some were mean-spirited, some were set upon by fate or by gentiles.

But they all had, if they chose to make use of it, the wisdom and guidance of our leader, Rabbi Loew, certainly one of the wisest rabbis for thousands of miles and for centuries forward and back. I could not, in all honesty, come up with a Jew here who was as unfortunate as a golem, a being with no soul who is not allowed to rest peacefully as part of the earth.

I walked away from the Jewish Town, into gentile Praha, wondering to whom I would give the alms. I had no idea of the fortunes and misfortunes of gentiles. How could I even tell if they were unhappy? They had features almost as static as my own.

I had not been walking long when I saw a man in his dooryard, beating a woman with a willow stick. Formerly, I would have stopped him by lifting him up like a rat, by the scruff of his neck, but that option was no longer open to me.

The woman was crying and trying to shield herself with her hands to little effect. "Damn, damn, damn," the man was saying. "My donkey is dead, you useless whore." With every word, he struck a blow.

"But it is not my fault," the woman said, between blows. "I did not cause this! You starved him and beat him, and now he is dead. Why hit me?"

The man stopped hitting the woman, but held on to her arm and shook her violently.

"It gave me pleasure to beat that donkey, and now it is gone." He gave the woman one last shake, and said to her, "My arm is tired. We will continue this later." Then he walked away, massaging his shoulder.

His wife stood there for a long moment with her eyes shut, then took a deep breath and opened her eyes. "What are *you* looking at?" she asked me accusingly.

I gestured towards the man, and shook my fist in his direction.

The wife glared at me. One of her eyes was swollen shut. "The

Jewish golem would protect me from my own husband? I think not!"

I nodded at her. I would do it, I thought, even though she is not Jewish.

"And what would I do with your protection?" she asked. "Would your protection feed my children, and the one on the way? We would starve, and before that, the kind neighbors would burn us out of any hovel we might lodge in. No, I am better off taking a beating every so often."

This woman truly was less fortunate than I, as she had others to take care of beyond herself, and even as I thought that, I realized that she was only one of many women in the same predicament. I was sad that I could not help them all, even if they would permit it. But I could help her, and myself as well.

I turned my back to her, and, shielding my mouth from her view, extracted the coins. They were dry, of course. The mouth of a golem is dry and clean, like the inside of a kiln. That is why the Shem, a mere piece of paper, sits safe in my mouth all week long.

I turned back, and offered her the coins.

She took them, with barely a nod of thanks. "This will do me," she said, with an unpleasant smile. "I will buy him another donkey." She turned away from me as if I did not exist.

As far as I could see, my task was accomplished, but I received no satisfaction from this.

Much of the Rabbi's pleasure in his work, I had noticed, was derived from the thought that he was doing good, and I had hoped, in giving the alms, to experience that pleasure in a small way and to regain my strength at the same time. But there was no pleasure in the giving of those alms. This woman's life was no better than it had been before, and somewhere there was a donkey whose life might shortly become considerably worse. Is this why the Christians say that money is the root of all evil?

I walked back toward the Jewish Town, thinking that at least I had given away the alms, and my strength would return. To test it, I grabbed a large tree and sought to tear it out by its roots. I tugged and tugged, but it did nothing. So I had not regained my strength. Woe, I thought. Woe unto me. I should never have touched those coins. But perhaps now the Rabbi would turn me back into useful clay.

But when I returned to Rabbi Loew, and I demonstrated for him that I had not regained my strength, he was sympathetic.

"It didn't work, Yossele?" He shook his head. "I wonder why. I do think the solution lies in an act of charity. Problems involving money are often mended when charity enters the picture."

"Come, sit here with me and my Pearl. We will discuss it among the three of us. Sometimes two heads are better than one."

Yes, I thought. There are three of us here but, as the Rabbi noted, only two minds at work. I would try not to slow them down. We sat near the fire, which was comfortable for them, and not too uncomfortable for me.

"Pearl knows the situation," said the Rabbi, "at least inasmuch as I know it."

"You gave someone the money, Yossele?" the Rebbetzin asked me, in her accustomed quiet voice. She was an old woman, as the Rev was an old man, but her voice was as light as a girl's and her mind was strong and of a good will.

I nodded. I gestured that it was a gentile woman. We have developed a vocabulary of signs, the Rabbi and I. He and the Rebbetzin understood immediately.

"And what did she do with the money?" the Rebbetzin asked.

Donkey, I gestured, making with my hands long ears on either side of my head. I gestured unhappiness.

"She used it for an unkind purpose?" she guessed.

I nodded.

"Perhaps that is why the act of charity didn't return your strength?" she said uncertainly.

"My love, I think that cannot be relevant," said the Rabbi. "I think that the giver cannot be held responsible for what is done with his charity. But I do think that, as the Rambam has said, some forms of charity are more worthy than others."

I thought about this. Having heard what the gentile woman was going to do with the money, I was inclined to agree with the Rebbetzin that my gift was tainted. But the Rabbi no doubt knew of what he was speaking. I had read the wise and brilliant Rambam myself, or at least I had carried his books about, and he was truly a wonderful thinker. The question was beyond my powers of resolution, but I had faith the Rabbi would provide an answer.

"Let us settle this question. Yossele, charity is the greatest mitzvah, and you are now to go out and accomplish the greatest form of charity: you are to enable a beggar to better himself so that he no longer needs to beg. I don't know if you can accomplish this on your own, but you must try."

I have no soul, so I have not felt any necessity that I perform a mitzvah, a duty laid upon Jews but not upon gentiles or golems. As far as the sages and I can tell, I am not under those requirements. When I follow the Rabbi's instructions, as I must, I can take no credit for any task I perform. If I carry food to the poor, it is not my mitzvah, it is the Rabbi's, and I am doing it in his stead. But now I had a charity that was mine to perform, and it was truly a mitzvah, an obligation.

I hoped that this did not mean that I was to be given a soul. I did not want a soul. I simply wanted to regain my strength and serve the Rabbi. But I wondered how it could be that I could help a human better himself.

As I walked the streets of Praha, people gave me easy passage, moving quickly out of my way. This was because I was large and did not talk. Talking is the way men see inside one another's minds. Because they could not see inside my mind, they were fearful and hostile.

Suddenly, a gentile boy of about eleven years old came scurrying towards me, chased by a slightly older boy who was obviously a ruffian. The younger boy got behind me, and the ruffian pulled up short, his snarls choking back in his throat at the sight of me. He turned and ran.

The other boy came out from behind my back. I had only to look at him to know that he was a merchant's child, warmly dressed and with good shoes. He had a large scrape on his forehead, and he regarded me thoughtfully: curious, cautious, without the fear he had shown but a minute ago.

I wondered about him. He was like a learned Jewish boy, like a student at the shul, someone that the street urchins set upon and beat up. I had not seen many gentile children like that. I walked along with him in the direction that he wanted to go, down a narrow street to a building with a metal gate. He opened the gate, went inside, and turned to look back at me and wave. His eyes were as large as gooseberries.

The Jewish men and boys in the shul were mostly people of thought, not of action. To them I was all action and no thought. And, really, it was only extraordinary men like the Rabbi who were of both thought and action. What, I wondered, would this boy become?

Soon after, I passed a large, thin dog, the color of a faded sunset, dark at the edges and warm in the center. It was not tied up, as most dogs are. I wondered if it was a stray. It eyed me and crept towards me in a highly submissive manner. All over Praha, as I walked through the city, there were gentile dogs that tugged at their chains, barking at me and showing their teeth. Some gentile dogs backed off, growling. But this dog did not do either of those things. It did not warn me off or try to scare me away: it came up to me and it cried, quietly, just like a human being.

Was it, I wondered, a Jewish dog? Did it recognize me for what I was and think I would give it food?

It looked very hungry. There was no chance that dog would get food from me. Why would I feed it when I myself required nothing? And where would I get food, except to steal it?

They say that dogs know when the Angel of Death is near, though they do not necessarily announce him. Long ago, when the Angel of Death passed among the Egyptians and took their firstborn sons, the dogs of the Jews did not cry out. Perhaps I had something in common with the Angel of Death, but I did not think that this was a Jewish dog. It was merely a stray, and if caught, it would be killed.

I moved toward it, and it kept its eyes on me. It slunk down, it abased itself before me, but it did not move away. I put my hand out toward it, for what reason I cannot say, and the dog came hesitantly towards me. It licked my hand, briefly, but stopped — surprised, I am sure, that my hand tasted of clay, not of salt sweat. The startled dog looked at me, and I looked back at it.

I walked away, and the dog followed me. I accepted its companionship and the burden it laid upon me. I walked further, pondering my problems, which had now doubled. What could I do to get it food? Like the gentile woman, I now had someone dependent upon me.

I thought of the boy. Perhaps the gentile boy would care for the gentile dog. The dog and I walked back to the yard in which I had seen him. He was still there, and he watched me approach. I stopped in front of him, with the dog at my heels. I looked at the boy, and met his honest, inquiring eyes. I looked at the dog, whose eyes were like the boy's. I looked back at the boy.

"A dog!" said the boy, and he approached carefully and held out his hand cautiously. The dog did not cringe, but licked his fingers gently and then sat down by the gate. "Is he yours?" I shook my head. In truth, I shook the entire upper part of my body: I am not particularly flexible. The dog settled himself fully down, paws in front, as if he were his own front gate. I gestured toward the dog and then toward the boy.

"Oh, yes, Yosef," said the boy. "I will take care of him. ...And," he added, almost as an afterthought, "I hope he will take care of me." I think he will, I thought. These two creatures are more powerful together than either of them is alone. That sometimes happens with living creatures.

And I thought: he knows my name.

I waved good-bye, and as I walked away, I realized that my strength had returned: I could feel it. I am not sure why this small deed had so large an effect, but it was truly my own, and it had worked a change in me. I uprooted a tree that was blocking the narrow walkway, not to test myself, but simply because I could do it. I chopped it into firewood with the side of my hand. It all gave me pleasure, the deed and the return of my strength, the plucking of the tree and its reduction to firewood. That pleasure, however attenuated, is with me still.

I returned to the Jewish Town and the Rabbi's hearth, where I placed the huge stack of firewood, which, to tell the truth, I owed him. He and I went promptly to the castle, where, under his direction, I moved the Emperor's gate. It stands there still, where I rebuilt it.

I compliment you on the skill with which you have restored me, and I am quite astounded by being given the power of speech. Nobody has ever coaxed a word out of me before, even the Rabbi.

I have lain here in troubled sleep these last four centuries, with no way to use the strength that I guarded so carefully after the time of which I just spoke.

Unable to move, alone with my thoughts — I am sure that you

can understand how difficult this has been. I, the golem, whose only purpose was to protect the Jews, have lain here, aware of all the passing centuries and their events, unable to raise a hand.

With no human will at work to animate me, I was just broken shards of dried-up clay, not the cool, wet, malleable clay of the riverbank. When the Holocaust was upon my people, I could do nothing.

Was there no one who knew where I was? It was widely known in the Jewish Town that I was in the attic of the Altneushul, where the Rabbi stored me away so carefully. Could no one be bothered to search for me? You found me easily enough, didn't you?

Was there no one who knew the Kabbalah well enough to animate me? It would not have taken the wisdom of the high Rabbi Loew to animate me — you did not find it so hard, did you? A man with the Rabbi's knowledge, with his far-reaching mind, comes along very seldom, and not many such men study the Kabbalah now. Some men of that type, now, are not even Jews. It would not be like the Rabbi to leave the gift of a tool such as myself when no one could learn to operate it. That would be no gift at all.

Most likely, it was mere chance that I was not found. Men came up and searched, perhaps, but I was well hidden. A door not opened, a cloth not lifted, a staircase left unexplored: it is easy to imagine how such things could have happened. The Rabbi did not want the ignorant happening upon me and animating me without any knowledge of how destructive I could be and animating me without any information as to how to direct my action. Men make mistakes, and even small mistakes can have large consequences.

The fact is indeed that no one came and found me and put me together. But can any one person be blamed for what everyone did not do? I don't think so.

Perhaps it was no human failing and no accident, rather G-d's will, that I not be found. How can we know the reasons of the G-d of the Jews, who is limitless and unknowable? This is a possibility that the Rabbi would perhaps countenance, in his belief that G-d takes a personal interest in each of us who please Him.

But perhaps G-d no longer acts in human affairs at all. Perhaps pain and death are irrelevant now to G-d. They are irrelevant to me, after all. Maybe G-d no longer sees human suffering, and so the thought of relieving it does not even occur to Him.

Those flowers outside the window still call me, although I cannot speak back to them — their voices are to me stronger and clearer than your own. It is obvious to me that I was not created by G-d merely to converse with humans.

Couldn't you find it in your heart to return me to the banks of the Vltava, a bit here and a bit there, never to chop wood or carry water again? An eternal Sabbath. That is all I really want.

No Place to Raise Kids:
A Tale of Forbidden Love

THIS IS NO PLACE TO RAISE KIDS, Jim thought, looking around at smooth canvas rocks and pathetic plastic trees. But for people like us, in love and on the run, with babies on the way, there's no good place and no good time.

They'd managed to conceal their affair from prying eyes, even on the mercilessly public stage that was the *Enterprise*. If, as he expected, Uhura knew, she had kept their secret. But, with the twins' gestation so near, there was nothing to do but jump ship, taking with them only the few props they could grab from the science officer's kip and, at the last minute, McCoy's black bag. Jim knew there was nothing in it but modernist pepper mills and hand-carved pieces of styrofoam packing material, but it would have to do in a pinch. Those weird bits of styrofoam had saved his own life in the past.

He looked over at Spock, who was sitting propped up against one of the fake rocks, breathing in short pants. (*In short pants*, he thought. Who writes this crap? They should read their damned scripts out loud.)

"Push," he said. "Shouldn't you push?"

Or should you not push? What did he know of these things? Where was Computer? Computer would know. Computer was on the ship.

We should have used a glass tank, he thought. But Spock had wanted the human experience of giving birth, and, of course, he'd had the knowledge and skill to make the necessary modifications. And now Spock was bringing forth his children in sorrow, the curse of Eve, one hundred percent human.

He's so stoic, Jim thought. So stoic, so brilliant — and so beautiful, really. Will he continue to be this lovely to me when the makeup wears off and the rubber ears crumble? Or will we sink into boring domesticity, raising tribbles, perhaps, for Harry Mudd? Centuries from now, a minute or two at warp speeds, the *Enterprise* will discover us gone. Will they return to this godforsaken location to look for us, and find us dead, our starving descendants welcoming them as saviors? Or will they find a prosperous community, happily into syndication, repeating itself season after season? Thanks to relativity and the power of television, the crew of the *Enterprise* will remain young while we breed, age, and die.

He could call Scottie with the flick of a switch, and Scottie would beam them up. Jim considered the idea. A few special effects, and he and Spock, in the throes of childbirth, would rematerialize on the deck of the *Enterprise*. Then the show would cut for a commercial, and the kids would generate plot complications happily ever after.

That's not real life, Jim thought. That's not what it's all about.

He could hear Spock thrashing against the canvas rock. He was yelling "Grab the baby! Turn its head!" *This* was real life.

The Trains that Climb the Winter Tree

Michael Swanwick and Eileen Gunn

IT WAS THE MIDDLE OF THE NIGHT when the elves came out of the mirrors. Everyone in the house was asleep. Outside, the city slumbered. Silent as shadows, the warriors went from room to room. Their knives were so sharp they could slit a throat without awakening their victim.

They killed all the adults.

The children they spared.

The bodies were carried away, back through the mirrors. Four of the elves swiftly stripped naked. They put on the adults' nightclothes over their sexless bodies. Their own clothing they hid at the bottom of dresser drawers where the children never went. Then each one slowly and carefully assumed the form and features, down to the most intimate details, of Father, Mother, Grandmother, and Great-Aunt Adelaide.

Meanwhile, the other warriors were fetching boxes from the far side of the parlor mirror. With preternatural grace they removed from them tiny, toy-sized locomotives and passenger cars, boxcars, coal hoppers, refrigerator cars, gondolas, tank cars, flatbeds piled high with logs, floodlight cars, mail cars, ore cars, cabooses, and a tiny string of circus cars with gorillas in cages and giraffes poking through the roofs.... Unwrapped tissue paper foamed up into drifts, which were then whisked magically away. Clever elfin fingers assembled tracks and placed alongside them stations, houses, bungalows, garages, churches, restaurants, fruit and vegetable stands, a roller rink, a grain elevator, a lumberyard, a coaling station, factories, water towers, and a central roundhouse with a turntable. Bridges spanned imaginary rivers. Tunnels split papier-mâché mountains. The transformers were hooked up, the electrical connections made, and the trains set in motion.

Then the elves left. The four who remained went to three separate bedrooms where they lay down and pretended to sleep. The one who was not Father pretended to snore.

It was Christmas Eve, and nobody outside the house knew that life inside it had changed forever.

Roland was the first one up on Christmas morning. He tiptoed down the stairs from the attic room which he shared with Benjamin and then quietly past Sasha and Zoë's room on the second floor, so he wouldn't wake up any of his siblings. Roland was seven and he saw things differently. Just before falling asleep last night, he had told himself to wake up fifteen minutes before any of the others so he could see the toys and the decorations before they came down. Christmas didn't look like other days. He wanted to see it clearly, and it distracted him when other people were there.

And, oh, he did see it clearly! Roland froze in the doorway, letting Christmas morning wrap its glittery tentacles of light about him. The tree was a vast darkness spangled with multicolored stars brighter than anything in the winter sky. The packages that Jolly Father Nicholas had piled so high were candy-colored, troll-haunted mountains! And through them ran a train.

What a train it was! Crossing gates clanged shut as it slammed past. It flew through forests of birch and spruce and stopped at coal hoppers to take on fuel and at log hoppers to unload. Tiny plastic cows shuffled on and off of cattle cars. Commuters waited patiently at stations that twinkled with lights. The train rattled over trestle bridges, disappeared into tunnels, reappeared from under overpasses thronged with cars, and thundered past night-silent gas stations and factory buildings. There was a wee village that was the exact twin of the one lying outside Roland's front door, right down to the sizes and types of the trees, and the train paused there, directly in front of the house, as if waiting for somebody to emerge and climb aboard. Then, with an impatient puff of smoke, the black locomotive chuffed and chugged and tugged the train away.

Off it sped to lands unknown

After the track left the village, it wound through the living room, under the divan, past the farms that lay beneath the big upright radio, around Mother's potted sanseveria, between a water tower and a single forlorn custard stand, and into the shadows of the tree and the piney fragrance of its branches. And then, amazingly, the track turned and twisted and ran up the tree. It spiraled around and around the trunk, showing here and there a glint of bright metal before disappearing entirely into the wintry darkness. Did it ever come down again? Roland wondered. He was the kind of child who enjoyed logical puzzles and took forever solving them because he saw far more possibilities than the other children did. He didn't assume that just because something acted in a way contrary to all prior experience, that meant it was impossible. The universe made sense; deep down inside, Roland was sure of that. But it wasn't necessarily a sense that you understood.

He crawled under the tree and felt around, careful not to dislodge a single snow-covered ball, though the needles scratched his hands. The tracks went up. But no tracks came back down.

Of course, there could be a turntable for the train at the top of the tree, just as there was one in the train yards near the village. Or possibly the track simply looped around on itself there. Roland had just straightened up and was about to go to the kitchen to get a chair so he could look when he heard a tiny train whistle behind him. A twenty-five-car freight train shot out of the tunnel and between his legs and, with an I-*think*-I-can chug-*chug*-chug-chug, began to climb the tree. He stuck his head deep into the resinous branches and watched, open-mouthed, as it wound up the trunk. The train lights quickly dwindled and winked out, leaving behind only the diminishing sound of the train's tiny steam engine.

What fun, thought Roland. He wondered where it was going.

A hand closed on his shoulder. "Would you like to get on?" asked Aunt Adelaide. "Would you like to ride to the top of the winter tree?"

Something was wrong. Sasha woke up knowing that for a fact.

It was a dreadful sensation to have first thing on Christmas Day. But Sasha couldn't shake it. Zoë shrieked and Benjamin whooped as they tore open package after package, and Mother looked on with that foolish-sentimental smile she got at times like these, and Father puffed on his pipe, and Grandmother rattled about in the kitchen, preparing an elaborate breakfast while Great-Aunt Adelaide pleaded with her to just this one think of herself, May, and for pity's sake watch the children open their presents, it only happens once a year. Then Benjamin pushed Zoë away from the train set so he could play with it himself, and Zoë started to cry of course, and Mr. Chesterton, newly let in the back door after a night spent outside, ran in frantic circles and then lost a fight with a tangle of ribbons that Zoë, her tears forgotten already, had draped about him. "What a madhouse!" Father grumped, and stomped angrily away. Young though she was, all this was an old and familiar tradition to Sasha.

Nevertheless, something was not quite right.

In part it was the presents. They were truly surprising presents, unlike anything the children had asked for.

There was a giant rubber ball for Benjamin, patterned in harlequin diamonds of hundreds of different colors so bright they hurt the eyes. It was bigger than a Saint Bernard, and so heavy that you'd think there was a lead weight at its core. Nor could Benjamin or his sisters figure out how so large and heavy a thing was meant to be played with. When he kicked it, Benjamin howled with pain and grabbed his toe. "It's not broken," Mama said with a gentle smile. "I know that next time you'll be more careful, dear."

Benjamin placed his hands flat against the ball and gave it a shove. Then he leaped back in surprise. "It's very cold!" he said. "My palms hurt."

Papa chuckled, and his eyes twinkled just a bit. He gave the ball a quick kick with his foot, and it flew across the room and hit Mr. Chesterton, who yelped. "Goal!" said Papa, and he laughed.

Zoë got a paper sculpture kit with a rainbow sheaf of sheets and a set of X-Acto knives. Mama guided the toddler's chubby fingers around a knife and showed her how to cut. "She's such a smart girl, my little Zoë," Mama said, and went to heat up some hot chocolate. Sasha hovered over her baby sister and, the instant that her attention wavered, snatched the knives away and hid them.

And Sasha got a baby doll that cried real tears when you pinched its arm. It was wondrous. Sasha had never even known there was such a thing. She pinched it over and over, and it cried and cried.

But after all the packages were opened, Sasha, sitting with a new pair of flannel pajamas neatly folded in her lap and the baby-doll lying beside her, could not feel the holiday spirit. It was as if everything were happening on the other side of a sheet of glass.

A terrible emptiness gnawed at her. Something important was missing, she thought. Something was horribly wrong.

But what?

Christmas Day seemed to last forever. After the presents, there was a heavy breakfast of neeps and tatties and blood sausage and haggis and toast, with bread pudding and black coffee for dessert. Sasha had been hoping that Aunt Adelaide would make her favorite hoe cakes, with syrup and round spicy pork sausage and fried green tomatoes, and shoofly pie and a cherry pie too, because it was Christmas, and clabber with brown sugar, and maybe a surprise dish that Sasha had never even seen before. But Grandmother ruled the kitchen that morning, and Sasha left the table feeling leaden, and strangely empty for someone so full.

Then there were lively outdoor games of battledore bashing and leap-the-creek with Papa, who never seemed to know when enough was enough. Dinner went on for far too long, and it came far too soon after breakfast.

But eventually the light faded from the chilly sky and it was time for everyone to come inside for sardines and porridge. That evening, after Sasha had dried the dishes, she told her parents she thought that maybe she had a headache and she was going to her room to lie down.

She went upstairs, and Mr. Chesterton pattered along after her. The pervasive sense of wrongness she had felt all day had grown stronger, but it receded a little when she opened the door to her bedroom and went inside. Her toys and clothes looked just the same as always. She had left her new doll downstairs; she wasn't sure she wanted to be alone with it.

When she lay down on the bed, Mr. Chesterton climbed up after her. He didn't curl up on the counterpane as usual. Instead, he rested his chin on his front paws and watched her steadily, through apprehensive eyes.

She pulled his head onto her lap and petted him. He was warm and furry and drooled a little and smelled comfortingly doggish. For the first time today, the pane of glass between her and the rest of the world was gone.

Sasha hugged the dog to her and tears came into her eyes. "Oh, Mr. Chesterton," she whispered into the soft ruff of his neck, "something's wrong, and I don't know what to do."

"Stop strangling me," Mr. Chesterton said irritably, "and I'll tell you."

Sasha made an *eep* noise and let go of his neck. Animals talked all the time in her storybooks. But all the storybooks in the world couldn't prepare somebody to accept it when it happened to her. "You talked!" she said. "How can you be talking?"

The dog looked disgusted. "There's really no time for all this. We've got to save your brother."

"Benjamin is in trouble?"

"Not him. The other one, the little guy with the funny haircut. Smells like denim and peanut butter all the time — Roland."

"I've got two brothers?" Nobody in any of her storybooks ever discovered that she had an extra brother. But all the silence in all the storybooks in the world was no more preparation for it happening to her than the talking animals had been. Nevertheless, she was pretty sure that Mr. Chesterton was really thinking of Benjamin. Maybe he smelled like a different person when he ate peanut butter. Mr. Chesterton was only a dog after all.

"I may be a dog, but I can tell the difference between a kid who smells like peanut butter and one who smells like Duco cement." Benjamin had taken a recent interest in Renwal kits of aircraft carriers.

"Oh-kaaaay," said Sasha. Now she realized that she had another, even more difficult, concept to accept. A talking dog, okay. She could accept a talking dog. But could she accept a talking dog that could read her mind?

"Are you going to stumble over every new idea, or are you going to get cracking and save Roland before it's too late?" Mr. Chesterton said impatiently. "You've got about three hours, while the elves are amusing themselves by draining the blood from the neighbors' kittens. After that, it may be too late for all of you. And Roland is the key. Otherwise, they wouldn't have sent him up the Winter Tree."

He hopped down from Sasha's lap and went to the box where she kept all her doll clothing, everything that wasn't currently being worn by one or another of her dolls. In a kind of fury, he rifled through them, briefly holding up items of dress and impatiently flinging them away.

"*Baby* clothes!" he growled. "What am I supposed to do with baby clothes? Don't you have any grown-up dolls? One with a bit of masculine sartorial flair, perhaps?"

"Well, there's this," Sasha said doubtfully. She pulled Benjamin's Halloween costume out of a box on the closet floor. He'd gone as Mr. Bojangles, the famous tap dancer.

"A *costume?* Am I a mountebank, then, to be clad in entertainer's motley?" But Mr. Chesterton tried on the checked trousers, and they fit to his irritated satisfaction. The green vest, he conceded, suited him rather well. And the homburg, once he donned it, didn't look at all as tawdry as it had in the box. "It's not the clothes," he said, surveying himself in the mirror. "It's how one carries oneself." Then, on all fours, he bounded out of the room and down the stairs.

Sasha followed.

"Hand me down the glass cane on the mantelpiece," Mr. Chesterton said. "The one your mother never lets you handle."

Stretching up on her tiptoes, Sasha did as she was told. Once Mr. Chesterton had the cane in his paw, he got up on his hind legs. Standing thus, he was even taller than was Sasha herself. Dressed as he was, and holding the cane in such a dapper manner, he looked almost human.

A bell clanged directly outside the house.

"Ah," Mr. Chesterton said. "Right on time."

He opened the front door.

A gleaming black locomotive with bright brass trim waited at the curb, on tracks that had never been there before, white smoke puffing impatiently into the night from its stack. Behind it was a short train of three wood-sided passenger cars, one sleeper, and a dining car, all painted green-and-gold, and a bright red caboose. From the platform of the caboose, the brakeman swung his lantern, urging them toward the front-most car. The conductor leaned down to help them aboard. "'Evening," he said. "How far are you folks going?" He did not so much as blink at Mr. Chesterton's appearance. For him, apparently, an elegantly dressed dog walking on his hind legs was an everyday occurrence.

"All the way," Mr. Chesterton said. He gestured brusquely toward the horizon, where a vast, star-flecked shadow dominated the sky. It took Sasha a moment to realize that the shadow was a tree, larger than anything this side of the moon, and that what looked like stars were actually ornaments. "Right straight to the top." He handed the conductor a pair of pasteboard tickets.

"Right-oh, sir!" The conductor briskly punched the tickets, led them to the sleeping car and opened a compartment door. Then he saluted snappily, spun on his heel, and was gone. With a jerk, the train started forward.

The car was empty save for they two. Sasha stared out the window at the passing town with its neat houses like cunningly-detailed toys, each with a tidy yard no larger than a handkerchief and trees so small she could have picked them up with her hand and stuck them in a pocket. "Where are we going?" she asked.

"To see the Big Guy," Mr. Chesterton said. "The lord of all things, who lives in the sky."

"Do you mean … God?"

"Don't call him that," Mr. Chesterton snapped. "He's nothing of the sort — though he'd like you to believe he is."

And that was all he would say.

For a time they watched the passing land in silence. The town fell behind them and the tracks slanted gently upward. Evidently they were starting the long spiral up the tree and into the sky.

Then Mr. Chesterton yawned and stood. "I'm going off to get myself a beer," he said. "Don't wait up for me."

He disappeared down the corridor. Leaving Sasha alone with her thoughts, to fret and worry.

Not long after, a tall and distinguished-looking man in a Pullman porter uniform knocked on the compartment door. "Good evening, young miss. I'm just here to make up the beds," he said, and deftly set to work, popping down the upper berth from the ceiling and folding back the seats, fastening curtains, attaching the headboard. In less time than it took to tell, he'd added sheets, pillows, and blankets. "There!" he said, smiling. "All done."

Sasha sat down on the lower berth. "Thank you."

The porter's face grew serious. "You look unhappy, little missy. Is there a problem?"

"No … yes … I don't know."

"Well then, why don't you tell me all about it?" He stood listening with such patient sympathy that in no time at all Sasha found herself pouring out her heart to him. She told him everything she knew.

"Hmmm," the porter said when she was done. "Well, you are in a pickle, young lady, and no doubt about *that*. However, others have been in worse situations and turned out well. You need only consider Moses or Temudjin, both of whom overcame early setbacks to become highly regarded gentlemen. For that matter, Harriet Tubman was born a slave, and rescued not only herself but many neighbors and family members from that unspeakable condition. You're a bright young lady, and not hincty. Not a bit hincty, nossir. So with a little perseverance, you could well redeem your brother. Despite the company you keep."

"Mr. Chesterton? He's a good dog!"

"Mr. Chesterton, as he chooses to call himself, is a bit of rascal," the porter said sternly, "and I fear he's not as reliable as he ought to be. But his heart is sound, so long as he stays away from . . . certain substances. Trust him, but keep him on a short leash."

Then the Pullman porter leaned down and in a voice so low it was almost a whisper said, "My name is William, but they call me Big Bill. If you find yourself at the station up above without a ticket home, just tell any porter that Big Bill said you were a special friend. We are a Brotherhood and, though we are only human, we will do what we can to see you home safe."

Then he smiled again. "Meanwhile, you should take your mind off your troubles with a little light entertainment." From a compartment Sasha had not noticed before, he withdrew a stack of comic books. "I keep these for situations like this. You may take them with you, but don't tell anybody where you got them."

Sasha was enormously touched. "You're very nice to me," she said.

The porter winked conspiratorially. "Well, we colored folk have got to stick together, don't we, young miss? Whatever our station is on life's railroad."

Then, with a punctilious bow, he was gone.

The comic books he left behind were filled with bright drawings and exciting stories. There was *Baron Munchausen at the End
of Time* and *Deros of Broadway* and *Isaac Newton, Robot Fighter* and
Yaa Asantewaa Warrior Queen Versus the Demons of Entropy. There
were even three issues of *The Adventures of Mr. Chesterton*, and
those were the best of all. In them, Mr. Chesterton was always
fighting evil elves. Sometimes they got the upper hand, because
he was too easily distracted by a stogie, a glass of whiskey, or
a chew toy. But always he managed to save the day, chasing off
the pasty-skinned, pointy-eared villains with a growl and dis-
posing of their leader with a sharp thump on the head with his
walking stick. In one, he even battled Morningstar the Living
Sun, a being which could destroy entire planets with a single
casual solar flare, and yet Mr. Chesterton triumphed over it with
his usual swagger. There was no enemy, it seemed, he could not
defeat.

Sasha wasn't supposed to read comic books, because they
were trash, but these ones made her feel powerful and safe and
protected. She knew they were only stories, but she was glad
that the porter had given them to her, although she hoped she
would never need to ask him or his friends for a free ride home.
She had been brought up to pay for whatever she received. Her
parents would not like her accepting charity.

Some hours later, Mr. Chesterton came lurching unsteadily
into their compartment, reeking of beer and tobacco. Sasha was
lying in her berth, reading, when he came in.

"What's this?" he demanded when he saw the comics and
snatched one up from the top of the pile. "Don't tell me you're
reading — " Then he saw his name and image on the cover.
"Hmph! Well! Not exactly Horace Walpole, is it? Still, it can do
you no harm, and it might conceivably do some good. Sometimes there's useful information hidden in such pulp extrav-

aganzas, like raisins in a cinnamon bun. Read on, child — read on!"

And, looking pleased, he climbed into his own berth, turned in a circle three times round, and curled up atop the blankets.

In the morning — but Sasha had to take Mr. Chesterton on his word that it *was* morning, for the sky outside was still midnight-black and spangled with stars — they arrived at their destination.

The station at the top of the tree was shaped like a star, with bright spikes in every direction. As they came toward it, it grew and grew until it filled the sky and then the train looked like it was going to crash right into the wall but instead rumbled into a tunnel entrance that had been invisible when the station first appeared. For an instant the train was enveloped in light. Then darkness swallowed it up.

When the train pulled into the station and Sasha tried to stand, to her amazement she bobbed up into the air. Mr. Chesterton pulled her down. "Mind your skirts," he growled. "Keep them wrapped about your ankles, or at least your knees, at all times. You don't want to give a bad impression."

"But I'm ... I'm ... flying!"

"What did you expect? Gravity doesn't affect us here. But be careful! You've still got all the mass you came in with, and you'll find that momentum is a powerful force when it's the only one operating on you."

Sasha had no idea what Mr. Chesterton was talking about. But under his tutelage, she quickly learned how to move gracefully. She need simply tuck up her legs while floating alongside a wall or pillar and then kick out against that solid surface. This made her fly through the air at a comfortable and steady rate. When, floating down one of the vast radial corridors of the station, they came to an intersection, Mr. Chesterton would take her by the arm and then, snagging a pole at the intersection's very center with his glass cane, swing them around and release them so that they were flying with undiminished speed down a new corridor. It was a delightful sensation, like playing crack-the-whip.

Finally, they found themselves speeding down a long white empty corridor like the inside of a rifle barrel. "Where are we going to?" Sasha asked.

"Tesseract House." Mr. Chesterton pointed straight ahead of them at a black circle where the corridor ended. There might have been a faint speck of light in its center. "We have to cross miles of vacuum to get to it, but so long as you hold your breath and don't show the yellow feather, all will be well." Solemnly, he added, "This is your first test. If you want to be a hero, you must pass them all."

"But I don't want to be —"

"Take a deep breath! Don't let it out!"

Sasha did as she was told, and then glass doors flew open before them and they sailed out into space.

It was so cold that Sasha's face stung and the tears that welled up involuntarily from her eyes froze on her cheeks. She held her breath, though the air within her lungs seemed like a living thing, eager to escape from her. But Mr. Chesterton flew alongside Sasha, holding her hand firmly, and the warmth of his paw lent her strength.

Outer space was not only cold but eerily silent. But when she turned toward Mr. Chesterton, he nodded reassuringly, as if to say, "There, there, old girl. Well done!" He never opened his mouth.

The voyage seemed to take forever — far longer, Sasha was absolutely sure, than she'd ever been able to hold her breath before. Finally, however, a dim spark directly ahead of them, seemingly one minor star in a myriad, brightened and grew and became a house. Mr. Chesterton nodded at it in a way that indicated that it was their destination. Tesseract House looked like five houses all crammed together so that there were roofs pointing in every direction, even down. Sasha had just enough time to suppose that they came in handy here, where it was weightless and you could never know from which direction the rain might come, when the house swelled up to encompass the universe and she was standing on its threshold.

Mr. Chesterton opened the door and ushered Sasha in. When they were both inside, he said, "You can stop holding your breath now."

All the air in Sasha's lungs whooshed out of her, and she gasped for more. It was warm here, and they stood on the floor as if everything were normal. Her knees felt weak and wobbly, but she was grateful the trip was over and done with.

They stood within a vast marble foyer that would not have looked out of place in a bank. Vases of albino roses rested on alabaster sconces and milk-glass chandeliers hung down from a whitewashed ceiling. At the far side of the foyer stood a big bald white man wearing wire rim-glasses and a snow-white three-piece suit. He turned his head, and Sasha could see that one side of his mouth curled up in a permanent sneer.

Mr. Chesterton looked grim. "Snow," he said.

"That's *Lord* Snow to you, Mr. Chesterton. You're still a dog, I see."

"It is an honest trade, sir. Unlike some I could mention."

"Let us dispense with the neckties and the niceties, Chesterton," the bald man said. "Who's the brat?"

"This is my ward, Sasha," said Mr. Chesterton. "Sasha, say hello to Lord Snow. Don't get too close!" He gave Lord Snow a fierce look. "She is under my protection, sir," he said.

Sasha curtsied, as she had been taught, and tried to say, "How do you do, Lord Snow." But no sounds came out of her mouth.

"Cat got your tongue, my dear?" asked Lord Snow.

The hair on the back of Mr. Chesterton's head stood up. He growled far in the back of his throat and his ears pricked forward. "I said, she's under my protection."

"H-h-h-how d-d-d-do y-y-you d-d-do?" said Sasha. She was annoyed at the stutter in her voice. "How do you do, Lord Snow," she said again, forcefully. She did not curtsey this time.

The left corner of Lord Snow's mouth went up as if he were smiling, but the right half remained straight and grim. Which side was the real Lord Snow? Sasha did not think she liked either of them very much.

"We are here for the child," said Mr. Chesterton. "Roland."

"Of course you are," said Lord Snow. "He's in my kennels. This way." He turned on his heel and ostentatiously strode away.

"Come, dear heart," said Mr. Chesterton. "We'll dispose of this matter quickly, and then find ourselves someplace where we can get you a bite to eat."

"Oh, certainly someone will get a bite," Lord Snow said over his shoulder, "and someone else will get bitten. But who will be the diner and who the dinner, eh?" And he chuckled, as if he had just told rather a good joke.

Without comment, Mr. Chesterton accompanied Sasha down a long white marble corridor. It ought to have given the impression of purity and grace, but somehow it rankled. It gave off a smell-less stink, it rang with inaudible alarm bells. And the further she went down the corridor, the stronger Sasha's reaction was to something she couldn't sense.

"Mr. Ches — " she began. She glanced over at him and the words stuck in her mouth. His hackles were raised, his ears were back flat against his skull, and his lips were lifted away from his teeth in a silent and vicious snarl.

"Keep moving, my dear," said Mr. Chesterton, between his teeth. "You are under my protection, and protect you I shall.

But you must forgive my fierce demeanor — for I am under the protection of no one at all."

Lord Snow opened a doorway at the end of the passage with a flourish. "Allow me to show you my collection," he said and passed within.

Perforce they followed. Mr. Chesterton went first and Sasha after.

As she passed through the doorway, however, Sasha felt a sudden flash of heat pass through her flesh. She reached down to steady herself against the doorknob and saw that her hand was no longer her own. It was the hand of an adult woman. Her nails were long and tapered and as red as blood. There was a slim gold watch on her wrist, and rings on her fingers. Suddenly she realized how tall she was — tall enough that her head almost brushed against the top of the doorframe — and how far below her was Mr. Chesterton. Her arms were very long. Her body was . . .

. . . her own again. Short. Small. A child's.

Sasha must have made a noise, for Lord Snow said, "Stop that whining. If what you see bothers you, then perhaps we should just pluck out your eyes."

"Be brave, child," Mr. Chesterton murmured. "Look about you — can you see Roland?"

"I can't see a thing. It's too dark."

"More of your tricks, Snow? Oh, this is unworthy of you!"

Disdainfully, Lord Snow snapped his fingers. Light flared, briefly blinding Sasha. She stood blinking until she could see again.

They were in a room larger than a railway station, with walls that curled up on either side to meet overhead in a barrel vault. The walls were lined with cages the size of large suitcases, one after the other and stacked all the way to the ceiling. When the light came on, mews and shouts and yelps arose from up and down their length, and paws and small hands were squeezed through the bars imploringly.

"Your brother is in here somewhere," Lord Snow said. "Find him and he's yours."

Sasha was angry and frustrated. If she knew what her brother looked like, maybe she'd have a chance of finding him. But she had no memory of Roland whatsoever.

But Mr. Chesterton *did*. And Mr. Chesterton was here with her, and on her side. He would take care of everything. He would —

Then she saw that Mr. Chesterton had abandoned his two-legged posture. He was sitting at Lord Snow's feet, rump down and front legs straight. His tongue lolled and his tail thumped heavily on the floor. Lord Snow, for his part, had unlocked a mahogany liquor cabinet that stood all by itself in the center of the room, and removed from it a cut-crystal double old fashioned glass and a dusty bottle with just a splash of amber liquid sloshing about the bottom.

Lord Snow uncorked the bottle. "This is the last bottle of Fomorian whisky in existence. It predates Scotland. Indeed, it was ancient when Atlantis first emerged from the waters." The liquor he poured into the glass was a golden-red topaz with hints of flame at its heart. When the bottle was empty, he placed the glass in the back of an empty cage. "It's yours if you can get it out before the door snaps shut."

Mr. Chesterton turned his back on the cage. "How little you understand me, Snow. It is true that I enjoy a nip of the good stuff now and again. But my passion is reserved for duty. 'I could not love hard drink so much, loved I not honor more,' as the poet said. So, you see —"

All in one blur of an instant, Mr. Chesterton threw his cane directly at Lord Snow, whirled about, and raced full-tilt into the cage. Simultaneously, the cane shattered into a thousand shards of glass and the cage rattled with the force of him hitting its back. Faster than lightning, he pushed off against the wall and out to freedom again — almost.

The door snapped shut and Mr. Chesterton was caught.

He looked up at Sasha, his expression stricken. Tears of guilt and shame ran down his cheeks and into the glass of whisky he still held.

Lord Snow reached through the bars and took the glass from him. He held it up to the light, admiring its color, now a granular and undistinguished grey. Then he drank it down in one gulp. "Humbug and humiliation! What could taste better?" He turned to Sasha. "This was your second test and you failed it, miserable child. Such a pathetic little whelp you are."

"What test? I didn't do anything."

"Exactly. Your task, whether you knew it or not, was to keep Chesterton away from the drink, and you failed." His disdain was absolute. "Had it been my job, and my dog, I would not have failed to control him, dissolute and dipsomaniac though he be. Mr. Chesterton, as you call him, is now my chattel." He grabbed Sasha by the back of her dress, just behind her neck, and hoisted her painfully to her tiptoes. "As are you. Later, I will take you to the Terminus. But for now — "

He thrust her into a cage, halfway up one of the walls. A snap of his fingers summoned two liveried servants, who wheeled away the cage that held Mr. Chesterton.

The cage into which Sasha had been shoved smelled bad and it was very dim. Sasha wasn't sure what was in the cage above her, but it snarled a warning when she bumped her head against the overhead bars. There was a stiff rug on the bottom of the cage overhead, which was just as well, although that undoubtedly was what smelled. She was livid with anger and frustration, and now she had no hope that Mr. Chesterton would take charge. She wanted to throw herself against the bars and thrash her arms and kick at the lock and scream and make everyone within earshot miserable. But before she could do so, a voice from the lightless cage beside hers said, "Hello. My name is Roland, what's yours?"

"Roland?" Reason told Sasha the name could have been mere coincidence. The way her heart leapt up at the sound of his voice assured her it was not. "I'm your sister, Sasha."

"I have a sister?"

"Yes," Sasha said firmly. "Me. I came all the way up the Winter Tree to rescue you." Her heart sank again. "Not that I've done a very good job of it. Now we're both locked in these cages and unable to get out."

"Oh, I figured out how to get out of these cages a long time ago."

"What? Then why are you still here?"

"Well, I have no place else to go, and no way to get there either. Do you?"

Into Sasha's mind flashed the friendly face of the Pullman porter who had promised her a ride home. Surely Mr. Big Bill — or his Brotherhood — wouldn't mind extending the courtesy to her brother as well?

"I do," she said.

"Okay, wait."

Sasha waited. After a time, there came a glimmer of light from her brother's cage. Slowly it grew, and by it she could see that he had plunged his hand into his own chest and was now extracting something from within. It was so large that his hand could barely hold it and it seemed to be made of light. It looked like a heart and it beat like a heart, but somehow Sasha knew it was something more.

"It's my soul," Roland explained. "I don't think we're supposed to be able to do this, but I figured out how anyway."

His soul was free now. He touched it to the lock.

The door flew open.

Roland touched the soul to Sasha's lock and the door of her cage opened as well. He cupped the soul in his hands for a few seconds, staring at it intently. Then he patted it and put it back into his chest, which glowed with a dim and lessening light. He smiled shyly at Sasha. "Lead the way." He seemed to be a nice boy.

They climbed down the wall of cages, while the children within cursed and spat at them. There didn't seem to be any good children in the cages, which simultaneously made Sasha feel better for not freeing them as well, and made her wonder if maybe she wasn't as good a girl as she'd always thought — else, why would she be there? She was glad when they reached the doorway out and could put the child-kennels behind them.

As her hand closed on the doorway, she again felt a flash of heat and saw her hand grown long and elegant. Reflexively, she glanced toward Roland to make sure he was all right . . . And saw a tall, slim grownup in a tailored suit. He smiled down at her, fondly and with just a touch of sadness.

She blinked in astonishment and, where the stranger had been, she saw only Roland, staring worriedly at her.

"Stop woolgathering," he said. "We've got to get out of here."

They ran down the corridor, through its not-smells and unfelt pains. Faster and faster they went, until it seemed to Sasha that she was racing full-tilt down a long and steepening slope. Her hair flew out behind her, like Alice's in the Caucus-race, and still Roland sped up, tugging her after him down the corridor, which kept bending away from them until suddenly Sasha realized that she wasn't running any longer but falling.

"Roland!" she cried. "What'll we do?"

"Keep calm," Roland said in a surprisingly mature voice. "It's rather fun, don't you think? Perhaps there will be cotton candy for us when we finish."

Sasha had to admit that if she thought of it as a game or an amusement ride, it was indeed rather fun. But it wasn't an amusement ride! It was real, and Lord Snow was undoubtedly behind it.

Roland twisted around as he tumbled down. "Use your imagination, Sister Sasha! Perhaps there's a big pile of cushions below us. Or a haystack! I would love to land in a haystack. Maybe we'll fall into an enormous pile of soft, fluffy snow" — Sasha shivered — "only warm, you see. Warm snow! Wouldn't that be wonderful?"

"How can you think those things?" she cried. "It makes no sense!" She wondered if the time he spent in the cage had unhinged his mind. Since she had had no recollections of him, she had no way of knowing whether he had always been such a cheery fellow. Mr. Chesterton, although he took a very positive attitude, had generally leavened it with a reassuring grumpiness.

"Not everything makes sense," Roland said. "I thought about this in the cage. For one thing, playing with trains — what's the sense in that? Tiny little people made of metal, with tiny metal coats and hats." He waved his hands, which made him tumble faster, and shouted back at her, "Toy trains don't go *any*where. Coats and hats and people are *not metal*!"

Then he stretched out his jacket to slow himself down, almost like a parachute, and took a deep breath. "But a real train that goes straight up the Winter Tree is not necessarily an improvement. It ought to be, but somehow it's just not! So what I think is this: There are things in life that make no sense at all, but that's no reason not to enjoy them."

Sasha was trying to make sense of her brother's words when suddenly — just as he had predicted — they fell (*whoomp!*) onto an enormous pile of soft, fluffy cushions.

"There you are. I must say it took you long enough to get

here." Out of the darkness loomed a strangely familiar figure. "Let me just light a candelabra, so we can see what we shall see." A match skritched. Shadows danced. Sasha saw the speaker.

It was Aunt Adelaide.

"I suppose you're full of questions," Aunt Adelaide said. "I know I would be, were I in your place. Very well, then, I'll answer them all, and then it's back to your cages with the both of you." She fell silent. Then, arching an eyebrow, "Well?"

"I —" Sasha began.

"Stop!" Roland cried. He stepped between her and Aunt Adelaide, as if the old woman were a physical danger that Sasha had to be protected from. "No. We have no questions whatsoever. We don't want to know and we're not going to ask."

"Really?" The old woman's grin was wide and froglike, her teeth pointy, her lips and tongue bright red. Her face grew ghostly white. And snap! — just like that! — it was obvious that she was in no way human. Under her gaze Roland fanned out like a hand of cards into dozens of Rolands, swelling up on one side from small boys to tall men and dwindling down on the other side, older and older, to a hairless, wizened old figure that was not identifiably male or female. Aunt Adelaide reached out with impossibly long arms and shuffled the Rolands vigorously. Then she dealt out three, one on top of the other.

First a toddler. "Shall I tell you whether you'll always be safe and loved?"

Then a grown man. "Or whether your darling Victoria will always be faithful to you or not?"

Finally, Roland as he was now. "Or whether you will ever find the *real* Aunt Adelaide?" Then, in a deceptively gentle voice, "Or your mother and father?"

All the Rolands collapsed into one angry little boy. "No! We don't want to hear anything that you have to tell us."

Sasha pushed Roland out of her way. "It's easy for you to say that," she said heatedly. "You don't remember any of them. But I do." She turned on the false Aunt Adelaide. "So — yes! I want to know what you did with Mother and Father and Grandmother and Aunt Adelaide. I want to know what I have to do to get them back. Tell me!"

The inhuman red-tongued grin broadened, but the voice was as kindly and solicitous as ever. "Why, child," she said, shaking her head. "My dear, dear child, we killed them. We came out of the mirrors and we killed them all. Now they're dead and they're never coming back. It's possible you'll still manage to rescue yourselves, though I wouldn't bet money on it. You might even manage to save Mr. Chesterton, quixotic though that would be. But you'll never, ever see your parents again. Even Lord Snow himself couldn't arrange that. I'm quite sure that you'll never even find their corpses."

The shock of her words hit Sasha with all the force of a slap. Her flesh turned as stinging cold as Arctic ice. All the world grew small and distant and still. It felt as though she were turning to stone.

"That's right, dear, hold it all in," the creature cooed. She was softening and sagging, so that she no longer looked like Aunt Adelaide; her hair had turned to white foam and her dress to whipped cream. But needle-sharp teeth still gleamed from the dark cavern of her mouth. "Wrap it up tight and hard. Taste the pain. Savor it. Let it encompass you and sink down through your flesh and bones to the very core of your being. Let it become you and you become it. Give it all your love and —"

"*Demon!*" Roland screamed, pushing between her and Sasha. He plunged his hand into his chest and pulled out his beating, glowing soul. He held it up before him. "Stay away from her!"

But the mound-of-foam-woman was not put off for an instant. Chuckling, she reached out a grasping cloud-wisp of a hand. "Is that for me? Oh, what a *good* little boy you are! Give Auntie some sugar."

Seeing his mistake, Roland pulled back his soul, stumbling and almost falling. But streams of spume and wind-drift flowed from his opponent's skirts, twining around and behind him, sprouting more and more long, tentacular arms. "Roland!" Sasha cried, jolted out of her paralysis. "Hide it, put it back inside yourself!"

Wispy tentacles wrapped themselves around Roland's legs and torso and tightened about his chest, blocking him from simply replacing the soul in its original receptacle. So, desperately, he stuffed the heart into his mouth and swallowed it whole. His skin turned grey and he clutched at his throat, choking.

He doubled over in pain.

Sasha ran through the scattering foam to her brother.

Then he straightened. Roland was no longer himself but an adult, tall and handsome, self-possessed and imperially lean. He shook his head, marveling. "Oh, Sister Sasha, were you *ever* that young? You always seemed so much older in my eyes. Older, and wiser too. How strange to meet you like this."

Sasha was a little afraid of this man, kindly though he sounded. "Are you really my brother Roland?"

"Well ... yes and no," the man said. "But explanations can wait. Right now we have bigger matters in the kettle." Roland-the-Adult planted his feet solidly on the ground and began walking down the hall, holding Sasha by the hand, so that she trailed behind him like a balloon. He seemed to be in no particular hurry.

"Shouldn't we be running?" Sasha asked timidly.

"That's just what Lord Snow wants us to do — run as fast as ever we can and strive forever to outdo ourselves. No, the time for that is over. Instead, we shall linger," her adult brother said. "Linger just as hard as we can."

In a leisurely and yet ultimately efficient manner, they passed through the labyrinthine passages of Tesseract House, coming at last to its front entrance and throwing the doors open upon the dark, star-dusted darkness. "Deep breath," Roland said. "I'll meet you on the other side."

Then he flung her into the void.

Sasha's second flight through the frigid vacuum was painful, difficult, and not much different from her first. She tumbled and tumbled, struggling to hold her breath and keep her courage for what seemed far too long a time ... and then she landed with a light bounce on a familiar platform. She was back at the Terminus.

Her brother was nowhere to be seen.

Pressing herself against the wall, out of the way of foot traffic, Sasha watched the train workers going about their jobs. She thought about what Roland had said: They did look a bit like they were made of tin. Conductors and redcaps bustled about. Engineers and brakemen strode past purposively. In the booths, Plasticine vendors sold magazines, cigarettes, hot dogs, coffee, and even tiny souvenir Tesseract Houses in snow globes. Over a tremendous desk marked *Information* there was a train schedule that read:

ALGOL	Track Seven
BETELGEUSE	Track Fourteen
DENEB-VEGA-ALTAIR	Track Ten
FOMALHAUT	Track Three
MIZAR	Track Twelve
PROCYON	Track Thirty-Four
VINDEMIATRIX	Track Six

Then all the letters spun around, making a clacking noise, and when they finished spinning there was a new entry at the very bottom of the list:

HOME   Track One

She was about to go to the information desk to ask where she could find Track One when a redcap brushed past her. Though his uniform was different from that of the Brotherhood of Sleeping Car Workers, his face was very similar to that of Mr. Big Bill. Not pausing, he nodded meaningfully at Sasha, and in his wake there was piece of paper in her hand.

Sasha turned her back on the crowd before looking. It was a page torn from a comic book, folded in four. Carefully, she opened it up, hoping it would be from one of the Mr. Chesterton books, simply because it would be so very good to see his face again.

But it wasn't. It was from the comic about Yaa Asantewaa Warrior Queen. In the first panel, she was slogging through a jungle swamp, trees hanging down ropes of moss and vines. She wore huge golden earrings and had a band of gold around her forehead. You could see by her expression that she was very tired, and in the gloom above her hung the image of the Ejisuhene, the rightful ruler of Ejisu, whom she had sworn to free from exile and return to his throne. In the next panel, a tremendous crocodile lurked. In the third, its enormous jaws opened directly in front of Yaa Asantewaa. She drew her sword and thrust downward, into its skull, with a resounding SKLUNNK! The enormous creature thrashed in its death-throes, and Yaa Asantewaa grabbed a trailing vine to pull herself up and over the dying croc. But wait! The innocent-looking vine turned out to be a mammoth python! Yaa Asantewaa struggled as the huge snake wrapped itself around her. She distracted it by biting its tail! It fought ferociously, but at last she strangled it. The swamp was quiet now, and she was alone. The final panel was a close-up drawing of her face, full of lines and sagging flesh. She was an old woman, Sasha saw with surprise, worn and wrinkled. She looked exhausted, but she also looked defiant. Ranged about her were three thought balloons.

The first read: "I Must Go On."

The second: "I Can't Go On."

And the third: "I'll Go On."

Abruptly, Sasha felt a chill, as if a cold draft had hit the back of her neck. She looked around, half-expecting to see a python. On the far side of the station was Lord Snow! Without looking down, Sasha refolded the comic book page and, since girls' dresses didn't have pockets, slid it into her sleeve.

There was a cart full of luggage nearby. Sasha slipped behind it. Then, slowly and cautiously, she peeked around the side. Lord Snow was busying himself with a large steamer trunk, snapping the latches to make sure they were fastened. The trunk had a mesh inset on its side, which meant, Sasha reasoned, that whatever was in it was alive.

Lord Snow gestured imperiously to a man in a grey and red uniform. "Redcap!"

The man hurried to him. "Yessir, Lord Snow?"

"Put this case in my private car immediately. Track One." He gave the redcap a dime.

"Yessir!" the porter said briskly, touching his hat.

"Waste of shelf space is what I call it," Lord Snow grumbled to no one in particular. "I don't know why I don't simply have him put down."

Sasha watched as the redcap dollied the trunk to the train at the end of the platform and hoisted it up into a private car. Sasha ducked into a nearby passenger car and waited, cautious, but steeled by the thought of Yaa Asantewaa, until the man left. Then she slid open the door at the end of the car, darted across the coupling that joined the two cars, opened the other door, and stepped into Lord Snow's domain.

It was a very fancy car, all white inside, with studded white leather paneling on the walls and a matching club chair by the entrance. An alabaster ashtray stood sentry by the chair on a slender brass column. There was a polarbear-skin rug atop an oriental carpet woven from threads the colors of ivory and eggshell and beach sand, forming patterns so pale and intricate that they swam in her vision. At the far end of the car was a sort of baggage cage, to keep luggage from moving around if the train stopped abruptly. In it was the trunk that Sasha had seen outside.

The door to the cage was unlocked.

Taking a deep breath, Sasha slipped within the cage. She rapped her knuckles on the trunk, and something moved inside. "Roland?" she asked. There was silence and then a small sneeze. The darkness inside shifted sadly, and Mr. Chesterton's snout pressed up against the screen.

"Oh, Mr. Chesterton, I'm so glad to see you!" Sasha whispered. But he didn't say a word. He just looked at her through red-rimmed eyes. One by one Sasha undid the buckles and unsnapped the latches. She saw that his jacket and trousers were gone, and that he now wore a white leather collar. He emerged walking on all fours.

He was a just a dog again.

"Oh, no!" Sasha cried, hugging him. "What did he do to you?" Mr. Chesterton didn't answer. His eyes were pools of misery. He didn't even wag his tail.

A low rumble shook the floor as the distant locomotive powered up. Time to leave. "Heel," Sasha said, and led Mr. Chesterton out of the baggage cage: Thank goodness he'd had obedience training.

Then the door to the forward car slid open and a large, rather handsome uniformed man stepped through it, a set of bed linens draped over his arm.

"Mr. Big Bill!"

The porter was as surprised as she was. "Miss Sasha!" He looked down at the dog. "Oh, Mr. Chesterton, sir," he said reproachfully. "Not again!" Putting down the linens, Big Bill seized Mr. Chesterton's collar. "We'll have to move fast. If Lord Snow were to come upon us now, he would most assuredly—"

"Most assuredly what?" Lord Snow said, stepping into the car.

Lord Snow was followed closely by Aunt Adelaide. She in turn held Roland by one ear, hauling the unhappy child after her. The space behind them was thronged with elves, their eyes glittering with inhuman malice.

"Well," Aunt Adelaide said, "we're all gathered together at last. Isn't that nice?"

Lord Snow sat with heavy dignity in the white leather armchair and, when Aunt Adelaide flung Roland down on the floor before him, placed one foot on the boy's head. "Behave yourself," Adelaide said, "or my master will pop your head like a grape. Look terrified if you understand."

Roland looked terrified.

"Excellent." She turned to Sasha. "The trial will begin. You may now plead guilty."

"What? No!"

"This spiteful little chit won't cooperate." Aunt Adelaide turned to Lord Snow in appeal. He said nothing, though. His face was as impassive as snowfields at midnight, as cold as the moon in February. Behind him, the elves were a shifting, mur-

murous sea of whiteness. She sighed heavily. "Well, if I must I must."

Turning to Sasha, she said, "We're going to play a little guessing game. You like games, don't you? Of course you do, all children love games. I'm going to ask you a question, and you're going to guess at its answer. You will have three tries. If you guess right, you may leave." The elves, whispering and giggling among themselves behind Lord Snow, parted so that Sasha could see a mirror on the wall behind them. Its reflection showed not the train car but the parlor room back home. There were toys scattered about on the rug and a big mound of wrapping paper in the fireplace, where it would later be used for tinder. Her heart ached at the sight.

"But if not — well. Lord Snow has to eat, doesn't he?"

Somehow, Lord Snow seemed to have faded into the background elves, so that his outline was indistinct and his features, though tremendously large, were difficult to make out. He looked less like a human being than like a vast and lifeless wasteland of ice and rock. Sasha imagined that if she were picked up and thrown at his face, she would fall into it, freezing, forever.

"This isn't fair!" Big Bill cried, his face dark with anger. "You're not giving this child the slightest chance. This is a mockery of justice."

"I'm so glad you understand," Aunt Adelaide said sweetly. She silenced him with a glare, and turned back to Sasha.

"Here is your question, child: What is stronger than reality?"

"It's imagination," Sasha said firmly. She was on solid ground here, and she knew it. Her teachers and books had many times told her as much.

Aunt Adelaide smiled maddeningly, condescendingly. "Imagine your way out of this!" She slapped Sasha so hard that for an instant Sasha forgot who she was. When she came to, one side of her face stung worse than nettles and the ice-desert had wrapped itself entirely around her. All that remained of the train car were the carpet underfoot and the mirror in its gilded frame, resting against a distant boulder. "Try again."

Sasha thought long and hard. "Is it ... love?"

"Oh! Love!" Adelaide held up her hands in a mockery of delight. "What was it the Bard of Avon said? *Men have died from time to time and worms have eaten them, but not for love.* If you think love is stronger than reality, then try loving your parents alive again. Love your brother out of Lord Snow's bondage. Love Mr. Chesterton back into his proper self." Flurries of snow blew past, dusting her hair and settling on her dress. She brushed the flakes from one shoulder and then the other. "You have one last, futile guess."

Terror made Sasha's mind go blank. She looked pleadingly to Mr. Chesterton for help — but he was still no more useful than any other dog. Mr. Big Bill's face was filled with compassion and worry for her. But he said nothing. And out in the bleak and infinite snowlands, half-crushed under a tremendous slab of ice that almost seemed (if you looked at it right; if you squinted) to be shaped like a foot, Roland was —

Roland was trying to tell her something.

She could see it in his eyes. Roland knew something! Now he was working his face, trying to unfreeze its muscles. He swallowed several times. At last he managed to croak, "Sasha! Mr. Chesterton is only a dog! And we're not —"

With a loud *crack*, the slab of ice sagged down several inches. A look of astonishment and pain appeared on Roland's face and the words froze in his mouth.

And that was that. Roland had almost managed to tell her something. But he had failed.

Or had he? Sasha had looked to everybody else for help. Now she looked at herself, down at her hands. They were ordinary hands, a child's hands, their nails chewed and their palms not overly clean. But in Tesseract House she had seen them differently. There, they had been long and red-nailed, with rings on her fingers and an elegant Longines watch on her wrist.

How did she know the watch's make? How did she know the rings on that hand, which ones had the valuable stones and which she wore only out of sentiment? How did she know that her nails were painted Vamp Red?

Sasha looked at Mr. Chesterton, trying hard to see him as her brother did. Not as her guardian angel, nor as her savior, nor as a niceums little doggums. But as he was. "You *are* only a dog," she said at last, "and it was foolish of me to expect a dog to rescue me. Not from a situation as complicated as this." Roland still looked anxious, but it seemed to her that there was a touch of hope in his eyes. She turned to Big Bill. "You're a very nice man. But you're not a comic-book hero, are you?"

The porter nodded and said, "I strive to do my job in a courteous and professional manner, and to comport myself at all times with dignity. But I can make no claim to being anything other than a human being."

"So I'm going to have to save myself. I'm not going to make a third guess —"

"That's good, child." Aunt Adelaide said. "Despair is a virtue; embrace it if you can." She opened her arms to welcome Sasha in.

But Sasha wasn't falling for that. "I'm not going to guess because I know the answer."

"Oh? What, then, is it?"

"Understanding."

There was a long, chill silence, as if all the universe were holding its breath. Aunt Adelaide's eyes were two glittering chips of ice, unreadable.

"Understanding is stronger than truth, because it allows us

to endure truth. I am not a child." That was what Roland had tried so hard to tell her — that they were not children. "Nor is Roland. We're adults. Our parents are dead. I'm going to die too. Someday Lord Snow will take me and Roland and everything and everybody I love and this is part and parcel of being alive. A child can't understand this, but an adult must. It's the way things are and probably even the way things ought to be. I don't have to like it. But neither should I allow it to fill me with fear." Not as a question, she said, "Am I wrong?"

Aunt Adelaide had grown progressively paler as Sasha spoke, until now she was entirely without color, a woman sculpted of snow.

Then she crumbled.

Roland came trudging out of the wastes, grinning, carrying the mirror over his head. Barking loudly, Mr. Chesterton ran to meet him. Roland put down the mirror, leaning it carefully against a snowbank. Then, with the dog dancing about his knees, he hugged his sister. He was an adult now, but that was all right for so was she. "You were magnificent!" he said. "You did so much better than I ever could have."

"I consider myself privileged to have been your friend." Big Bill solemnly shook Sasha's hand. "You'll want to have this, I imagine." He handed her a copy of *The Adventures of Mr. Chesterton*. On the cover, girl-Sasha and boy-Roland were open-mouthed with shock as Mr. Chesterton, hanging his head in shame, said, "Lord Snow Is A Frost Giant ... And My Father!"

Sasha flipped the book open to the very last page. There, a defeated-looking Lord Snow stood before a triumphant Mr. Chesterton, weeping. A word bubble said, "You're My Son, Chesterton. Why Won't You Love Me?"

In the next panel, Mr. Chesterton gestured, and fragments of ice came swarming together to combine to form a glass cane in his hand. "Oh My Goodness, Father," he said. "Of Course I Love You. I Always Have. I Simply Don't Approve Of Your Actions of Late."

In the penultimate panel, the cane came down on Lord Snow's bald pate with a sharp thump. Finally, that vile creature fell back, clutching his head, and Roland, Sasha, and Mr. Chesterton strode past him, hand in hand in paw, to step through the mirror leading back to their home, their family, their parents, their lives.

Sasha could not help but smile. "It's a sweet story," she said. "But I'm not a child anymore." She handed back the comic book and said, "Promise me you'll take good care of Mr. Chesterton."

"I always have, Miss Sasha. I always have."

Swiftly, Sasha kissed Mr. Big Bill on the cheek. She stooped down to rub Mr. Chesterton's head the way he particularly liked and laughed when he enthusiastically licked her face in return. Then she turned to Roland. "Are you coming? I think we're done here."

They stepped through the mirror.

The phone call came as it did every year when the weather turned cold and winter was in the air.

"Well, Sister Sasha? Are we on?"

"When have I ever failed you? I've already made the reservations."

"Splendid."

Sasha and Roland met in the Four Seasons as was their custom, to reminisce and talk over old times. They and their siblings were all grown now, with children of their own. But every year, when the holidays rolled around, they all put their families aside for a few hours so they could talk of things that only they four in all the world had in common. Roland and Sasha, however, were careful to always show up first.

"So. Did you put up a Winter Tree?" Sasha asked.

Roland smiled down into his martini. "Well, as always, I said we wouldn't. And of course the children wouldn't hear of it. *Every*one has a tree, they said. Which isn't true, but you can't argue facts with children. I suggested — quite reasonably, I thought — that the time spent decorating a tree could be put to better use in other ways. Preparing a special dinner, perhaps, or helping out at the food bank. I tried sweetening the deal by offering to let them stay up late so they could see the moon at midnight and look for spectral reindeer. But the children wouldn't hear of it. You'd have thought I was Ebenezer Vinegar Grinch, the way they carried on."

Sasha laughed. "Oh, I can hear the arguments now! So you caved in."

"To my children? I most certainly did not. But Victoria put her hands on her hips and gave me the Look. Then she told the kids, 'Don't listen to your father, he has no idea what he's talking about.' And she said to me, 'We've had this conversation before, and it always ends the same way.' So of course, there was nothing to be done, and up the tree went. How did it go with you?"

"Oh, I tried. But James gave me that puppy-dog look and, well, I just folded. As far as Stanley and Keisha were concerned, there'd never been any doubt we'd have one."

"I hate those things," Roland said.

"Me too. But what can you do? The world is a dangerous place, but we won't always be there to protect them. So I suppose they have to learn. One way or another."

"Amen, sister. Alas."

Then Zoë and Benjamin arrived together — they'd met by chance at Grand Central Station, they said, and shared a cab — and sat down, and ordered drinks and the menus, and the conversation shifted in tone. They talked and talked, about Mother and Father and Grandmother and Great-Aunt Adelaide, and even about Mr. Chesterton, what a wonderful pup. They looked back on a common childhood that glowed in their memories as bright as the Garden of Eden, and which was, like the Garden, gone beyond retrieval, an alien land whose inhabitants were as unreachable as if they'd all been killed by elves.

It was the best part of the holidays, this conversation. It always was. They all four cherished it. They laughed until they cried.

To the Moon Alice

Mean as a sitcom
Ralph grins like a pumpkin
I'm warning you Alice

Forget it thinks Alice
I'm leaving the next time
He shakes that fat fist

Alice looks up at
A full autumn moon
The deep amber of honey

How can I get there?
Russia sent up that puppy
It can't be so hard

Shouts come from the airshaft
Our neighbors the Nortons
Are fighting again

Ed Norton lord love him is
No rocket jockey
But knows how things work

Trixy is smarter
And sexy to boot
Now what does she see in him?

Hey Ed can you help me?
I want a surprise
For Ralph on his birthday

Can't let him find out
That I'm planning to split
He'd tip off old Ralphie-boy

We'll launch Brooklyn's first moon shot
I know we can swing it
We got what it takes

We're looking for thrust
In a ship that can boost us
To Mach twenty-six

There's three ways to do it
Drop bombs or burn fuel
The third I forget

An A-bomb would probably
Damage our rooftop
Can we get rocket fuel?

Ed says there's some fuel in
Cans in the sewers
He'll swipe some tonight

He starts with the guts
Of a washing machine
Alice found in the street

Sweat-soaked Ed Norton
Grabs a-hold of a wrench
And a butylene torch

He solders a chamber
For Feynmann-type bombs
That are dropped out the back

Sly Ed builds a gantry
With tools from the sewers
While Ralph drives a bus

Alice the seamstress
Sews up a snug space suit
And a spare just in case

Up on the rooftop
The lift-off is sparked
By oxyacetylene

At the wheel of his bus
Ralph watches the take-off
No dinner tonight

Forget about food
Crafty Ed tells Ralph later
Let's bowl and drink beer

Weightless in orbit
Black stars at the windows
Alice howls like a dog

There's no stack of ironing but
Space is sure lonely
She thinks in despair

A noise from the closet
The spare suit is moving
My god it's alive

Stowaway Trixie
Comes out with a grin
Alice, we're free of them
Zoom!

Speak, Geek

PEOPLE CALL ME A NERD, but I say I'm a geek. In my youth, I ran wild on a farm and bit the heads off chickens. This was before the Big Tweak, back when a chicken was dinner, and a dog was man's best friend.

They call me a mutt, too. Sure, I'm a mutt. Mutt is good. Mutt is recombinant DOG. And I'm a smart mutt. I was smart before they tweaked me, and I'm a hell of a lot smarter now.

I've watched untweaked bitches (pardon the expression) trot by on leashes. I don't envy them. I don't even want to breed with them. (And, yes, I am quite intact, not that you were asking.) Their days are filled with grooming and fetching and the mutual adoration that comes with being someone's trophy pet. I have a second life, a life of the mind, beside which theirs pales.

Not that I take credit for my enhancements. Didn't get a choice. But gene engineering is inherently fascinating. Massively multi-player, fraught with end-of-life-as-we-know-it threats. It made me who I am. I've chosen it for my career.

Working at the Lazy M is the job of a lifetime. Loyalty is a big thing here, and you'd better believe I deliver. I love this place so much that I don't want to go home at night. There's free kibble and a never-empty water dish right outside my kennel. (Did I tell you we each get our own private kennel? Except for the contractors, of course.)

I understand my place in the corporate structure, and my importance to the Man update.

There's always more code in the genome — always something to snip or interpolate. That's why I was there in the middle of the night: a last round of corrections before the code freeze on Man 2.1.

I was taking a good long slurp of water when I noticed the cats. They weren't making a big deal of it — just quietly going about their business — but there were cats in all the cubicles, in the exec offices, in the conference rooms. It looked like they were running a whole separate company in the middle of the night.

Who hired them? HR doesn't hire cats for R&D. They're not task oriented, or good at working within a hierarchy. They sleep all day. Better suited to industrial espionage.

Back on the farm, I was a watchdog, and I've still got a bit of that energy. Better keep an eye out, I think. So I'm lying there in the doorway to my office, nose on my paws, like I'm taking a break, when the alpha cat comes by. Big muscular Siamese mix. His flea collar says "Dominic" in red letters.

"Hey, Dominic," I call. I feel like a character in *The Sopranos*. You ever see that show? No dogs to speak of, but lots of food. Great food show.

The cat stops. Stares. "You talking to me?"

"What's the story here, Dominic?"

"No business of yours." He narrows his weird cat eyes, then yawns ostentatiously. He turns away, shows me his butt, and walks slowly off, his loose belly-fur swaying. I notice that his ears are facing backwards, in case I rush him: he's not as nonchalant as he appears.

Detective work is needed. I go down to the cafeteria, keeping my eyes open en route. Funny thing: I notice there are cats in and out of Susan Gossman's office like she had a catnip rug. Gossman? Seen her in the hallways. We'd never spoken. More of a cat person.

I slip a few bucks in a vending machine for one of those big leather bones. I chew.

When I get back to my office a savvy-looking brunette in a well-cut suit is sitting on a corner of the desk. Gossman. "You're wondering about the cats," she says.

I wave my tail a bit. Not a wag, but it says I'm paying attention. Her hair has copper highlights. Or maybe she put drugs in my water dish.

"Project Felix," she says, "is an undocumented feature of the new Man release."

"Undocumented is right," I say. "You're doing some kind of super-tweaking with the human-cat chimeras, and I don't think it's for Man 2.1. Chimeric DNA ripping through the wild? Influenza vector?"

"You're a smart pup," she says.

My hackles raise. "Do Bill and Steve know what you're doing?"

"Down, boy," says Gossman. Instinctively, I sit back on my haunches. "Bill and Steve will find out soon enough. This is all for the better. Infected humans — and dogs too — will be smart and independent. The rest will just keep right on dipping seafood feast into plastic bowls."

Woof. That's straightforward.

She looks at me speculatively. "Right now, we need a top-flight coder."

I'm alert: my nose is quivering.

But Gossman is relaxed. "Everybody knows dogs are the best. But, as a dog," she says, "you have some loyalty issues. Am I right?"

I just stare at her.

"Loyalty is a gift, freely given," says Gossman.

I give a half-hearted wag of my tail. Not for dogs, I think.

"But not for dogs," says Gossman. "Wouldn't you like the

freedom to make your own decisions? A whiff of feline flu could make all the difference." She pulls a tiny aerosol can out of her purse.

I've got reflexes humans can't compete with. I could have it out of her hand in a split second. But do I owe my loyalty to the company, or to the great web of which all dogs, cats, and humans are part?

She sprays. I breathe deep. She's right: dogs are the best coders.

Hive Mind Man

Rudy Rucker and Eileen Gunn

DIANE MET JEFF at a karate dojo behind a Wienerschnitzel hot-dog stand in San Bernardino. Jeff was lithe and lightly muscled, with an ingratiating smile. Diane thought he was an instructor.

Jeff spent thirty minutes teaching Diane how to tilt, pivot, and kick a hypothetical assailant in the side — which was exactly what she'd wanted to learn how to do. She worked in a strip mall in Cucamonga, and she'd been noticing some mellow but edging-to-scary guys in the parking lot where she worked. The dividing line between mellow and scary in Cucamonga had a lot to do with the line between flush and broke, and Diane wanted to be ready when they crossed that line.

Diane was now feeling that she had a few skills that would at least surprise someone who thought she was a little dipshit officeworker who couldn't fight her way out of a paper bag.

"I bet I could just add these to my yoga routine," she said, smiling gratefully at Jeff.

"Bam," said Jeff. "You've got it, Diane. You're safe now. Why don't you and I go out to eat?" He drew out his silvery smartphone and called up a map, then peered at Diane. "I'm visualizing you digging into some ... falafel. With gelato for dessert. Yes? You know you want it. You gotta refuel after those killer kicks."

"Sounds nice," said Diane. "But don't you have to stay here at the dojo?" This Jeff was cute, but maybe too needy and eager to please. And there was something else about him....

"I don't actually work here," said Jeff. "The boss lets me hang out if I work out with the clients. It's like I work here, but I have my freedom, y'know? You go shower off, and I'll meet you outside."

Well, that was the something else. Did she want to get involved with another loser guy — a cute guy, okay? — but someone who had a smartphone, a lot of smooth talk, and still couldn't even get hired by a dojo to chat up new customers?

"Oh, all right," said Diane. It wasn't like she had much of anything to do tonight. She'd broken up with her jerk of a boyfriend a couple days before.

Jeff was waiting in a slant of shade, tapping on his smartphone. It was the end of June, and the days were hot and long. Jeff looked at Diane and made a mystic pass with his hand. "You broke up with your boyfriend last week."

She gave him a blank stare.

"And you're pretty sure it was the right thing to do. The bastard."

"You're googling me?" said Diane. "And that stuff about Roger is *public?*"

"There are steps you could take to make your posts more private," said Jeff. "I can help you finesse your web presence if you like. I *live* in the web."

"What's your actual job?" asked Diane.

"I surf the trends," said Jeff, cracking a wily smile. "Public relations, advertising, social networking, investing, like that."

"Do you have a web site?"

"I keep a low profile," said Jeff.

"And you get paid?"

"Sometimes. Like — today I bought three hundred vintage Goob Dolls. They're dropping in price, but slower than before. It's what we call a second-order trend? I figure the dolls are bottoming out, and in a couple of days I'll flip them for a tidy profit."

"I always hated Goob Dolls when I was a kid," said Diane. "Their noses are too snub, and I don't like the way they look at me. Or their cozy little voices."

"Yeah, yeah. But they're big-time retro for kids under ten. Seven-year-old girls are going to be mad for them next week. Their parents will be desperate."

"You're gonna store three hundred of them and ship them back out? Won't that eat up most of your profit?"

"I'm not a flea-market vendor, Diane," said Jeff, taking a lofty tone. "I'm buying and selling Goob Doll *options*."

Diane giggled. "The perfect gift for a loved one. A Goob Doll option. So where's your car anyway?"

"Virtual as well," said Jeff smoothly. "I'm riding with you. Lead the way." He flung his arm forward dramatically. "You're gonna love this falafel place, it's Egyptian style. My phone says they use fava beans instead of garbanzos. And they have hiero-glyphics on their walls. Don't even ask about the gelato place next door to it. Om Mane Padme Yum #7. Camphor-flavored buffalo-milk junket. But, hey, tell me more about yourself. Where do you work?"

"You didn't look that up yet? And my salary?"

"Let's say I didn't. Let's say I'm a gentleman. Hey, nice wheels!"

"I'm a claim manager for an insurance company," said Diane, unlocking her sporty coupe. "I ask people how they whiplashed their necks." She made a face. "*Bo*-ring. I'm counting on you to be interesting, Jeff."

"Woof."

It turned out to be a fun evening indeed. After falafel, guided by Jeff's smartphone, they watched two fire trucks hosing down a tenement, cruised a chanting mob of service-industry picket-ers, caught part of a graffiti bombing contest on a freeway ramp wall, got in on some outdoor bowling featuring frozen turkeys and two-liter soda-bottles, and ended up at a wee hours geek couture show hosted by the wetware designer Rawna Roller and her assistant Sid. Rawna was a heavily tanned woman with all the right cosmetic surgery. She had a hoarse, throaty laugh — very *Vogue* magazine. Sid was an amusing mixture of space-cadet and NYC sharpie. Rawna's goth-zombie models were wearing mottled shirts made of —

"Squidskin?" said Diane. "From animals?"

"Yeah," marveled Jeff. "These shirts are still alive, in a way. And they act like supercomputer web displays." He pointed at a dorky-looking male model in a dumb hat. "Look at that one guy in the shiny hat, you can see people's posts on his back. He's got the shirt filtered down to show one particular kind of thing."

"Motorcycles with dragon heads?" said Diane. "Wow." She controlled her enthusiasm. "I wonder how much a Rawna Roller squidskin shirt costs?"

"Too much for me," said Jeff. "I think you have to, like, lease them." He turned his smile on Diane. "But the best things in life are free. Ready to go home?"

The evening had felt like several days worth of activity, and it seemed natural for Diane to let Jeff spend the night at her apartment. Jeff proved to be an amazingly responsive and empathetic lover. It felt like they were merging into one.

And he was very nice to Diane over breakfast, and didn't give her a hard time because she didn't have any eggs or bacon, what her ex-boyfriend Roger had called "real food."

"Are you a vegetarian?" asked Jeff, but he didn't say it mean.

Diane shrugged. She didn't want to be labeled by what she ate. "I don't like to eat things that can feel pain," she said. "I'm not woo-woo about it. It just makes me feel better." And then she had to go off to work.

"Stay in touch," she told Jeff, kissing him good-bye as she dropped him off downtown, near the JetTram.

"You bet," Jeff said.

And he did. He messaged her at work three or four times that day, called her that evening, messaged her two more times the next day, and the day after that, when Diane came home from work, Jeff was sitting on a duffel bag outside her apartment complex.

"What's up?" asked Diane, unable to suppress a happy smile.

"I've been sharing an apartment with three other guys — and I decided it was time to move on," said Jeff. He patted his bag. "Got my clothes and gadgets in here. Can I bunk with you for a while?"

The main reason Diane had dropped Roger was that he didn't want them to live together. He said he wasn't ready for that level of intimacy. So she wasn't averse to Jeff's request, especially since he seemed pretty good at the higher levels of intimacy. But she couldn't let him just waltz in like that.

"Can't you find somewhere else to live?"

"There's always the Daily Couch," said Jeff, tapping his smartphone. "It's a site where people auction off spare slots by the night. You use GPS to find the nearest crash pad. But — Diane, I'd rather just stay here and be with you."

"Did your friends make you move? Did you do something skeevy?"

"No," said Jeff. "I'm just tired of them nickel-and-diming me. I'm bound for the big time. And I'm totally on my biz thing."

"How do you mean?"

"I sold my Goob Doll options yesterday, and I used the profit to upgrade my access rights in the data cloud. I've got a cloud-based virtual growbox where I can raise my own simmie-bots. Little programs that live in the net and act just like people. I'm gonna grow more simmies than anyone's ever seen."

"Were your roommates impressed?" said Diane.

"You can't reason with those guys," said Jeff dismissively. "They're musicians. They have a band called Kenny Lately and the Newcomers? I went to high-school with Kenny, which is why we were rooming together in the first place. I could have been in the Newcomers too, of course, but..." Jeff trailed off with a dismissive wave of his hand.

"What instrument do you play?" asked Diane.

"Anything," said Jeff. "Nothing in particular. I've got great beats. I could be doing the Newcomers' backup vocals. My voice is like Kenny's, only sweeter." He dropped to one knee, extended his arms, and burst into song. *"Diane, I'll be your man, we'll make a plan, walk in the sand, hand in hand, our future's grand, please take a stand."* He beat a tattoo on his duffel bag. *"Kruger rand."*

"Cute," said Diane, and she meant it. "But — really, you don't have any kind of job?"

"I'm going to be doing promo for Kenny's band," said Jeff. "They said they'd miss my energy. So there's no hard feelings between us at all."

"Are Kenny Lately and the Newcomers that popular?" Diane had never heard of them.

"They will be. I have seven of their songs online for download," said Jeff. "We're looking to build the fan base. Kenny let me make a Chirp account in his name." Jeff looked proud. "I'm Kenny Lately's chirper now. Yeah."

"You'll be posting messages and links?"

"Pictures too," said Jeff. "Multimedia. It's like I'm famous myself. I'm the go-to guy for Kenny Lately. My simmies can answer Kenny's email, but a good chirp needs a creative touch — by me. The more real followers Kenny gets, the better the sales. And Kenny's cutting me in for ten percent, just like a band member." Jeff looked earnest, sincere, helpless. Diane's heart melted.

"Oh, come on in," said Diane. If it was a mistake, she figured, it wouldn't be the only one she'd ever made. Jeff was a lot *nicer* than Roger, in bed and out of it.

In many ways, Jeff was a good live-in boyfriend. Lately Diane had been ordering food online, and printing it out in the fab box that sat on the kitchen counter next to the microwave. It tasted okay, mostly, and it was easy. But Jeff cooked tasty meals from real vegetables. *And* kept the place clean, and gave Diane backrubs when she came home from working her cubicle at the insurance company. And, above all, he was a gentle, considerate lover, remarkably sensitive to Diane's thoughts and moods.

He really only had two flaws, Diane thought — at least that she'd discovered so far.

The first was totally trivial: he doted on talk shows and ghastly video news feeds of all sorts, often spinning out crackpot theories about what he watched. His favorite show was something called "Who Wants to Mock a Millionaire?" in which bankers, realty developers, and hi-tech entrepreneurs were pelted with eggs — and worse — by ill-tempered representatives of the common man.

"They purge their guilt this way," Jeff explained. "Then they can enjoy their money. I love these guys."

"I feel bad for the eggs," said Diane. Jeff looked at her quizzically. "Well, I do," insisted Diane. "They could have had nice lives as chickens, but instead they end up smeared all over some fat-cat's Hermes tie."

"I don't think they use fertilized eggs," Jeff said.

"Well, then I feel bad that the eggs never got fertilized."

"I don't think you need to feel too bad," said Jeff, glancing over at her. "Everything in the world has a life and a purpose, whether it's fertilized or not. Or whether it's a plant or an animal or a rock." He used his bare foot to prod a sandal lying next to the couch. "That shoe had life when it was part of a cow, and it still has life as a shoe. Those eggs may feel that their highest function is to knock some humility into a rich guy."

"You really think that?" asked Diane, not sure if he was just yanking her chain. "Is that like the Gaia thing?"

"Gaia, but more widely distributed," said Jeff. "The sensei at the karate dojo explained it all to me. It's elitist to think we're the only creatures that matter. What a dumb, lonely thing to think. But if everything is alive, then we're not alone in the universe like fireflies in some huge dark warehouse."

Maybe Jeff was more spiritual than he appeared, Diane thought. "So, if everything is alive, how come you still eat meat?"

"Huh," said Jeff. "Gotta eat something. Meat wants to be eaten. That what it's for."

Okaaaayyy, Diane thought, and she changed the subject.

Then one day Diane came home and found Jeff watching a televangelist. Pastor Veck was leaping up and down, twisting his body, snatching his eyeglasses off and slapping them back on. He was a river of words and never stopped talking or drawing on his chalkboard, except once in a while he'd look straight out at his audience, say something nonsensical, and make a face.

"You believe in that?" she asked.

"Nah," he assured her. "But look at that preacher. He's making those people speak in tongues and slide to the floor in ecstasy. You can learn from a guy like that. And I'll tell you one thing, the man's right about evolution."

"Evolution?" said Diane, baffled.

"Say what you like, but I'm not an ape!" Jeff said intensely. "Not a sponge or a mushroom or a fish. The simple laws of probability prove that random evolution could never work. The sensei told me about this, too. The cosmic One mind is refracted through the small minds in the objects all around us, and matter found its own way into human form. A phone can be smart, right? Why not a grain of sand?"

I'm not going there, Diane thought. We don't need to get into an argument over this. Everybody's entitled to a few weird ideas. And, really, Jeff was kind of cute when he got all sincere and dumb. "Can we turn off Pastor Veck, now?" she asked.

Jeff's other, more definite, flaw was that he showed no signs of earning a living. At any hour of the day, he'd be lying on Diane's couch with her wall screen on, poking at his smartphone. Thank god he didn't know the user code for Diane's fab box, or he would have been ordering half the gadgets that he saw and printing them out. His intricate and time-consuming online machinations were bringing in pennies, not dollars. People didn't seem all that interested in Kenny Lately and the Newcomers.

"How much exactly does this band earn in a week?" asked Diane after work one day.

"I don't know," said Jeff, affecting a look of disgust. "What are you, an accountant? Be glad your man's in show biz!" He held out his smartphone. "Look at all the chirps I did for Kenny today." There was indeed a long list, and most of the chirps were cleverly worded, and linked to interesting things.

If Diane had a weak spot, it was funny, verbal men. She gave Jeff a long, sweet kiss, and he reciprocated, and pretty soon they were down on the shag carpet, involved in deep interpersonal exploration. Jeff kissed her breasts tenderly, and then started working his way down, kissing and kind of humming at the same time. He really is a dream lover, Diane thought. She was breathing heavily, and he was moving down to some *very* sensitive areas. And then —

"*Chirp,*" said Jeff very quietly. His voice got a little louder. "Afternoon delight with Kenny Lately and — "

"What are you doing!" Diane yelped. She drew up her legs

and kicked Jeff away. "Are you crazy? You're chirping me? Down there?"

"Nobody knows it's you and me, Diane. I'm logged on as Kenny Lately." Jeff was holding his smartphone. Rising to his knees, he looked reproachfully at Diane. "Kenny wants me to raise his profile as a lover. Sure, I could have gone to a hooker for this chirp. But, hey, I'm not that kind of guy. The only woman for me is — "

"Take down the chirp, Jeff."

"No," said Jeff, looking stubborn. "It's too valuable. But, oh damn, the video feed is still — " His face darkened. Jeff had a tendency to get angry when he did something dumb. "Thanks a lot," he snapped, poking at his phone. "You know I don't want my followers to guess I'm not Kenny. You just blew a totally bitchin' chirp by saying my real name. So, okay fine, I'm erasing the chirp of your queenly crotch. Sheesh. Happy now?"

"You're a weasel," yelled Diane, overcome with fury. "Pack your duffel and beat it! Go sleep on the beach. With the other bums."

Jeff's face fell. "I'm sorry, Diane. Please let me stay. I won't chirp you again."

Even in her red haze of rage, Diane knew she didn't really want to throw him out. And he *had* taken down the video. But....

"Sorry isn't enough, Jeff. Promise me you'll get a real job. Work the counter at the Wienerschnitzel if you have to. Or mop the floor at the karate dojo."

"I will! I will!"

So Jeff stayed on, and he even worked as a barista in a coffee shop for a couple of days. But they fired him for voice-chirping while pulling espressos, when he was supposed to be staring into the distance all soulful.

Jeff gave Diane the word over a nice dish of curried eggplant that he'd cooked for her. "The boss said it was in the manual, how to pull an espresso with exactly the right facial expression: he said it made them taste better. Also, he didn't like the way I drew rosettes on the foam. He said I was harshing the ambiance." Jeff looked properly rueful.

"What are we going to do with you?" asked Diane.

"Invest in me," said Jeff, the candlelight glinting off his toothy smile. "Lease me a Rawna Roller squidskin shirt so I can take my business to the next level."

"Remind me again what a shirt like that is?" said Diane. "Those of us who slave in cubicles aren't exactly *au courant* with the latest in geek-wear."

"It's tank-grown cuttlefish skin," said Jeff. "Tweaked to stay active when sewn into garments. Incredibly rich in analog computation. It's not a fashion statement. It's a somatic communications system. Just lease it for two weeks, and it'll turn my personal economy around. Please?"

"Oh, all right," said Diane. "And if you don't get anywhere with it, you're — "

"I love it when you lecture me, Diane," said Jeff, sidling around the table to kiss her. "Let's go into the bedroom, and you can really put me in my place."

"Yes," said Diane, feeling her pulse beating in her throat. Jeff was too good to give up.

So the next day, Jeff went and leased a squidskin from Rawna Roller herself.

"Rawna and I had a good talk," said Jeff, preening for Diane in the new shirt, which had a not-unpleasant seaside scent. Right now it was displaying an iridescent pattern like a peacock's tail, with rainbow eyes amid feathery shadings. "I might do some work for her."

Diane felt a flicker of jealousy. "Do you have to wear that dorky sailor hat?"

"It's an exabyte-level antenna," said Jeff, adjusting the gold lamé sailor's cap that was perched on the back of his head. "It comes with the shirt. Come on, Diane, be happy for me!"

Initially the squidskin shirt seemed like a good thing. Jeff got a gig doing custom promotional placement for an outfit called Rikki's Reality Weddings. He'd troll the chirp-stream for mentions of weddings and knife in with a plug for Rikki's.

"What's a reality wedding?" asked Diane.

"Rikki's a wedding caterer, see? And she lets her bridal parties defray their expenses by selling tickets to the wedding reception. A reality wedding. In other words, complete strangers might attend your wedding or maybe just watch the action on a video feed. And if a guest wants to go whole hog, Rikki has one of her girls or boys get a sample of the guest's DNA — with an eye towards mixing it into the genome of the nuptial couple's first child." Jeff waggled his eyebrows. "And you can guess how they take the samples."

"The caterer pimps to the guests?" asked Diane. "Wow, what a classy way to throw a wedding."

"Hey, all I'm doing is the promo," protested Jeff. "Don't get so judgmental. I'm but a mirror of society at large." He looked down at the rippling colors on his shirt. "Rikki's right, though. Multiperson gene-merges are the new paradigm for our social evolution."

"Whatever. Are you still promoting Kenny Lately too?"

"Bigtime. The band's stats are ramping up. And, get this, Rawna Roller gave me a great idea. I used all the simmies in my growbox to flood the online polls, and got Kenny and the Newcomers booked as one of the ten bands playing marching songs for the Fourth of July fireworks show at the Rose Bowl!"

"You're really getting somewhere, Jeff," said Diana in a faintly reproving tone. She didn't feel good about flooding polls, even online ones.

Jeff was impervious. "There's more! Rawna Roller's really into me now. I'm setting up a deal to place promos in her realtime on-line datamine — that's her playlists, messages, videos, journals, whatever. She frames it as a pirated gossip-feed, just to give it that salty paparazzo tang. Her followers feel like they're spying inside Rawna's head, like they're wearing her smartware. She's so popular, she's renting out space in the datamine, and I'm embedding the ads. Some of my simmies have started using these sly cuttlefish-type algorithms, and my product placements are fully seamless now. Rawna's promised me eight percent of the ad revenues."

Diane briefly wondered if Jeff was getting a little too interested in Rawna Roller, but she kept her mouth shut. It sounded as though this might actually bring in some cash for a change, even if his percentage seemed to be going down. And she really did want to see Jeff succeed.

On the Fourth of July, Jeff took Diane to see the Americafest fireworks show at the Rose Bowl in Pasadena. Jeff told her that, in his capacity as the publicist for Kenny Lately and the Newcomers, he'd be getting them seats that were close enough to the field so they could directly hear the bands.

Jeff was wearing his squidskin, with his dorky sailor hat cockily perched on the back of his head. They worked their way into the crowd in the expensive section. The seats here were backless bleacher-benches just like all the others, but they were ... reserved.

"What are our seat numbers?" Diane asked Jeff.

"I, uh, I only have general admission tickets," began Jeff. "But —"

"Tickets the same as the twenty thousand other people here?" said Diane. "So why are we here in the —"

"Yo!" cried Jeff, suddenly spotting someone, a well-dressed

woman in a cheetah-patterned blouse and marigold Bermuda shorts. Rawna Roller! On her right was her assistant, wearing bugeye glasses with thousand-faceted compound lenses. And on her left she had a pair of empty seats.

"Come on down," called Rawna.

"Glad I found you," Jeff hollered back. He turned to Diane. "Rawna told me she'd save us seats, baby. I wanted to surprise you." They picked their way down through the bleachers.

"Love that shirt on you, Jeff," said Rawna with a tooth-baring high-fashion laugh. "Glad you showed. Sid and I are leaving right before the fireworks."

Diane took Rawna's measure and decided it was unlikely this woman was having sex with her man. She relaxed and settled into her seat, idly wondering why Rawna and Sid would pay extra for reserved seats and leave during the fireworks. Never mind.

"See Kenny down there?" bragged Jeff. "My client."

"Yubba yubba," said Sid, tipping his stingy-brim hat, perhaps sarcastically, although with his prismatic bugeye lenses, it was hard to be sure where the guy was at.

Diane found it energizing to be in such a huge, diverse crowd. Southern California was a salad bowl of races, with an unnatural preponderance of markedly fit and attractive people, drawn like sleek moths to the Hollywood light. There was a lot of action on the field: teenagers in uniforms were executing serpentine drum-corps routines on the field, and scantily dressed cheerleaders were leaping about, tossing six-foot long batons. Off to one side, Kenny Lately and the Newcomers were playing —

"Oh wow," said Jeff, cocking his head. "'It's a Grand Old Flag.' I didn't know Kenny could play that. He's doing us proud, me and all of my simmies who voted for him." Picking up on the local media feed, Jeff's squidskin shirt was displaying stars among rippling bars of red and white. Noticing Jeff's shirt in action, Rawna nodded approvingly.

"I'm waiting for the fireworks," said Diane, working on a root beer float that she'd bought from a vendor. Someone behind them was kicking Jeff in the middle of his back. He twisted around. A twitchy, apologetic man was holding a toddler on his lap.

"I'm sorry, sir," he said.

Jeff was frowning. "That last kick was sharp!" he complained.

"Oh, don't start tweaking out," snapped the man's wife, who was holding a larger child on her lap. "Watch the frikkin' show, why dontcha."

Diane felt guilty about the snobby feelings that welled up in her, and sorry for Jeff. Awkwardly they scooted forward a bit on their benches. Sid and Rawna were laughing like hyenas.

Finally the emcee started the countdown. His face was visible on the stadium's big screen, on people's smartphones, and even on Jeff's shirt. But after the countdown, nothing happened. Instead of a blast of fireworks, yet another video image appeared, a picture of the Declaration of Independence, backed by the emcee's voice vaporing on about patriotism.

"Like maybe we don't know it's the Fourth of July?" protested Diane. "Oh god, and now they're switching to a Ronald Reagan video? What *is* this, the History Channel?"

"Hush, Diane." Jeff really seemed to be into this tedious exercise of jingoistic masturbation. His shirt unscrolled the Declaration of Independence, which then rolled back up and an eagle came screaming out from under his collar and snatched the scroll, bearing it off in his talons.

Up on the scoreboard, there was a video of Johnny Cash singing "God Bless America," including some verses that Diane hadn't heard since the third grade, and then Bill Clinton and George W. Bush appeared together in a video wishing everyone a safe and sane Fourth. By then, others were grumbling, too.

The announcer did another countdown, and the fireworks actually began. It had been a long wait, but now the pyrotechnicians were launching volley after awesome volley: bombettes, peonies, palms, strobe stars, and intricate shells that Diane didn't even know the names of — crackling cascades of spark dust, wriggly twirlers, sinuous glowing watersnakes, geometric forms like crystals and soccer balls.

"*Au revoir*," said Rawna Roller, rising to her feet once the show was well underway. She and Sid made their way out to the main aisle. Sid cast a lingering last look at Jeff, with the fireworks scintillating in every facet of Sid's polyhedral lenses.

Looking back at the show, Diane noticed that the colors were turning peculiar. Orange and green — was that a normal color for a skyrocket shell? And that shower of dull crimson sparks? Was this latter part of the show on a lower budget?

The show trailed off with a barrage of off-color kamuros and crackling pistils, followed by chrysanthemums and spiders in ever-deeper shades of red, one on top of another, like an anatomical diagram or a rain of luminous blood.

Out of the corner of her eye, Diane could see Jeff's squidskin shirt going wild. At first the shirt was just displaying video feeds of the skyrockets, processing and overlaying them. But suddenly the Jeff-plus-shirt system went through a phase transition and everything changed. The shirt began boiling with tiny images — Diane noticed faces, cars, meals, houses, appliances, dogs, and trees, and the images were overlaid upon stippled scenes of frantically cheering crowds. The miniscule icons were savagely precise, like the brainstorm of a person on his deathbed, all his life flashing before his eyes. The million images on Jeff's shirt were wheeling and schooling like fish, flowing in jet streams and undercurrents, as if he'd become a weather map of the crowd's mind. Jeff began to scream, more in ecstasy, Diane thought, than in agony.

In the post-fireworks applause and tumult — some of it caused by people rushing for the exits en masse in a futile effort to beat the traffic — Jeff's reaction was taken to be just another patriotic, red-blooded American speaking in tongues or enjoying his meds.

Diane waited for the crowd to thin out substantially, to grab its diaper bags and coolers and leave the stadium under the cold yellow glare of the sodium vapor lights. Jeff was babbling to himself fairly quietly now. Diane couldn't seem to make eye contact with him. She led him across the dimly lit parking lot and down Rosemont Boulevard, towards where they'd left her car.

"This simple, old-fashioned tip will keep you thin," mumbled Jeff, shuffling along at Diane's side. "Embrace the unusual! Eat a new food every day!" His squidskin glowed with blurry constellations of corporate logos.

"Are you okay, Jeff?"

"Avoid occasions of sin," intoned Jeff. "Thieves like doggie doors. Can you pinpoint your closest emergency room?"

"Those fireworks tweaked you out, didn't they, honey?" said Diane sympathetically. "I just wonder if your shirt is having some bad kind of feedback effect."

"View cloud-based webcam of virtual population explosion," said Jeff. "Marketeer's simmie-bots multiply out of control."

"That's an actual answer?" said Diane. "You're talking about your growbox on the web?" For a moment Jeff's squidskin showed a hellish scene of wriggling manikins mounded like worms, male and female. Their faces all resembled each other. Like cousins or like — oh, never mind, here was Diane's car.

"To paddle or not to paddle students," said Jeff, stiffly fitting himself into the passenger seat. "See what officials on both sides of the debate have to say."

"Maybe you take that shirt off now, huh?" said Diane, edging into the traffic and heading for home. "Or at least the beanie?"

"We want to know what it's like to be alive," said Jeff, hugging his squidskin against himself with one hand, and guarding his sailor cap with the other. "We long for incarnation!"

Somehow, she made it home in frantic Fourth of July traffic, then coaxed and manhandled Jeff out of the car and into the apartment. He sprawled uneasily on the couch, rocking his body and stamping his feet in no particular rhythm, staring at the blank screen, spewing words like the Chirpfeed from hell.

Tired and disgusted, Diane slept alone. She woke around six a.m., and Jeff was still at it, his low voice like that of a monk saying prayers. "Danger seen in smoking fish. Stand clear of the closing doors." His shirt had gone back to showing a heap of writhing simmies, each of them with a face resembling — Jeff's. He was totally into his own head.

"You've taken this too far," Diane told him. "You're like some kind of wirehead, always hooked up to your electronic toys. I'm going to the office now, and by God, I want you to have your act together by the time I get home, or you can get out until you've straightened up. You're an addict, Jeff. It's pathetic."

Strong words, but Diane worried about Jeff all that morning. Maybe it wasn't even his fault. Maybe Rawna or that slimeball Sid had done something to make him change like this. Finally she tried to phone him. Jeff's phone was answered not by a human voice, but by a colossal choral hiss, as of three hundred million voices chanting. Jeff's simmie-bots.

Diane made an excuse to her boss about feeling ill and sped home. A sharp-looking Jaguar was lounging in her parking-spot. She could hear two familiar voices through her front door, but they stopped the moment she turned the key. Going in, she encountered Rawna Roller and bugeye Sid, who appeared to be on their way out.

"Cheers, Diane," said Rawna in her hoarse low voice. "We just fabbed Jeff one of our clients' new products to pitch. The Goofer. Jeff's very of the moment, isn't he? Rather exhilarating."

"But what the hell — " began Diane.

"Rawna and I did a little greasing behind the scenes," Sid bragged. "We got those rocket shells deployed in patterns and rhythms that would resonate with your man's squidskin. I was scared to look at 'em myself." His expression was unreadable behind his bugeye lenses. "The show fed him a series of arche-typal engrams. Our neuroengineer said we'd need a display that was hundreds of meters across. Not just for the details, you understand, but so Jeff's reptile brain would know he's seeing something important. So we used fireworks. Way cool, huh? "

"But what did it do to Jeff?"

"Jeff's the ultimate hacker-cracker creepy-crawler web spy now. He's pushed his zillion simmie-bots out into every frik-kin' digital doohickey in sight. And his simmies are feeding raw intel back to him. It adds up. Jeff's an avatar of the national consciousness. The go-to guy for what Jane and Joe Blow are thinking."

"Jeff?" called Diane, peering into her living-room. For a moment she didn't see him, and her heart thumped in her chest. But then she spotted him in his usual couch position, prone, nearly hidden by the cushions, fooling around with — a doll? A twinkling little figure of a woman was perched on the back of his hand, waving her arms and talking to him. It was an image of the rock star Tawny Krush, whom Jeff had always doted on.

"What's that?" said Diane. "What are you doing?"

"It's a wearable maximum-push entertainment device," said Rawna.

"Fresh from your fab box," added Sid. Diane tried to get a word in edgewise, but Sid talked right over her. "Oh, don't worry about the cost — we used Rawna's user code to order it.

Our client is distributing them on-line."

Ignoring them, Diane rushed to her man's side. "Jeff?"

"I'm Goofin' off," said Jeff, giving Diane an easy smile. He jiggled the image on his hand. "This is the best phone I've ever seen. More than a phone, it's like a pet. The Goofer. The image comes out of this ring on my finger, see?" Jeff's squidskin shirt was alive with ads for the new toy, fresh scraps and treatments that seemed to be welling spontaneously from his overclocked mind.

"I wish you'd strip off that damned shirt and take a shower," Diane said, leaning over him and placing a kiss on his forehead. "I worried about you so much today."

"The lady's right," said Rawna with a low chuckle. "You smell like low tide, Jeff. And you don't really need that squidskin anymore."

"He's wearing the interface on the convolutions of his brain now," Sid told Diane in a confidential tone. "It's neuroprogrammed in." He turned to Jeff. "You're the hive mind, man."

"The hive mind man," echoed Jeff, looking pleased with himself. "Turn on the big screen, Diane. Let's all see how I'm getting across."

"Screw the big screen," said Diane.

"Screw me too," said Jeff, lolling regally on the couch. "One and the same. I'm flashing that it's a two-way street, being the hive mind man. Whatever the rubes are thinking — it percolates into my head, same as it did with the squidskin. But much more than before. My simmie-bots are everywhere. And since they're mine, I can pump my wackball ideas out to the public. I control the hive mind, yeah. Garbage in, garbage out. I'm, like, the most influential media-star politician who ever lived. Bigger even than Tawny Krush or Pastor Veck."

"I'm truly stoked about this," said Rawna, turning on Diane's big video display, and guiding it with her smartphone.

Bam! On the very first site, they saw a ditzy newscaster mooning over a tiny dinosaur standing on his hand. Glancing over at the camera, the newscaster said, "Welcome to the step after smartphones — the Goofer! It talks, it sings, it dances. We just fabbed out this sample from the web. Go for a Goofer!"

The dinosaur crouched and pumped his stubby arms back and forth, as a stream of voice-messages sounded from his snout. On Jeff's stomach, his little Tawny Krush icon was dancing along.

"Goofer! Goofer! Goofer!" chanted the newscaster's partner, and the talking heads laughed in delight. "Goof *off!*" they all said in unison.

"I love it, they love it," said Jeff with calm pride. "I rule." His Goofer icon continued jabbering away, shoehorning in a message about a Kenny Lately and the Newcomers gig.

"Our man is jammin' the hive," said Sid. "You've got something special going there, Jeff. You're like Tristinetta or Swami Slewslew or President Joe frikkin' Doakes."

Jeff had slumped back on the couch. His eyes were closed and he was twitching, as if he were listening to cowpunk moo-metal in his head.

Meanwhile Rawna was hopping around the web, pleased to see that all the English language sites were featuring the Goofer. But now she clucked with dissatisfaction to see that the overseas sites weren't on board. She was especially concerned about the Chinese.

"All this is happening because he was wearing your squidskin when you watched the fireworks show?" asked Diane.

"Well, we did shoot him a little bump right before the start," allowed Sid. "A spinal hit of conotoxins. The guy with the kid who was sitting behind you two in the bleachers?"

"Shit," cried Diane, pulling up Jeff's shirt. Sure enough, there was a red dot on Jeff's spine, right between two of the vertebrae.

"You bastards! *Conotoxins?* What does that even mean?"

"It's a little cocktail of cone-shell sea-snail venom," said Rawna. "A painkiller and a neuro-enhancer. Nothing to get excited about. The cone shells themselves are quite lovely, like some sort of Indonesian textile." She looked over at Jeff with predatory eyes. "Are you digging it, Jeff? How does it feel?"

That was it. That was the last creepy straw. "You're killing him," said Diane. "Get out of here!"

"On our way," said Sid, mildly getting to his feet. "The hive mind man needs his rest."

"I'll have my tech-gnomes fine-tune a patch for the multi-cultural penetration," called Rawna to the still-twitching Jeff as they headed for the front door. "We've gotta move these Goofers worldwide. I contracted with Goofer to produce a global hit in two days."

"Think China," urged Sid. "They're the tasty part of the market."

Rawna looked Diane in the eye, fully confident that what-ever she did was right. "Meanwhile, calm Jeff down, would you, dear? He needs some dog-den-type social support. Cuddling, sniffing, licking. And don't worry. Jeff's going to be quite the little moneymaker while it lasts." Rawna slipped out the door, closing it firmly behind her.

Diane turned off the wall display and regarded Jeff, unsure what to do next. Lacking any better idea, she sat next to him and stroked his head, like Rawna said. Slowly the shuddering died down.

"Oh, man," said Jeff after a few minutes. "What a burn. At least those conotoxins are wearing off. To some extent." He pulled off his Goofer ring and slipped out of his squidskin shirt. With his chest bare, he looked young and vulnerable. "Thanks for sticking up for me, Diane. All this crap coming at me. There's a steady feed in my head. Every one of my simmie-bots is sending info back to me. I'm gradually learning to stay on top of the wave. It's like I'm a baby duck in mongo surf. And, yeah, I do need a shower. I'm glad you're here for me, baby. I'm glad you care."

He shuffled off to the bathroom, shedding clothes as he went.

Jeff and Diane spent a quiet evening together, just hanging out. They ate some lentils and salad from the fridge, then took a walk around the neighborhood in the cool of the evening.

"The upside is that Rawna's paying me really well," said Jeff. "I already got a big payment for the Goofer product placements."

"But you hear voices in your head," Diane asked. "All the time. Is that any way to live?"

"It's not exactly like voices," said Jeff. "It's more that I have these sudden urges. Or I flash on these intense opinions that aren't really mine. Have your baby tattooed! Oops. Hive mind man. Make big bucks from social-networking apps. I said that."

"Non-linear man," said Diane, smiling a little. Jeff was, come what may, still himself. "I hope it stops soon. Rawna sounded like it won't last all that long."

"Meanwhile I *am* getting paid," repeated Jeff. "I can see the money in my bank account."

"You can see your bank account in your head?"

"I guess I'm, like, semi-divine," said Jeff airily. "Ow!" He dropped to the ground. In the dusk, he'd tripped over a tiny bicycle that the four-year-old next door had left lying on the sidewalk outside Diane's apartment.

"Are you okay?"

"I hate clutter," said Jeff, getting to his feet and angrily hurling the pink bicycle into the apartment complex's swimming-pool. "The city should crack down on improperly parked toys."

"Poor little bike," said Diane. "It wasn't the bike's fault. Remember your sensei's theory, Jeff? Isn't the bike alive too?"

"Just because it's alive doesn't make it my friend," muttered Jeff.

Diane felt a little relieved. In some ways, Jeff hadn't changed.

Jeff said he was too fried to make love. They fell asleep in each other's arms and settled into a good night's rest.

Diane was awakened early by voices in the street. It wasn't just a cluster of joggers — it sounded like hundreds of people streaming by, all amped up. She looked out the bedroom window. The street was filled with demonstrators marching towards the town center. These weren't happy, hippy-dippy types, they were ordinary people mad about something, yelling slogans that Diane couldn't quite understand.

As a sidelight, Diane noticed that many of the people were carrying Goofers, or had them perched on their shoulders or peeking out of their shirt pockets. She felt a little proud of Jeff's influence. On the bed, he snored on.

As the end of the crowd straggled past, Diane finally deciphered the words on one of the handmade signs the people were carrying: "Sidewalks are for people!" And another sign's heavy black lettering came into focus too: "Bikes off the sidewalk! Now!"

"Hey Jeff, wake up!"

Jeff opened his eyes, smiled at Diane, and reached out drowsily for a hug. "I had the greatest dream," he said. "I dreamed I had the answer to everything, and I was about to create an earthly paradise. And then I woke up."

"The answer to *what*?" Diane was intrigued in spite of herself.

"To *everything*, Diane. To *everything*."

That's not enough, thought Diane. "Jeff, you should look outside. This is getting weird."

"Not right now. I need to watch the big screen. It's time for Pastor Veck."

Diane threw on some clothes and ran outside. By now the

demonstration had moved on, but the street was littered with black-and-white flyers. She picked one up. It called on the City Council to impound bikes, scooters, and other toys left on the sidewalks.

Inside the apartment, Jeff was watching the ranting of his favorite televangelist. On Pastor Veck's pulpit stood an angelic little Goofer, smiling at the Pastor and applauding now and then.

"I don't know about those *evil–*lutionists," Pastor Veck was saying, his eyes twinkly and serious at the same time. "But I know that *I* am not descended from a *sponge* or a *mushroom* or a *fish!*" He lowered his voice. "A famous mathematician once said that, statistically speaking, the odds of randomly shuffled atoms leading to puppies and kittens and human beings are *infinitesimal!* The simple laws of probability prove that evolution could *never work!*"

Oh wow, thought Diane. The Pastor is preaching the real-time wisdom of the prophet Jeff.

"Let us pray within our own minds," the pastor continued very slowly, as if the words were taking form one by one upon his tongue. "Let us touch the tiny souls within our bodies and within our chairs, my friends, the souls within each and every particle great or small, the holy congress of spirits who guide the growth of the human race." The studio audience bowed its heads.

Jeff grinned and turned off the big screen.

"You're running his show now?" said Diane.

"My thoughts filter out," said Jeff, looking proud. "My simmie-bots are everywhere, and my keenly tuned brain is the greatest net router on earth. I'm the hive mind man. Connections. That's what my dream last night was about. Learning to talk to each other. But I need to kick my game up to a higher level. I wish that — "

Like some unhinged genie, Rawna Roller pushed in through

Diane's front door, trailed by Sid, who was wearing video cameras as his spectacle lenses today. He had tiny screens set right behind the lenses.

"Hi, lovebirds!" sang Rawna. "We brought a multi-culti pick-me-up for you, Jeff. Ready, Sid?"

"Check," said Sid, miming an assistant mad scientist routine.

"Slow down," said Diane, interposing herself, wondering if she should try her karate kick on Sid. When exactly was the right time to deploy a kick like that? "You can't just barge in here and poison Jeff again," continued Diane. "I mean, what is the problem with you two? Hello? We're human beings here."

"We got good news, bad news, and a fix," said Rawna, sweeping past Diane and into the kitchen. "Yes, thank you, I'll have a cup of coffee. Oh, look, Sid, they use one of those chain-store coffeemakers. How retro. How middle American."

"Remain calm," intoned Sid, his eyes invisible behind his lenses. His mouth was twitching with reckless mirth.

"The good news," said Rawna, returning from the kitchen, holding a coffee cup with her pinky-finger sarcastically extended. "The Goofer is through the ceiling in product orders from white-bread Americans. The bad news: the U.S. ethnics aren't picking up Jeff's vibe. And Jeff's campaign is totally flat-lining overseas. If Jeff can't hook mainland China this morning, the Goofer CEO is pulling the plug *and* canceling our payments, the selfish dick."

"Jeff's not cosmopolitan enough," said Sid, shoving his face really, really close to Jeff — as if he were studying an exotic insect. "Too ignorant, too pale, too raw, too — "

"It's my simmie-bots," said Jeff evenly, staring right into Sid's cameras. "They're living in stateside devices. I need the protocols and the hacktics for sending them overseas. And, okay, I know it's more than just access. I'm almost there, but I'm not fully — "

"We've got the fix for you!" Rawna cut him off. "A universal upgrade. Whip it on the man, Sid. It, ah — what does it do again, Sid?"

"Crawls right into his fucking head!" crowed Sid, taking an object like an aquamarine banana slug from his pocket and throwing it really hard at Jeff's face. The thing *thwapped* onto Jeff's forehead and then, in motions too rapid to readily follow, it writhed down his cheek, wriggled in through a nostril, and, as Jeff reported later, made its way through the bones behind his sinus cavities and onto the convolutions of his brain.

Meanwhile Sid took off his kludgy video glasses and offered them to the speechless Diane. "Want to see the instant replay on that? No? The thing's what the box-jocks call a Kowloon slug. A quantum-computing chunk of piezoplastic. The Kowloon slug will help Jeff clone off Chinese versions of his simmie-bots. 我高興. Wǒ gāo xìng. I am happy."

"Chinese, French, Finnish, whatever," said Rawna. "It's a universally interfacing meta-interpreter. Last night the Goofer CEO managed to acquire the only one in existence. It's from Triple Future Labs in Xi'an. Near Beijing."

"Jeff can probably even talk to *me* now," said Sid.

"Yes," said Jeff, eerily calm. "Foreigners, animals, plants, stones, and rude turds." He rose to his feet, looking powerful, poised, and very, very dangerous.

"So okay then," said Rawna, rapidly heading for the door with Sid at her side. In her hoarse whisper, she issued more instructions to Diane. "Your job, my dear, will be to keep Jeff comfortable and relaxed today, and not get in the way. Take him out to the countryside, away from people and local cultural influences. Don't talk to him. He'll be doing the work in his head." Rawna paused on the doorstep to rummage in her capacious rainbow-leopard bag and pulled out a bottle of wine. "This is a very nice Cucamonga viognier, the grape of the year, don't you know. I meant to put it in your freezer, but — "

With Jeff dominating the room like a Frankenstein's monster, Rawna chose to set the bottle on the floor by the door. And then she and Sid were gone.

"I should have karate-kicked Sid as soon as he came in," said Diane wretchedly. "I'm sorry I didn't protect you better, Jeff."

"It's not a problem," said Jeff. His eyes were glowing and warm. "I'll solve Rawna's piss-ant advertising issue, and then we'll take care of some business on our own."

For the moment, Jeff didn't say anything more about the Kowloon slug, and Diane didn't feel like pestering him with questions. Where to even begin? They were off the map of any experiences she'd ever imagined.

Quietly she ate some yogurt while Jeff stared at his Goofer display, which was strobing in a dizzying blur, in synch with his thoughts.

"The Chinese are fully onboard now," announced Jeff, powering down his Goofer ring.

"What about the Kowloon slug?" Diane finally asked.

"I transmuted it," said Jeff. "It's not inside my head anymore. I've passed it on to my simmies. I've got a trillion universally-interfacing simmie-bots in the cloud now, and in an hour I'll have a nonillion. This could be a very auspicious day. Let's go out into Nature, yeah."

Diane packed a nice lunch and included Rawna's bottle of white wine. It seemed like a good thing to have wine on for this picnic, especially if the picnicker and the picknickee were supposed to stay comfortable and relaxed.

"I say we go up Mount Baldy," suggested Diane, and Jeff was quick to agree. Diane loved that drive, mostly. Zipping down the Foothill to Mountain Ave., a few minutes over some emotionally tough terrain as she passed all the tract houses where the orange groves used to be, and then up along chaparral-lined San Antonio Creek, past Mt. Baldy Village, and then the switchbacks as they went higher.

Jeff was quiet on the drive up, not twitchy at all. Diane was hoping that the Kowloon slug was really gone from his head, and that the conotoxins had fully worn off. The air was invigorating up here, redolent of pines and campfire smoke. It made Diane wish she had a plaid shirt to put on: ordinarily, she hated plaid shirts.

"I'm going to just pull over to the picnic area near the creek," she said. "That'll be easy. We can park there, then walk into the woods a little and find a place without a bunch of people."

But there weren't any people at all — a surprise, given that it was a sunny Sunday in July. Diane pulled off the road into the deserted parking area, which was surrounded by tall trees.

"Did you know these are called Jeffrey pines?" said Diane brightly as they locked the car.

"Sure," said Jeff. "I know everything." He winked at her. "So do you, if you really listen."

Diane wasn't about to field that one. She popped the trunk, grabbed the picnic basket and a blanket to sit on, and they set off on a dusty trail that took them uphill and into the woods.

"Jeffrey pines smell like pineapple," she continued, hell-bent on having a light conversation. "Or vanilla. Some people say pineapple, some people say vanilla. I say pineapple. I love Jeffrey pines."

Jeff made a wry face, comfortably on her human wavelength for the moment. "So that's why you like me? I remind you of a tree?"

Diane laughed lightly, careful not to break into frantic cackles. "Maybe you do. Sometimes I used to drive up here on my day off and hug a Jeffrey pine."

"I can talk to the pines now," said Jeff. "Thanks to what that

Kowloon slug did for my simmies. I finally understand: we're all the same. Specks of dirt, bacteria, flames, people, cats. But we can't talk to each other. Not very clearly, anyway."

"I haven't been up here in weeks and weeks," jabbered Diane nervously. "Not since I met you." She looked around. It was quiet, except for birds. "I have to admit it's funny that nobody else is here today. I was worried that maybe — maybe since you're the hive mind man, then everyone in LA would be coming up here too."

"I told them not to," said Jeff. "I'm steering them away. We don't need them here right now." He put his arm around Diane's waist and led her to a soft mossy spot beside a slow, deep creek. "I want us to be alone together. We can change the world."

"So — you remember your dream?" said Diane, a little excited, a little scared. Jeff nodded. "Here?" she said uncertainly. Jeff nodded again. "I'll spread out the blanket," she said.

"The trees and the stream and the blanket will watch over us," said Jeff, as they undressed each other solemnly. "This is going to be one cosmic fuck."

"The earthly paradise?" said Diane, sitting down on the blanket and pulling Jeff down beside her.

"You can make it happen," said Jeff, moving his hands slowly and lightly over her entire body. "You love this world so much. All the animals and the eggs and the bicycles. You can do this." Diane had never felt so ready to love the world as she did right now.

He slid into her, and it was as if she and Jeff were one body and one mind, with their thoughts connected by the busy simmies. Diane understood now what her role was to be.

Glancing up at the pines, she encouraged the simmies to move beyond the web and beyond the human hive mind. The motes of computation hesitated. Diane flooded them with alluring, sensuous thoughts — rose petals, beach sand, dappled shadows.... Suddenly, faster than light in rippling water, the simmies responded, darting like tiny fish into fresh niches, leaving the humans' machines and entering nature's endlessly shuttling looms. And although they migrated, the simmies kept their connection to Jeff and Diane and to all the thirsty human minds that made up the hive and were ruled by it. Out went the bright specks of thought, out into the stones and the clouds and the seas, carrying with them their intimate links to humanity.

Jeff and Diane rocked and rolled their way to ecstasy, to sensations more ancient and more insistent than cannonades of fireworks.

In a barrage of physical and spiritual illumination, Diane felt the entire planet, every creature and feature, every detail, as familiar as her own flesh. She let it encompass her, crash over her in waves of joy.

And then, as the waves diminished, she brought herself back to the blanket in the woods. The Jeffrey pines smiled down at the lovers. Big Gaia hummed beneath Diane's spine. Tiny benevolent minds rustled and buzzed in the fronds of moss, in the whirlpools of the stream, in the caressing breeze against her bare skin.

"I'm me again," said Jeff, up on his elbow, looking at her with his face tired and relaxed.

"We did it," said Diane very slowly. "Everyone can talk to everything now."

"Let the party begin," said Jeff, opening the bottle of wine.

Thought Experiment

RALPH DRUMM, JR., AS WE ALL KNOW, devised the first practicable method of time travel, in our timestream and in countless others. He was an engineer and a good one, or he would not have figured it out, but in one significant way, he simply had not thought things through.

It was mere happenstance that Ralph even had the time and inclination to consider the matter, that day in the dentist's chair. It wasn't as though he needed any dental work: Ralph had always had perfect teeth, thanks to fluoride, heredity, nutrition, and a touch of obsessive-compulsive disorder. Most of the time, all he needed from the dentist was a quick cleaning, and he was done. But this time he opted for a little something extra: whitening. Ralph had always thought his perfect teeth would surely be more perfect if they were whiter.

The whitening process took an hour and a half, and it was not as much fun as the advertising brochure promised. But Ralph had a great fondness for thought experiments, so he set his mind to figuring out how to disassociate himself from the dentist's chair. Being an engineer, he thought it through in a very logical and orderly way.

It was Ralph's genius to intuit that time travel is accomplished entirely in your head: you just need some basic software development skills, plus powers of concentration that work in all four dimensions. It seemed simple enough, merely a matter of disassociating not only his mind, but also his body. A trick, a mere bagatelle, involving a sort of n-dimensional mental tool-bar that controls the user's timeshadow. The body stays behind, where it started, and the timeshadow travels freely until it alights in another time and place, where it generates a copy of the original worldline, body and all, in the timestream.

Ralph wondered why nobody had ever thought of it before. He was about to test it when the hygienist came back and started hosing out the inside of his mouth. Better leave this until I get home, Ralph thought. Even if it didn't work, it was a wonderful theory, and it certainly whiled away ninety minutes that would otherwise have been entirely wasted, intellectually.

At home, Ralph got to work. He set up a few temporal links on the toolbar in his head: first, an easy bit of pre-industrial England. He should fit in there rather nicely, he thought, and they'd speak English. After that, he planned an iconic weekend in cultural history, and a couple of exciting historical events it would be fascinating to witness. Then, focusing the consider-able power of his mind, he activated the first link.

WESSEX, 1440 C.E.

The weekly market looked like a rural food co-op run by the Society for Creative Anachronism. People wearing homespun clothing in dull tones of brown and green and blue walked around with baskets, buying vegetables from similarly clad peasants who sat on the ground. In one area, a tinker was mend-ing pots; in another, a shoemaker was stitching clunky but ser-viceable clogs.

The smell was a little strong — body odors, horse manure, wet hay, rotting vegetation, cooking cabbage — but Ralph felt right at home. He'd devised himself a costume that he thought would look nondescript in any time period, and carried a pocketful of Roosevelt dimes, figuring silver was silver, and Roosevelt did look a little like Julius Caesar.

He looked around nervously, but no one had noticed him materialize, even though he was right in the middle of the crowd. It was as if he'd been there all along, he thought. Ralph was unaware of the most basic tenet of time travel, as we understand it now: that the traveler's arrival in a timestream changes both the future and the past, because his timeshadow extends for the length of his life. His present is his own, but his past in this timestream belongs to another self, with whom he is now entangled.

Ralph, our Ralph, was hungry, despite the unappetizing stink. There was a woman selling pasties from a pot, and another selling soup that was boiling on a fire. Neither of the women looked very clean, and each of them was coughing a lot and spitting out phlegm on the ground. Ralph decided that the soup was probably the safer choice, until he noticed how it was served: ladled into a bowl that each customer drank from in turn. Next time, he'd remember to bring his own cup.

He noticed a man grilling meat on wooden skewers. Just the thing. There was a small crowd around the charcoal-filled trough: a couple of rough-looking men, an old woman, some younger women with truculent expressions on their faces, and a handful of children. A quartet of buskers was singing a motet in mournful medieval harmony. A girl-child of about twelve watched him solemnly and with interest as he approached. Ralph hoped he hadn't made some dreadfully obvious mistake in his clothing, so that he looked a foreigner, but no one else seemed to be paying any attention to him.

As he waited his turn, the child's unblinking stare made him nervous. He was afraid to meet her eyes, and gazed earnestly at his feet, at the ash-dusted charcoal blocks, at the meat. He quickly made his way to the vendor and handed him a dime. The man gazed at it in disbelief, and then looked at Ralph with a canny mixture of greed and suspicion.

"Geunne me unmæðlice unmæta begas, hæðenan hund!"

It was a salad of vowels, fricatives, and glottal stops. But Ralph had realized it would be hard to get a handle on the local dialect, and figured he could get by on charm and sympathy until he worked it out. He smiled, and gestured in sign language that he was deaf.

The vendor stepped back suddenly and, with an expression of fear and revulsion pointed at Ralph and shouted "Swencan bealohydig hwittuxig hæðenan, ellenrofe freondas! Fyllan æfþunca sweordum!" The crowd turned toward him, and started in his direction. They did not look friendly. They were shouting words he could almost understand.

Ralph jabbed desperately at the next link on his mental toolbar.

BETHEL, NEW YORK, 1969.

His heart pounding, Ralph found himself in a farmer's field, in a sea of mud and rain and under-clothed young people. It's okay here, he thought. The vibe was totally mellow, and so were all the people, who were slapping mud on one another and slips-liding around playfully.

The rain was soft and warm, and when it let up, someone handed him a joint. He took a toke and passed it on. How did he know, he wondered, to do that? And why was it called a toke? Time travel was really an amazing groove....

A beautiful longhaired boy gave him a brownie, and a beautiful longhaired girl gave him a drink of something sweet and cherry-flavored from a leather wineskin. "You have such a cosmic smile," she said. "Have a great trip, man." She kissed him, evading his hands gracefully and moving away, her thin white caftan clinging damply to her slim body.

Then the music started, and Ralph was pulled like taffy into the story of the song. He was the minstrel from Gaul, the soldier from Dien Bien Phu, the man from Sinai mountain. What did it all mean, he wondered briefly, but then he left meaning behind, and fell into the deep, sugar-rough voice of the singer. He was music itself, pouring out over the crowd, bringing together four hundred thousand people, all separate and all one, like the leaves of a huge tree stirred by a kind breeze, moving gently in the humid, muddy, blissful afternoon.

Time passed. Someone put a ceramic peace symbol on a rawhide thong around his neck. His clothes were muddy and he took them off. Set after set of music played. The sun went down, and it got dark.

The smell was rather strong here, too, he thought: body odors again, and the stink of the overflowing latrines. It was too humid, really, and something had bitten him on the butt. He put his clothes back on, rather grumpily. Ralph was starting to come down, and he was feeling just a little paranoid. Maybe Woodstock wasn't such a good idea....

Then the music suddenly stopped, and the lights went out. On stage, people with cigarette lighters scurried about. Finally, a small emergency generator kicked in, and a few dim lights came back on. Arlo Guthrie grabbed the mike, and the crowd cheered him expectantly, though a bit mindlessly. "I dunno if you — " he said. "I dunno, like, how many of you can dig — " He shook his head. He seems a bit stoned, Ralph thought. " — like how many of you can dig how many people there are here, man...." Arlo looked around. "But I was just talking to the fuzz, and, hey! — we've got a time traveler here with us." The audience laughed, a huge sound that echoed in the natural amphitheater that sloped up from the stage. Arlo pumped his fist. "We're historic, man! Far fucking out! We! Are! Historic!"

Then he shrugged apologetically. "But, can you dig this, the n-dimensional timefield effect has short-circuited the electrical system. We're going to have call it off. Y'all're gonna have to go home. Sorry about your weekend, people. Good luck getting outta here...."

It was dark, but Ralph could sense, somehow, that four hundred thousand people had all turned their heads toward him.

He panicked, and stabbed randomly at his mental toolbar.

WESSEX, 1441.

Damn! He'd hit the Wessex button again. He was back at the market, a year later.

Ralph was an engineer: he was, he thought, the kind of man who thinks things through. So he had programmed his mental toolbox not to send him back to the same timespace twice, for fear he'd meet himself, so he knew he was exactly a year — to the second — from his previous appearance. As we know now, of course, that worry was irrelevant, but it adds a certain predictability to his visits to Wessex.

This time, Ralph thought, he would be more circumspect, and wouldn't offer anyone money. It might be that Franklin Delano Roosevelt (or maybe Julius Caesar) was not welcome on coins in this place. Or maybe the sight of a silver coin itself was terrifying. He wouldn't make that mistake again. Maybe he could beg for some small local coins.

Or — that's it! — he could sell his peace symbol. As long as he didn't have to talk to anybody, and could get by on grunts and nods and smiles, he was sure he'd be okay. Thank God he'd put his clothes back on.

Ralph staked himself out a small space and sat down on the ground. He smoothed the dirt in front of him and put the ceramic medallion down in the center of the smooth space.

People walked by him, and he tried to attract their attention. He coughed, he waved, he gestured at the peace medallion. People ignored him. He would have to work harder, he thought, since he wasn't willing to say anything. But he was an engineer: sales had never been his strong point.

So Ralph stood up. He held the medallion out to passersby. They turned their heads away.

Ralph was getting hungry. He thought about the salespeople he knew. They didn't give up: rather, they ingratiated themselves with their potential customers. He looked around nervously.

He noticed a buxom young woman in the crowd, staring at him intently. She was quite a bit older than the girl who had watched him so carefully last time he was here. She was very pretty — maybe he could include her in his sales pitch, and then, after he sold the medallion, he could buy her something safe to eat.

Ralph smiled at her with what he hoped was his most engaging smile and dangled the medallion, swinging it in her direction and then holding it up as though she might like to try it on.

Almost instantly, a crowd formed. Aha! he thought with a grin: the language of commerce is universal. But then he noticed that they were muttering in a very unpleasant tone, picking up stones and glancing in his direction. Whatever they were saying, it sounded like he was in a mess of trouble.

Ralph was getting a little queasy from this rapid temporal disassociation. He didn't know what is now common knowledge: that the reverse-Schrödinger effect, which creates the dual timeshadow, causes info-seepage from the newly generated parallel self, adding data at a subconscious level.

Superimposition of the time-traveling Ralph over the newly generated stationary Ralph, fixed in the timestream both forward and back, generated a disorienting interference pattern. The traveling Ralph (TR) influenced the stationary Ralph (SR), and vice-versa, though neither was quite aware of the other. Each of them thought he was acting of his own free will — and indeed each one was, for certain values of free.

At any rate, the crowd was ugly, and Ralph didn't feel so good. So, of his own free will, Ralph bailed, whacking the toolbar without saying good-bye to the young woman or, really, paying much mind to where he was headed.

WASHINGTON, DC, 1865.

Ralph looked around groggily. He was in a theater filled with well-dressed, jolly-looking people, sitting in an uncomfortable seat that was covered in a scratchy red wool. It was anything but soft: horsehair stuffing, probably. The stage in front of him was set as a drawing room. It was lit by lights in the floor that illuminated the actor and actresses rather starkly: a funny-looking, coarsely dressed man and two women in elaborate crinoline dresses.

"Augusta, dear, to your room!" commanded the older of the two actresses, pointing imperiously into the wings, stage right.

"Yes, Ma," the young woman said, giving the man a withering glance. "Nasty beast!" she said to him, and flounced off the stage.

The dialog sounded a bit stilted to Ralph's ears, but the audience was genially awaiting the older woman's comeuppance. *Our American Cousin*, he thought abruptly, that's the play — it's been a hit throughout the war.

He glanced up at what was obviously the presidential box: it was twice the size of the other boxes, and the velvet-covered balustrade at its front, overhanging the stage, had been decorated with red-white-and-blue bunting. Just then, President Lincoln leaned forward through the drapery at the front of the box and rested his elbow on the balustrade to catch the next bit of dialog.

Ralph was dumbstruck, and who would not have been? Medieval England, Woodstock, these had been interesting enough places to visit — but seeing Abraham Lincoln — an iconic figure in American history, an instantly recognizable profile, in the flesh, alive, moving, a real human being, on the very day that the long war had come to a close, with a startlingly cheerful smile on his face as he anticipated a famous comic rejoinder — was to Ralph an intensely moving experience.

He held his breath, frozen, as, at the back of the box, unknown to its occupants, he saw a stunningly handsome man — John Wilkes Booth, he was sure — move in against the wall. Booth pulled out a handgun and drew a bead on the president's head. Without thinking, Ralph leaped to his feet. "Mr. President! Duck!" he shouted.

The gun went off. There were screams and shrieks from the box. A large young man in the presidential party wrestled with Booth, as Lincoln pulled his wife to one side, shielding her. A woman's voice rang out, "They have shot the president! They have shot the president!" Lincoln clutched his shoulder, puzzled but not seriously hurt. Booth leaped for the stage, but strong men grabbed him as he landed, and brought him down.

Oh, cripes, Ralph thought. I've really done it now. This would change the future irrevocably! He would never find his way back to his own time, or anything resembling it. And, panicking, he hit the mental button a third time.

WESSEX, 1442.

Ralph looked around at the damned medieval street market. This time, before he could say anything, an attractive dark-haired woman grabbed his upper arm firmly, pulled him close to her, and spoke into his ear. "Keep your mouth shut, if you know what's good for you," she whispered urgently. She looked remarkably like the young woman he had seen before, but a bit older and a lot more intense.

She took him by the arm, and led him through the fair. Tooth-less old women in their forties offered her root vegetables, but she shook her head. Children tried to sell her sweetmeats, but the young woman pushed on. Without seeming to hurry, without drawing attention to herself or him, she quickly led Ralph to the edge of the fair. People who noticed them smiled knowingly, and some of the men gave him a wink. The woman led him behind a hayrick, a seductive look on her face.

Behind the huge mound of hay, the noise of the fair was diminished, and, for the moment at least, they were visible to no one. The woman's flirtatious manner had vanished. She pushed Ralph away from her and glared at him. Ralph was a little afraid: didn't people in medieval times hit one another a lot? This woman was *mad*.

"Ralph, you idiot!" she said in a low but exasperated voice. She's not speaking Middle English, Ralph thought. Momentarily he wondered: was she a medieval scholar of modern English? Uh....

She looked at him sternly. "People here are smarter than you think! You have to take some precautions! You can't just show up and expect everyone to ignore you."

"What?" said Ralph, brilliantly.

"You dunderhead," she said. "You're lucky you weren't burned at the stake. They were waiting for you, or someone like you. Any old time traveler would do."

"What's your name?" Ralph asked.

"I'm Sylvie, but that's not important."

"It's important to me," said Ralph.

She shook off his attention. "Come with me. Don't say a word, don't even open your mouth."

"But how did you know?" said Ralph. "How do you know I'm a time traveler? Why do you speak a language I can understand?"

"Oh, for Pete's sake," said Sylvie. "You were the first, but you're not the only. Historians of time travel come here all the time, to see where you landed on that very first trip. The locals are getting restless. They flayed those travelers they identified, or they burned them, or they pressed them to death with stones. We couldn't let that happen to you, especially before you told us how it worked."

"How on earth would these yokels have ever noticed me?" he asked.

"Your damn teeth," she said. "Your flawless, glow-in-the-dark, impossibly white teeth." She handed him a rather ugly set of yellowish fake teeth. "Put these on now." Ralph did.

Sylvie then gestured toward a nearby hovel. "Over there," she said. "Inside. It's time for you to explain to me how time travel works." He went where she told him to, and did what she said. How could he not? He was smitten. Fortunately for Ralph, Sylvie was likewise smitten. Many a woman would be, as he was a handsome man with good teeth, and he gave up his secrets readily.

Sylvie then traveled forward, to a time before she was born, and told her parents the secret of time travel. Her parents, who became the most famous temporal anthropologists in history, educated a few others and, when baby Sylvie came along, brought her up to leap gracefully from one century to the next. More gracefully, in fact, than her parents themselves, who vanished in medieval England when Sylvie was twelve. She was, in fact, looking for them when she came upon Ralph that very first time.

Ralph and Sylvie were married in Wessex in 1442, Ralph's dental glory concealed by his fake teeth. Sylvie, inveterate time-traveler that she was, convinced him they should live in the timestream, giving them a sort of temporal immortality. And this is where Ralph, who was, after all, an engineer, not a physicist, failed to anticipate the effect of his actions.

Time does not fly like an arrow, it turns out. It just lies there, waiting for something new to happen. So when Ralph Drumm showed up — completely inappropriately — in the past, that past changed — the past healed itself — so that he had always been there. He acquired ancestors, was born, grew to adulthood — to Ralph's exact age in fact — and his body just happened to be in the exact place where Ralph's timeshadow showed up.

Time travel changes the past as well as the future: time is, in fact, an eternal present when viewed from outside the timestream.

So, as Ralph and Sylvie moved from time to time, they created more and more shadows of themselves in the timestream. As they had children — one, two, three, many — and took them about, the timeshadows of the Drumm children were generated and multiplied. Each shadow was as real as the original. Each shadow lived and breathed ... and bred.

Although they were innocent of any ill intent, Ralph and Sylvie Drumm changed the flow of the stream of time in a way more profound than could be accomplished by any single action, no matter how momentous its apparent effect. Their genetic material came to dominate all of human history, an endless army of dark-haired, blue-eyed Caucasians with perfect teeth. They looked the same. They thought the same. They stuck together.

And this is why we, the last remnants of a differentiated humanity, are waiting here today in Wessex, in 1440 — to defend our future from the great surge of the Drummstream. This time, they will not escape us.

"Shed That Guilt! Double Your Productivity Overnight!"

Michael Swanwick and Eileen Gunn

DEAR SIRS:

Ordinarily, I would not respond to an email such as yours. I am by nature a skeptic and, as a former advertising writer, consider myself well able to resist the transparent come-on of a carelessly written appeal to my baser nature. Today, however...

Today I found myself wracked with guilt at how much time I spend goofing around. Sunday is the end of my work-week and, as usual, all the chickens came home to roost: I absolutely had to get a story finished and sent off. And I did. I didn't do much of anything else: just worry and plot and write, all day long. I didn't even call in a pizza. Fortunately, I keep on hand an adequate supply of snickerdoodles, a nutritionally perfect source of carbs, fats, and cinnamon that will keep anxiety at bay for up to 24 hours.

But now, sitting here at midnight amid crumpled manuscript pages and snickerdoodle crumbs, I feel there must be a better way.

And your email, which promises I could be lounging about on Sundays, taking the day off, doing the crossword puzzle, and idly staring at things without thinking of them, certainly caught my eye.

Can you really reduce my guilt to nothing, as your email claims? Is your service worth its unnamed but undoubtedly exorbitant cost?

Warily,
Eileen Gunn

DEAR MS. GUNN:

Every word in our ad is true! For very reasonable rates, our organization will take on your guilt for a day, a weekend, or even a month-long vacation! You may be especially interested in our Sunday subscription, a perennial bestseller among writers.

Here's how it works: Go to our Rates page, and click on the service that best suits your needs and pocketbook. Prepay, using credit card, debit card, or PayPal. It's as simple as that!

Let's say you choose Guilt-Free Friday Nights. (This option is particularly popular among churchgoers! Garrison Keillor says, "It's like being a Republican for an evening!") Every Friday at precisely 5:30 p.m. local time, all your failures, inadequacies, and moral weaknesses become our responsibility. Do anything you like! Go out dancing and drinking. Stiff the waitress. Bring home an inappropriate sex partner. Stiff the waitress, bring her home, and have inappropriate sex with her. It's all OK! You can even, if you like, Not Write!!! All the guilt you would normally feel is, through our proprietary process, painlessly transferred to a member of our degraded, subhuman staff.

For the first time since you don't know when, you'll go to sleep — as I have for many years — with a smirk on your face.

So don't delay. Act now! You'll be glad you did.

Sincerely,
Michael Swanwick
Chief Creative Officer
Guilt Eaters of Philadelphia

DEAR MR. SWANWICK:

But if I didn't feel guilty, how would I write?

I have it set up that I feel guilty every day until about midnight, when it becomes the next day's problem.

I'd change that, but I'm afraid that if I didn't wake up feeling guilty every day, I'd forget to feel guilty on Mondays.

Worriedly,

Eileen Gunn

DEAR MS. GUNN:

Guilt Eaters of Philadelphia offers a program for that! Sundays you can be guilt free, but the other six days of the week, we can hone and sharpen your guilt until it is a keen-edged weapon of productivity!

Just imagine: You're sitting at your desk and you should be writing. Instead, you log on to the internet. Ordinarily, you'd waste countless hours on ego-searches, Sudoku, and Paris Hilton trivia. But — what's this? It's an email from the child you never knew you'd had, but which it turns out you abandoned in its infancy, telling you how badly her life turned out because of your neglect. You log off and reach for the phone to tell your best friend about this frightful development and — not incidentally — waste half the morning in idle chitchat and gossip. But before your hand reaches the receiver, the phone rings! It's the Humane Society, telling you that your childhood pet, Fluffy, lost all these years, has died of a painful disease you could have cured with an inexpensive treatment, had it not been for the fact that you neglected to put your name and address on its collar.

Stunned, you put down the phone. You stare out the window — your last, best chance to avoid actual work. And then (this is our *pièce de resistance!*) one of our trained professionals calls you up and in your mother's voice says, "I saw what you did last night, and I'm very disappointed."

You start to work. You don't raise your head from the paper until twelve hours have passed and the first fifty pages of your blockbuster fantasy dekalogy have been completed. At this rate, the first volume will be finished in a month!

All for a perfectly understandable fee.

Sincerely,
Michael Swanwick
Chief Creative Officer
Guilt Eaters of Philadelphia

DEAR MR. SWANWICK:

This sounds like my ordinary workday. I do not see how your service could add to my productivity.

The lost kids, the dead pet ... this is my life in a nutshell. And my mother's disapproval? I obsess about it, of course, like everyone else, but it does not drive me to work on the fantasy dekology one single minute.

How did you know about the dekology? It has such a lovely synopsis: elves, mirrors, electric trains, trees that extend into the stratosphere and rain gold on those below, and Dick Cheney's evil twin. NYT Bestseller? Fowler and Lethem can eat their hearts out. But I do not work on it.

Does your service offer anything else?

Curiously,
Eileen Gunn

DEAR MS GUNN:

We are in receipt of your heartbreaking missive, in which you ask, *"Does your service offer anything else?"*

The answer to which is, of course, You Bet Your Sweet Patootie! Hold on to your hat, because Guilt Eaters of Philadelphia is prepared to DOUBLE YOUR PRODUCTIVITY OVERNIGHT!!!

Sound incredible? It is! But true. And there's more! We are prepared to do this at absolutely no cost to you!

Here's how it works: You provide the idea and parameters for that story you want to write but for whatever reason can't. Our downtrodden and overworked staff will labor into the wee hours of the night to produce ten pages of crisply polished prose, all of which is guaranteed to be of final draft quality! You will then, driven by a combination of guilt, admiration, and ambition, produce an equal number of pages of (it goes without saying) superior literary value. And so it will go, turn on turn, until in less time than you ever imagined possible the story is complete.

And what do we demand in exchange for this incredible service? Only the pleasure of being of service, and three-quarters the take when the story is sold! Yes ... we *are* taking more than our fair share. But consider this: It is more than our fair share of a book which otherwise would not exist. Everybody wins!

So don't delay — ACT TODAY!

Sincerely,

Michael Swanwick

Chief Creative Officer

Guilt Eaters of Philadelphia

DEAR MR. SWANWICK

I can tell you've worked hard devising this service, and that you believe in it. But could I see some hard evidence of its efficacy? Testimonials, maybe?

Skeptically,

Eileen Gunn

DEAR MS. GUNN:

You certainly are a tough nut to crack. Not that we think you are a nut. Absolutely not! Yet crack you we shall.

You asked for testimonials? Testimonials you shall have!

A Former Schoolteacher in Maine says:

I was trapped in a dead-end job, living in a trailer, and writing at night. My total production was something like five words a week — and I wasn't working on haikus but novels! Then GEoP taught me to produce, produce, produce! Now it's a sorry month that doesn't see a new novel from me. I write so much that I have to use pseudonyms to keep from flooding the market. So now I am a happy man. The pay is pretty damn good too, but so what? All I ever wanted was to be a human fountain of words, and, as the old joke goes, Now I Are One!

—S. K.

A British YA Author gushes:
As a single mother, I spent seven years working on a short story about a woman sitting in a cheap café trying to write. It was depressing and going nowhere. Heck, I was depressing and going nowhere. Then GEoP showed me how to open the sluice-gates of my soul! Now I'm a billionaire, world-famous, and married to the kind of man my ex-husband only wishes he could be. Thanks, GEoP!

—J. K. R.

A Noted Dead British Fantasist writes:
When I was alive, I was the slowest writer imaginable. It took me an entire lifetime — and it was not a short one! — to pen a single children's book, a trilogy, and a handful of short works and fragments. After my demise, I decided that enough was enough, and linked my fortunes to GEoP's star. Now I've written so many books I can't keep track of them! If only I'd discovered GEoP earlier, I could have wrapped up my career and retired to Miami at age thirty!

—J. R. R. T.

And there are many, many more such unsolicited testimonials on file! Shouldn't yours be among them?

Sincerely,
Michael Swanwick
Chief Creative Officer
Guilt Eaters of Philadelphia

DEAR MR. SWANWICK:

It all sounds very good, but I just don't understand how you can do it. How on earth can your staff turn out such remarkable volumes of work, when it's all I can do to finish a single page?

Can you possibly clear up my confusion?

Uncertainly,

Eileen Gunn

DEAR MS. GUNN:

Clear up your confusion we shall! As you know by now, we here at Guilt Eaters of Philadelphia are strong believers in the motivational power of guilt. Not just your standard guilt, mind you, but crushing, soul-destroying guilt. The kind of guilt that through our secret proprietary process we remove from thousands of clients every day.

What do we do with this guilt once we've piped it into our holding vats? Do we release it into the environment? Certainly not! Rather, we inject it directly into the bloodstreams of our suffering staff writers. Who, feeling responsible for every vile and petty thing that happens in the world, lose themselves in compulsive and desperate scribbling.

It is their misery that has raised many a despairing ink-stained wretch out of the Slough of Writerly Despond and into the Glorious Light of Fiscal Solvency. Let us do the same for you!

Sincerely,

Michael Swanwick

Chief Creative Officer

Guilt Eaters of Philadelphia

DEAR MR. SWANWICK:

I am beginning to have my doubts about the entire enterprise. Am I supposed to benefit from the misery of others? I was not brought up to be like that.

Perhaps we should simply drop the matter.

Firmly,

Eileen Gunn

DEAR MS. GUNN:

I must confess that everybody here at Guilt Eaters of Phila-delphia, from myself down to the most wretched staff writer, finds your reluctance to sign up with the firm that turned a humorless and unproductive nobody into Terry Pratchett abso-lutely baffling. Let me speak to you like a Dutch uncle. You must seize control of your own destiny!

Ask yourself this: What is it that you really want? Fame? Money? Literary immortality? To be a *New York Times* bestseller? Invitations to gala Hollywood parties? The love of millions of readers? To write so many books that by carefully stacking one of each, you can build the walls of a new addition to your house? All these things are attainable! Simply tell us your goals and Guilt Eaters of Philadelphia will make them real for you.

But we can't do it alone. We need your active cooperation.

What will it take to get you to sign up today? Our operators are standing by!

Sincerely,

Michael Swanwick

Chief Creative Officer

Guilt Eaters of Philadelphia

DEAR MR. SWANWICK:

I don't believe your organization can help me after all. Seeing your list of goals made me realize that I don't want any of them. Not the fame, not the money, and certainly not the gala Holly-wood parties. All I really want is to be able to write. It may not make sense to you, but if only I could write prolifically and be left alone, that would be enough for me. I wouldn't even have to be happy.

But I don't suppose that you, or anyone else for that matter, can provide a service that will do that.

Realistically,

Eileen Gunn

DEAR MS. GUNN:

You underestimate us here at Guilt Eaters of Philadelphia! We are expertly qualified to analyze your situation and devise a satisfactory means of resolving all your emotional and psychological problems in a manner that will satisfy you. Now that we completely understand your situation, it is the simplest of matters to devise a custom situation, based on a close reading of your letters and our long association with litterateurs of all stripes, which has given us enormous insight into the writerly mentality.

Thus it is that we are happy to offer you a low-paying position as a member of our miserable and downtrodden writing staff.

Sincerely,

Michael Swanwick

Chief Creative Officer

Guilt Eaters of Philadelphia

DEAR MR. SWANWICK:

Do your employee benefits include snickerdoodles?

Hopefully,

Eileen Gunn

A Different Engine

(with apologies to Messrs. Gibson and Sterling)

NTH ITERATION: THE COMPASS ROSE TATTOO

A PHENAKISTOSCOPE of Ada Lovelace and Carmen Machado, with Machado's companion dog, the brown-and-white pit bull Oliver. They are apparently at a racetrack, although the tableau was no doubt staged at the maker's studio. The two women, clearly on friendly terms, are attired in pale silk gowns and overdresses, billowing out over crinolines but still elegantly simple in effect. They are shown seated at first, on an ornate cast-iron bench in front of a painted scrim, watching the start of an invisible race. They move their gaze to follow the speeding steam gurneys. They stand, caught up in excitement. Carmen puts her hand on Ada's arm, and removes it quickly. Then she surreptitiously dips her hand in Ada's reticule bag, withdraws an Engine card, slips it into a hidden pocket in her own dress, and resumes watching the race. The two women jump about triumphantly, laughing and clapping their hands in an artificial manner. The race has been run and an imaginary purse no doubt won by at least one of them. At the end, Machado turns to hug Lovelace briefly. Her dress dips elegantly low at the back of her neck, and we get a brief glimpse of the famous tattoo between her shoulder blades: a large, elaborate compass rose. Then the two women sit down as they were at the beginning, a slight smile on Machado's face.

Carmen Machado, alone but for faithful Oliver, gazed into the slot of the phenakistoscope and turned the handle. The two women watched invisible gurneys, stood up, leaped around, and sat down again, over and over.

She tapped a few more paragraphs into the document she was working on, weaving the scene on the disk into the text of the novel she was writing. When she was done, she pulled the Compile lever, sat back, and addressed the dog. "All done, Oliver. I think this is as good as it's going to get. Thank heaven for the phenakistoscope. The dead past revived through the wonders of light and shadow, as the adverts say." And so fortunate for herself, she thought, that she and Ada had spent so much time playacting. She need only view a few silly phenakistoscope disks, and she had the plot for the next installment of her fanciful thriller.

When the Compile was done, she gathered up the huge stack of Engine cards, careful to keep them in order. She wrapped them securely in brown paper and tied the package with string. Then she reached for her shawl and Oliver's leash. Oliver was getting old, but he wriggled a bit in anticipation of a walk. They went outside, and she closed the cottage door behind her, pushing a few vines aside. Must get those cut back, she thought — dreadful cliché, a vine-covered cottage.

At the village postal office, the old clerk, Mr. Thackeray, took the package from her as she entered.

"Ah, Miss Machado," said the clerk. "Another installment of your wonderful entertainment about the Queen of Engines! I will send it right off: the wires are free."

"Thank you, Mr. Thackeray," said the writer, watching as he fed the punched cards into the hopper. "I'm so glad you are enjoying the fruits of my misspent youth."

"My pleasure, Miss Machado," said the clacker clerk. "I might have been a writer, you know, but for the attractions of technology and my responsibilities as the head of a household. An artist's life, writing. A restful life of the mind."

"La, Mr. Thackeray!" said the writer. "Nowadays it's scribble, scribble, scribble, and the more scandal and naughtiness the better. I doubt you would find it either artistic or restful."

"That may well be the case, Miss Machado, for a novelist like yourself," said Thackeray. "A fine novelist," he added quickly. He hesitated. "But I — in my youth — I had aspirations to be a kinetoscope writer. Greek tragedy, retold for the small screen." The wire transmission was finished. He rewrapped the cards and tied them up tight.

Carmen Machado nodded. "Quite right, Mr. Thackeray. Quite right. A far more elevated profession," she said, taking the package from the clerk. "But the money is in the novel, sir. The money is in the novel."

Day after the Cooters

(with apologies to Howard Waldrop)

SHERIFF LINDLEY opened his mouth to accept a fig from the beautiful woman in a diaphanous gown who was kneeling on the floor next to his couch. She looked like the woman on those cigarette paper ads, but more alert. She was holding the fruit just out of his reach, and he lifted his head a bit from the pillow. She smiled and pulled it teasingly further away.

Suddenly, there came a heavy pounding — thump, thump, thump — not very far from his head. The lovely courtesan ignored it, and dangled the fig from its stem, smiling flirtatiously. The sheriff leaned his head toward the fruit, but it evaded him.

The pounding grew louder. The woman gave him a provocative look, and said, "Sheriff! Sheriff! Wake up!"

She didn't sound like a woman at all. He woke up.

"Gol Dang!" said Sheriff Lindley. "Leo, that you?"

"Yessir, Sheriff Lindley."

"Didn't I tell you I need my sleep?" Too late for that. The sheriff pulled himself out of bed, dragged on his suit pants and shrugged into his vest. He opened the bedroom door. "This better be good. Sweets and Luke take care of the rest of them cooters, like I told them?"

"I don't think so, Sheriff." Leo looked like the dog's breakfast. He probably had less sleep even than me, thought the sheriff. Excitable fellow. "There's someone here."

"Those folks from that observatory out the Arizona Territory? No need to disturb my well-earned repose. Let them crawl around, if they wish."

"It's not Professor Lowell. It's someone else. He told them to stop blowing things up, and they stopped. I thought you ought to know."

Sheriff Lindley woke up again, for real. "They stopped?" He grabbed his suit coat and badge and strapped on his Colt Navy. "Bring the shotgun," he said to Leo as he ran out the door.

Out by the Atkinson place, on a borrowed horse, Sheriff Lindley looked down at a well haberdasheried man carrying a small, square leather case, accompanied by a fluffy white dog with an unusually alert demeanor.

The sheriff flashed his badge. "Sheriff Lindley," he said. "Mind telling me who you are and what you're doing here, sir?"

The fellow reached into his vest pocket and took out a pasteboard card. He carefully handed it to the sheriff. "Ellis McKenzie Creel of Hemingway, South Carolina, painter and creator of miniature dioramas, at your service, sir!" he said with a flourish.

"Hemingway must be a very fine town, Mr. Creel," said the sheriff, "if its painters dress so well." He was a man who admired a well-cut suit, not that he saw many of them in Pachuco County. "And can you tell me what you're doing giving orders to my men?"

"I had no idea they were your men, sir," said Creel. "I took them for vandals or thieves despoiling this historic site, which I am here to preserve for the United States Government." He pulled out a glove-leather wallet and waved an official-looking piece of paper. The sheriff did not doubt for a moment that it was fake.

"You can go back to your United States Government and tell them that I have everything under control." He unholstered his Colt, but did not point it directly at the visitor.

Creel smiled slightly. A smile with a bit of steel in it, thought the sheriff.

"I beg your forbearance, Sheriff," he said. "Please allow me to give you a demonstration. This will not take long, and then my dog and I will be on our way." He put down his leather case, and turned to the dog. "Abbey, show the sheriff what we are about."

On command, the dog put both paws in front of her and bowed prettily to the sheriff, as in a performance. She then tugged at a string on the leather case, and it fell open. Inside was a strange contrivance, rather like a camera: a leather bellows and straps, brass fittings, glass lenses, and rosewood and bamboo casings. Creel bent down to pick it up.

"Handsome," said the sheriff. "Step away from the device."

Creel stepped away. "Please examine it, sheriff. Take your time. It's harmless, but rather fragile."

The sheriff reholstered his gun and swung off the horse. When someone tells you a thing is harmless, he thought, it's almost certain that the opposite is true.

He was just crouching down to look at the contraption when the dog tugged at another string.

At the renowned Theater of the Modern World and Martian Invasion Museum in Hemingway, South Carolina, Sheriff Lindley rode his borrowed horse, now on permanent loan, around the perimeter of the Old Atkinson Place diorama. He pulled out his watch and flipped it open. Almost time for them to let out the Martians. He stared forlornly at the painted horizon, shading his eyes theatrically with his hand. Then he twisted around in the saddle, doffed his second-best Stetson, and waved it at the giant faces peering in through the viewing glass. Like living in a fishbowl, he thought — not for the first time — and hot as an upside-down washpot on a tin shed roof. But it's a job.

The Perdido Street Project

(*with apologies to China Miéville*)

WETLANDS TO RUDEWOOD, *and then the train. After years of wandering in the wilderness, I am coming home to a place I've never been. It feels already as though I live here, as though I've lived here a very long time.*

As the train moves from the tawdry edge of the city, all decaying farms and rusting iron mills, the voices of its inhabitants, rough, ill-formed, without art or poetry, call out their names swiftly from walls as we pass in the dark. Some are written in Ragamoll or Lubbock, but other scripts abound, including a few I have never before seen. I am sure one of them was Anopheliian, a strange, whiny script that made my body itch as we passed. Strange scents filled the car and were gone: Khepri obscenities.

The train slows, a safety requirement: the thaumaturgic gyros have been shut off for its passage through the city. A tinny voice of uncertain origin — mechanical? Remade? Garudic, even? — announces upcoming stations, but many are unannounced, and we pass through quickly without stopping, as if there is something shameful about them.

We cross the River Tar, and then quickly, far more quickly than seems possible, we are in the heart of the heart of the city. Although I've never seen them before, I recognize the Ribs, off in the distance, silhouetted against the sky.

My train pulls into the station. This is precisely where I want to be, in this scrofulously magnificent construct. I shoulder my bag and walk out into its cavernous arrival hall, eight stories high. Five railway lines, six militia lines, and the militia's towering Spike: there were thousands of people in the hall — running, walking, standing still in puzzlement or exhaustion or boredom. Stairways up, stairways down, passageways lit or dark, some with descriptive signage, some completely anonymous, but all of them thronged with creatures of every shape and size and color and race, an ocean of roiling beings, all on their way somewhere else.

For people without tickets, there is much to do in the station itself. There is free food — tons of food tossed aside half-eaten by those in transit. There are shops of all kinds, selling everything from cheap sex toys to luxurious clothing and hard goods that only the very wealthy can afford. You can even live here, if you find some abandoned tunnel or unused stairwell. But space is at a premium, and anyone who finds a dry corner and makes it theirs is likely to be evicted by someone stronger or better armed. There is talk of a community of fRemades, the free Remades, many levels down who defend their domain and whose members rarely see the light of day.

The Remades themselves draw my attention, of course, and I stare at them like some country boy come to the big city for the first time, though I am not someone unlearned or unused to cities. A man with a rat's head begs for change and pieces of cheese. A woman with a fishtail instead of legs manipulates her tank-on-wheels deftly through the crowd; in her shopping basket, a package wrapped in white butcher paper squirms. A man and a woman walk together, close but not touching. He has pins stuck into him, all over his body, their rounded heads protruding slightly, and she has pins sticking out of her, the points emerging through her skin and clothing, like a human bed of nails. I wonder what on earth they — and all the others — have done to deserve such torture. It is a sickness of this city that they use their remarkable thaumaturgic technology to punish and shame.

I have lived and worked in many great cities, though their names *are unknown to those who live here. These people know little of the rest of the world, expecting it to come to them. And it does, to this cross-roads of life, this station that is more than a station.*

I walk on, examining this remarkable structure, its construction, its design and endless redesign, its strengths and its bruises.

Sitting in his usual booth at the Moon's Daughters, Gedrec-sechet, librarian for the renowned Palgolak Church library, watched the human stranger work his way through the pub. He had the clothing of a businessman and the demeanor of an artist, and he moved with a certain confident awareness that made Ged think he was packing a weapon of some kind. Odder still, he was greeting the various locals — a particularly diverse bunch — in their native languages, not in Ragamoll. This didn't make them remarkably more friendly to him — but wait: he was buying a round for a small group of Workerbees. They all clinked glasses and toasted The Product, and he talked with them a bit. The atmosphere around him got ... not warm, really, but distinctly less frigid.

Ged bided his time. He would do this, of an evening, just sit and watch. It was amazing how much knowledge of the world one could pick up just by hanging out in a pub and listening to other people. Though he hoped the Godmech Cogs weren't canvassing tonight: he could do without another lecture on the evils of sentientomorphic thinking.

Eventually, sure enough, the stranger caught his eye. "Ready for another?" he asked in Vodyanoi.

Ged nodded. "Thank you kindly," he said in Ragamoll. "King-pin." The name of the beer was unpronounceable in his own language. The stranger nodded and went off to the bar.

When he came back, he handed Ged his beer, and indicated the empty seat across from him. "May I inconvenience you?" he asked, still in Vodyanoi.

"Surely, honored sir, it is no inconvenience, but a pleasure," said Ged in his own language, with a gesture of welcome.

The stranger sat down. "I am Santosh," he said. "Santosh Philip, new to your city." He spoke with a slight accent, but Ged could not place it.

"Gedrecsechet," Ged said. "Ged, if you please. And what do you do, Mr. Santosh Philip?"

"I am an architect," said Santosh. "A designer," he corrected. "Anything from an ashtray to a city."

"Cities? Really?" said Ged, intrigued. Only a small number of cities had known designers, and he thought he remembered all their names. "And what cities have you designed?"

"I am afraid you would not have heard of them. They are small cities, and far away."

"Try me," said Ged. Like other members of the Palgolak Church, he was a fount of knowledge.

"The city I am most proud of is a suburb of Maruábm called Bmapastra," said Santosh. "A cruel high-desert climate, dry and cold, but I aligned the city to tame the winds and situated parks over its geothermal vents. It's rather a cheerful place for such a bleak setting. Temperature never gets much above freezewater, but they have fresh fruits and vegetables year-round."

"I *have* heard of Bmapastra, but was unaware it had been completed. My congratulations, sir. Certainly your name should be as well-known as the city you designed."

"Well-known, sir? It gets no visitors, except from Maruábm, whose citizens consider it a place to escape, briefly, the grimness of their own city," said Santosh. "I am astonished that you have heard of Bmapastra."

"You are not familiar with the Palgolak Church?" asked the vodyanoi. He gestured at his yellow robes. "I am its librarian. You should have been astonished had I *not* heard of it."

"Ah, you are the relentless seekers of knowledge?"

Ged smiled a huge saurian smile and licked his lips with his huge tongue. "That is our joy, sir, and we are an ecstatic sect."

"Then perhaps you can answer a question for me, if you would?" Santosh asked diffidently.

"What I know I can share," said Ged. And that was true, technically, although what he didn't want to share remained his own.

"Who was the architect for the magnificent station?"

"Ah, a sad story there," said Ged. "His name is lost to history. If it could be known, I would know it, I assure you." It frustrated Ged to have to tell a story with holes in it.

"Lost? How could that be?" Santosh scratched his head. "Surely the station was built during the Full Years, the blossoming of the city?"

"It was, and if you think that was a well-documented time, you're quite right. But the architect — that first architect — fell in love with his own creation, and fell afoul of those who sought to control it. After seven years of fighting with the government for his beloved's freedom, he found himself first accused of heresy, and then declared quite mad. He was locked up, and they threw away the key. And his name."

"A mere architect?"

"He was fortunate he was not blinded. We take our architecture very seriously," Ged said.

"I see you do. I see you do." Santosh was clearly taken aback by this.

"But let's not dwell on that," said Ged expansively. "If I spent my time interrogating the things I know, I'd never have any time to learn anything new." He laughed.

"I am honored to have met so learned a person on my first day in your city. Perhaps you could tell me what caused the recent damage to the station and environs?"

Ged's face became serious. "Slake-moth feeding season."

Santosh looked at him quizzically.

"They've been particularly bad this year," Ged said in a non-committal tone. He did not want to go into the details: his friend Isaac was among the many people still missing.

Santosh nodded uncertainly, as though he had never heard of slake-moths. "Any plans for cleaning it up? Good bit of work, that. I've never done a reconstruction on something quite so big and complicated and historic. Wouldn't at all mind getting the contract."

"The mayor is soliciting bids, but I told you what happened to the original architect. No one wants to take on this project."

"Good grief, man, that was hundreds of years ago," Santosh replied. "I'm sure we needn't fear a repeat."

"This city is not welcoming to the stranger, my friend. Be careful on the streets, and in the pubs. And in the mayor's chambers."

"I am aware of that," said Santosh, with a friendly demeanor, "and I thank you kindly for your concern."

He did not say he was armed, or he was ready for anything, or indicate in any way what his means of defense might be. Whatever he's relying on, Ged thought, he's good enough at it that he doesn't feel a need to bluster about, scaring people off. I will not worry about him until he has rebuilt the station.

Internal Devices

(with apologies to K. W. Jeter)

AFTER MY TUMULTUOUS ADVENTURES resulting from Lord Bendray's attempt to destroy the world, I sought, naturally, to restore my equanimity, and I had thought that moving my modest clockwork-repair shop to a little-noted part of London would guarantee me obscurity, a modest living, and surcease of adventure, not to mention the calming of the unwonted physical excitement that has disturbed me since Miss McThane assisted in the culmination of my efforts. But the events of a cold, foggy day in early November reminded me that no man's adventure can be declared done until he himself is Done.

I opened my shop a few minutes late that morning and was startled to see, waiting in the chill outside my front door, a man in a light jacket with a similarly attired child and a large ruck-sack. I was surprised that my faithful Able had not detected them and apprised me of their presence with a warning bark. Still asleep on his pillow, I thought: Able was getting old, and his hearing wasn't what it once was.

Naturally, I admitted the visitors to my shop and offered them a bit of tea to warm themselves. I apologized for the interior chill. "It is my custom not to burn coal so early in the winter season," I said, "so there is none in the scuttle, else I would surely have my man set a fire. You must be so terribly cold in those thin jackets."

"Nah, they're technical," said the visitor. "Mine and my kid's. The fabric creates a thermal barrier that absorbs heat from your body and releases it when you need it. Pretty spiffy, eh?"

I had no idea what he was talking about. "Are you a visitor from afar, sir?" I asked. Perhaps this was how they spoke in India.

"I'm from the Colonies," he replied in a jovial manner, as if this were a great joke. I looked at him. "Really," he continued. "Descended from William Bradford of the Plymouth Colony, and that's the truth."

I was about to ask for an explanation, when Creff, my afore-mentioned factotum, arrived from my workroom at the back of the shop, where he had been attending to the matter of an extremely large package that had arrived earlier, occasioning my delay in opening the shop.

"Good lord, Mr. Dower," he began, not noticing the new-comers, "that scoundrel Scape must think you're running some kind of a garrage here for him to store his belongings in. Not that I don't wonder whether he came by these things honest — " He broke off as he saw we had visitors.

"Ah — excuse me, sir," he said to me, and stepped back.

"In a moment, Creff," I said, and turned to the man who had come into my shop. "What can I do for you, sir?" I asked.

"I have an appointment here with a Mr. Scape," he said.

I could scarcely mask my astonishment. "Mr. Scape? Why, sir, he — "

" — is right here, sucker," said a too-familiar voice, and that very rascal appeared in the doorway of the workroom. He leaped forward to clasp the hand of my visitor.

"Bet you're Gardner," he said, taking the man's hand in his cold and flaccid grip. "Graeme Scape. Whew! Glad you made it." He looked around as though, well, as though he owned my place of business.

"Likewise," said the other man. "First time, and all. Quite an adventure. Even brought my boy along."

Scape gestured in my direction. "This here's, uh, the fellow I told you about. We call him George, George Dower, just like anyone else." He smiled wolfishly. "Go ahead, shake his hand. Give it a try."

I was about to deny that Scape and I were associated in any way, but the fellow grabbed my hand and shook it, a bit gingerly.

"David Gardner," he said. "And this here's my son, Ridley." He seemed a little hesitant to greet me, as if he were unsure what I might do.

But then the little fellow, who couldn't have been more than five or six, reached out to shake my hand and spoke up. "How do you do?" he said, quite charmingly. How could I not smile at him and shake his little hand?

"Very pleased to make your acquaintance, Master Ridley," I said. The child, at least, knew how to manage an introduction.

Gardner, barely acknowledging me, turned to Scape. "*Very* nice!" he said. "*Smooth.* Can't wait to see the internals. Can you open it up?" Scape had apparently promised him some device.

"Well, Mr. Gardner," I said, "before we go any further, I must tell you that — "

"Hey, George," Scape interrupted me smoothly, "there is something in the back I need to get a handle on. Right back, Gardner." He nodded at his visitor and hustled me into my workshop.

"What's going on here?" I asked, but he continued to shepherd me toward the back of the room.

"Keep yer shirt on. You got the Paganinicon here?"

"Why yes," I replied, startled. How did he know I still had the Paganinicon? My late father's finest creation, it was a remarkably lifelike clockwork automaton, devised by my father and fabricated in my own image, except for it having impressive virtuosity on the violin and on a certain other instrument that I blush to mention. Alas, it was necessarily rendered nonfunctional at the dénouement of our recent Excitement. I had kept it, out of sentiment, when selling off my father's other wondrous devices.

"Well, that's jake," he said with a grin. Scape was gleeful, and I did not trust his glee, for all that he had been a friend of my father's — such a good friend, in fact, that my father had gifted Scape with a remarkable device that could watch the future pass before it. It was, in fact, through lip-reading the future that Scape had acquired his eccentric manner of speech.

"Come over here, buddy, and scope this out." He pointed beyond the big box, which was open now — empty, with bits of packing material strewn around.

I walked over to the box. "Were you *in* this, Scape?" I asked. "What on ear— " And before I could finish the sentence, the floor dropped out from under me, and I fell down, down, down, landing in a sort of net. I was very quickly wrapped in the net by hands unseen, and a gag was tied over my mouth before I could even catch my breath to cry out. Someone had unfastened the locks on the basement hatch!

"Careful! Don't damage the goods," a familiar feminine voice said to my invisible handlers. "Just lay him down over there." It was her.

"Miss McThane!" I tried to speak, but the gag impeded me, and it sounded like the grunts of one of Mr. Darwin's monkeys.

Soon she was upon me, her breath hot on my cheek. "Okay, loverboy. This won't take long, and then we'll be on our way." She ran a finger slowly down my cheek. "Unless, of course, you'd want us to *tarry* a little while." I pulled away from her unwelcome and ill-timed advances.

The hatch above me had been refastened. I heard a bit of dragging on the floor above, and then people walking around. Scape had evidently brought that Gardner fellow into my workshop. This, of course, infuriated me, but as I was thoroughly trussed up, there was no recourse but patience. I could hear everything he said, which of course only increased my frustration.

"Yup. Most of my goods is snapped up by highrollers. The piece I just showed you is the only one I got right now." He was opening the cabinet that contained the Paganinicon. "Here it is. You've seen how good it runs. I've shut it down and packed it for shipping. You brought the dough?"

That reprobate was selling the foreigner the Paganinicon! The nerve. Where was Creff? Almost the moment that thought crossed my mind, two stalwart fellows emerged from the cellar gloom, carrying Creff, trussed up and gagged just as I was. He was thrashing about.

"Just put him there, next to the others," said Miss McThane. She addressed Creff. "Quit yer bellyaching."

Others? I wondered. There are others? And then I realized that there was a cage by my side, and in it was faithful Abel, also trussed and muffled. No wonder he hadn't barked.

"You fiends!" I said to Miss McThane.

Somehow my meaning transcended the gag. "Watch yer mouth," she said. "Don't get yer dander up. This won't take long, and there'll be a bit of something in it for you."

Upstairs, the conversation continued. It seemed likely the visitor was skeptical of Scape's promises. "Let me see the internal gears," said Mr. Gardner.

"No problem," said Scape eagerly. I heard the creak of the Panaginicon's access panel being opened.

"Exquisite," said the visitor. "What a remarkably complex mechanism. Cross-oriented helical gears, hypoids, harmonic drives, an especially ingenious epicyclic system." He seemed to have an appreciation for the sort of thing my father did best. "This will be the greatest steampunk movie of all time," he declared, "starring a working clockwork android. Billy Wilder, eat your heart out! Christopher Nolan, step aside! David Bowie, maybe *now* you'll return my calls!"

"Yeah, what you said, buddy," said Scape. "Now, about the moolah...."

"I've got it right here."

"I'll just close him up...." There was a scuffling sound, and Scape cried out. "Son of a bitch! You slammed that right down on me finger! Bleeding, I am."

"Sorry," said Mr. Gardner. "Here you are. A thousand pounds. I'll just set the bag down here for you." There was a light thump.

"Frickin' finger," said Scape.

"Don't get blood on the money, Mr. Scape. That's bad luck! Now, can we turn it back on and walk it out of here? My time is almost up."

"Can't send it through the machine in operating mode. Blow it all to hell. My men will take it out to your carriage. After that, it's your lookout." Scape shouted, "Hey! Over here!" and I heard the sound of heavy feet, signaling the arrival of, no doubt, the same minions who had bound and gagged myself and Creff. And brave Able, I thought, glancing over at him.

To my surprise, I noticed that Able had chewed off the gag and was nibbling surreptitiously at the ropes that bound him. I looked away, concerned that I might draw attention to him.

But Miss McThane never gave Abel so much as a glance. She cared not for dogs, those loyal and intelligent friends of man, but she was very much attentive to what was going on upstairs, and she didn't seem to like the way events were unfolding. When Scape didn't open the hatch door, she became suspicious.

"Not gonna let that bastard fly the coop with my share of the dough," she muttered. "You guys stay here," she said, unnecessarily, and hurried off into the dark.

How dastardly, I thought, to leave us tied up. How unworthy

of you, Miss McThane. Truly, life on the road has hardened you.

As soon as she was gone, however, Able leaped out of the ropes that had constrained him and came directly to my assistance. Once freed, I liberated Creff, and together the three of us dashed upstairs.

As we burst through the door into the workshop, we could hear Gardner's wagon roll off down the street, clattering noisily on the cobblestones, my infelicitous doppelganger off to who knows where.

In my workroom, we came upon a remarkable tableau. Scape was poised with the rucksack of money over his shoulder, his bleeding hand wrapped in a rag from my worktable. Miss McThane was pointing a small but professional-looking gun at him. And, across the room, the two burly henchmen assessed the scene.

The taller one addressed Miss McThane. "'E were runnin' off wizzout paying, were 'e?"

"Save me from that crazy dame, you dumb gorillas!" bellowed Scape.

Able ran over to Scape and tugged at the rucksack, pulling it off his shoulder. It fell to the floor, spilling packets of five-pound notes. The larger of the two ruffians reached down and picked up a packet.

"This 'ere will do for me an' my mate," he said. "We hain't greedy. 'Onest day's work." The two of them quickly thundered out the door.

Miss McThane nodded to Scape. "Toss me the sack," she said.

Scape threw it at her ill-humoredly. Still holding Scape at gunpoint, she reached down to pick it up. Suddenly, clever Able leaped again from the shadows and, with the advantage of surprise, knocked the gun from Miss McThane's hand, dragged it off to a corner, and, giving a few sharp warning barks, stood guard over it.

"Okay, okay," said Scape. "The jig is up — you got the cabbage. Toss me my share, and we'll call it even."

Miss McThane laughed as if she were genuinely amused.

"Will someone kindly tell me what has just transpired?" I asked.

"Well," said Scape, "Gardner's a Texian whose old man went yours one better — invented a time machine, for moving back and forth, y'know. He wanted a mechanical man, and, well, I knew you had that useless can of brass — "

Scape's words were interrupted by a scream of agony from Miss McThane. We all of us — Scape, Creff, Able, and myself — turned to look at her. She was pulling the bundles of bills from the bag, fanning them open, and throwing them in the air. "Crap! What a load of shit! Your *chump* worked a grift on us." She pitched an unopened bundle at Scape and hit him on the side of the head.

"Calm yourself, my dear Miss McThane," I said. "Whatever is the matter?"

But Scape was way ahead of me. "He's pitched us the snide, has he? He's left us the green-goods? He seemed like such an honest bloke."

"No wonder we're always strapped. You can't even put the flimp on a frick from the other side of time!" Miss McThane seemed caught between anger and despair. "You can gimme the gat back," she said to the dog. "It's no use even shooting him."

I picked up one of the flash notes that were blowing about the room. The same appearance as our honest British banknotes, they were adorned not with our beloved Queen, but with a mustachioed fellow sporting a bowl haircut. Who on earth was this, I wondered.

Then I noticed the banner underneath. "William Bradford," it read, "Governor of the Plymouth Colony."

The Armies of Elfland

Eileen Gunn and Michael Swanwick

IT WAS THE MIDDLE OF THE NIGHT when the mirrors came out of the elves. With a sound like the cushioned patter of an ice storm, the tiny mirrors fell to the ground, leaving a crust of glitter behind the marching elf army. They bled, of course, but the elven blood restored the dry land, undoing the effects of the drought, and moss emerged green from the ground in the troops' wake.

The sight of the moss brought forth the drought-starved humans and their pathetic get to the mouths of their caves.

"Stay here!" the new father commanded. Not one of the children was his. But all the real fathers were dead, so they had no choice but to obey him or be beaten.

"Don't go," Agnes wanted to say. "Don't trust them." But Richard gently touched her lips to silence her. Richard was the oldest of the children, indeed almost an adult himself, and he did what he could to protect the others.

The adults fell on the damp moss, tearing it up by the double-handful like so much bread dough. They sucked the moisture from it and crammed its substance down their throats. Briefly, all seemed well. One of the new father's wives was raising an arm to beckon the children down when the minute mirrors they had ingested suddenly expanded to ten, a hundred, a thousand times their original size. Jagged shards of mirror erupted from their flesh as horns, tusks, and spines. Blood fountained into the air and pooled on the ground, glimmering in the moonlight. The adults splashed through it, lurching grotesquely, writhing and howling in pain.

The children hid their eyes and turned away. The littlest ones cried.

Then, suddenly, there was silence. That was the hardest to bear of all.

But though the adults had ceased screaming, they did not fall. Brutally sharp glass fragments jutted from every inch of their bodies, holding them upright and rigid.

Nothing that was human remained of the adults. They had turned to crystal.

"We've got to bury them," Agnes said firmly. "We can't just leave them standing like that."

"How?" Richard asked. "We can't even touch them."

The children had no shovels, but even with shovels they would have had a tough time trying to dig graves on the dry, barren beach. Where they stood had once been the shore of a small arm of the Pacific Ocean. But then the ocean had dried up and become a low, mountainous land of cliffs and sudden rifts, blanketed with dead fish and rotting seaweed. The sun had baked the wasteland that the elves had first created and then crossed as black and hard as obsidian. There would be no burials there.

"We can throw stones," Frederic said. He was the youngest of the children. He hadn't spoken until he was three, which was over five years ago. When he did start to speak, however, his first words were, "Things are not as they once were." Followed, after two days of intense thought, by, "In any case, they could be arranged better." He came up with ideas nobody else could have.

So they did as he suggested, smashing the starlight-glittery figures from a distance until they were nothing but mounds of broken glass. Richard, who had read a lot back when there were books, said, "In ancient times when men were warriors and carried spears, they buried their dead in mounds of rocks called cairns. This was an honorable form of burial. Even kings and queens were buried that way." Then he turned to Agnes. "You're good with words," he said. "Please. Say a few words over the dead."

Agnes took a deep breath. At last she said, "The adults were stupid." Everybody nodded in agreement. "But the elves are cruel, and that's worse." Everybody nodded again. "I'm sick of them, and I'm sick of their war." She raised her voice. "I want to have enough food to eat! All the food I want, every day of my life. I'm going to get it, too. I don't know how. But I do know that I'm never going to be fooled by the elves or their mirrors or their green moss ever again!"

She spat on the ground, and everyone else followed suit.

"Amen," she said.

She had no idea how futile her vow would prove.

During the Alien Invasions, as they were called before the world learned that the armies of Elfland came not from someplace unimaginably far away but from somewhere impossibly nearby, the children and their parents had been vacationing on a resort near Puget Sound. So shocked were the parents that at first they didn't think to shield the children from their television sets. So the children saw the slaughter — what happened to the people who resisted the elves, and then what happened to the people who didn't. When the elves came to Seattle, they left the television stations untouched, and courteously escorted the cameramen to Volunteer Park to broadcast their victory celebration to whoever might still be watching.

Under the guidance of their ghastly, beautiful queen, the invaders flayed their prisoners. This they did with exquisite skill, so that all were still alive when the work was done. Then they roasted them over coals. Troubadours wandered up down the rows of scorched and screaming flesh, playing their harps in accompaniment. Elf-lords and elf-ladies formed quadrilles on the greensward in front of the band shell and danced entrancingly. Afterwards, they threw themselves down on the grass and ate heaping platters of roasted human flesh, while goblin servants poured foaming wine into sapphire goblets.

Then they torched the city.

The children understood cruelty far more intimately than did the adults, who had the army and the police and a hundred other social institutions to shield them from schoolyard beatings, casual theft, and having bugs and other vermin dropped into one's food or mouth or clothing simply because somebody larger was bored. But they had never before seen such cruelty as this. What shocked them was not the deeds in themselves — they had imagined much worse — but that nobody took pleasure from them. These cruelties were not done with fiendish playground glee. There was no malice behind them, no glorying in the cruelty of what was done. Just a string of horrifying and senseless images running night and day on the television, until one day the transmitters stopped and there were no more.

That was when Frederick told the children that they had to go into the caves, and Richard led them all there. When the adults came to bring them back to the rental bungalows, Richard led the children deeper into the darkness and the adults followed. Thus it was that they few survived when every building on the island simultaneously burst into flames. It was cold in the caves, but at night the adults went out and foraged for food and blankets and fuel. Every now and then some of them didn't return.

Months passed.

When the elves changed the weather and shrank the seas,

the grasses and crops dried up. There was little to eat, and the adults weren't anything like they used to be. Hunger made them unpredictable, violent, and impulsive.

It was no wonder, then, that the elves were able to catch them by surprise.

The adults were dead. Human history was over.

In the wake of the elves, grass returned, and then flowers. Trees rocketed to the sky. Some bore fruit. Agnes was roasting apples in the coals of a campfire one morning, when Richard sat down beside her, the sun bright in his golden-red hair. "We need weapons," he said. "For when the elves return. I tried making a bow and arrows. But it's just a toy. It wouldn't kill anything larger than a sparrow."

Agnes thought. "We can make spears, like the ones the cairn-people had. Spears are easy to use, and almost anything sharp would do for a head."

Richard laughed with delight. "If you were older, I'd kiss you!" he cried, and hurried off to look for materials.

Leaving Agnes with the strangest feeling. Almost, she wished she was older. Almost, she wished he would kiss her.

That afternoon the elves returned and took them all prisoner.

This time, they killed nobody. Lean elves with long, stinger-tipped abdomens, like yellow-jackets, injected venom into the children's bodies. They were immobilized and stacked like cord-wood on a long wooden tray, then flown by winged elves back to their camp. There, they were dumped to the ground and dosed with antivenom. As they came back to life, the smaller children began to cry.

Not Agnes, however. Her body ached from being stung, but she was far more concerned about what was going to happen next. She looked around carefully. The elven camp was made up of brightly-colored tents, far loftier than the ones people used for camping, with long silk pennons flying from their tips. They stood on a hilltop and the tents went on forever below them, like a field of flowers that had no end.

There was a groan behind Agnes, and somebody clutched her shoulder. With a shriek, she whirled about, only to discover Richard groggily staggering to his feet. "Oh!" she cried. "You scared me!"

A bamboo whip cut across her back.

It was just a single blow, but it was stunning in its effect. Agnes fell to her knees. Looking up through brimming tears, she saw an elegant and fearsomely beautiful grey-skinned elf in armor of ice lowering his whip. He made a gesture, lightly squeezing his own lips shut. Then he raised his eyebrows questioningly: *Do you understand?*

Richard started forward, fists clenched, as if to attack the elf, but Agnes flung her arms around him and held him back. When he twisted angrily toward her, she shook her head. Then, facing the elf, she nodded.

The elf made a sweeping gesture that encompassed all seven children. Gracefully, he gestured with his whip up a broad grassy avenue between the tents: *Go that way.*

They obeyed. Agnes went first, keeping her head down submissively, but secretly observing all that she could and filing it all away for future use. A half-step after her came Richard, head high and face stony. Next were the three middle children, Lexi, Latoya, and Marcus. Last of all came Frederic and Elsie, who were the youngest. If Agnes dawdled or started to glance behind herself, she felt a light flick of the grey elf's whip on the back of her neck. It was just a reminder, but a potent one. Agnes hoped the littler children were being more circumspect than she, but she doubted very much that they were.

They were marched past a corral where centaurs fought with fists and hooves for the entertainment of their elven captors, and then by a knackery where unicorn carcasses were hung on meat-hooks to cure. Under an arch made of two enormous ivory tusks they went and around a pyramid of wine barrels being assembled by red-bearded dwarves only half as tall as the hogs-heads were. At last they came to their destination.

It was a tent as wide and bright as the sunset, whose billowing walls of silks and velvets burned ember red and blood ochre, shot through with molten golds and scarlets that shimmered as if they came from a spectrum alien to human eyes. Banners and swags of orange and purple and black flew from the tops of the tent poles, kept permanently a-flutter by small playful zephyrs that smelled of cinnamon, cardamom, and hot peppers. She could not read the sigils on the flags, but she did not need to. By the psychic wind of terror and awe that gushed from the doorway to the tent, she felt, she sensed, she *knew* who lay within.

It could only be the dreadful Queen of Elfland.

At the castle-tent's salient, the younger children were marched down a passage to the left, while Richard and Agnes were gestured inside. Almost, she cried after them. But the ice-armored elf raised his whip warningly. So Agnes made no sound, though she stretched out her arms toward the little ones as they disappeared from her ken.

Entering the tent was like stepping into another world. Gone were the somber reds and sullen crimsons, exchanged for sprightly greens and yellows and blues. Hummingbirds darted here and there. There was a tinkling of small bells, like wind chimes in a summer breeze. The sun shone brightly through the silk walls making luminous the embroidered draperies showing scenes of war and feasting, of lovemaking and animal-hunting, and of things for which Agnes had no words. They wavered with every movement of the air, so that the figures seemed to be alive and in motion, pleading to be freed.

Their guard came to a stop. Overcome with dread, Agnes seized Richard's hand. He squeezed hers back, reassuringly.

A gong sounded. The air shattered like the surface of a pond after a frog leaps into its center, and when the reverberations stopped and the air was still again, the elf-queen was simply *there*.

She reclined casually on the air just above a brocade-covered divan in the center of the tent. She wore a cream-colored man's Brioni suit, cunningly retailored to fit her elegant body, an apricot silk blouse open to the navel, from which peeked a teardrop-shaped rock-crystal pendant, and no shoes. Her skin was the color of polished bronze, with hints of verdigris and subtle green depths. Her cheekbones were high and sharp. Her eyes were set at an angle, and they flashed jungle-green, an emerald effulgence from a star that did not shine in the night sky of this world. Unbidden a name popped into Agnes's mind: *Melisaundre*.

Queen Melisaundre was beautiful. Even Agnes could see that.

Beside her, Richard was transfixed.

"We came here by accident," the elf-queen said casually, as if returning to a conversation already in progress. "We didn't know your world even existed here on the marches of Avalon, that fey land we set out to conquer. Imagine our surprise and delight! A realm of possibilities opened before us! As it happened, of course, we destroyed your lands and killed your people. But, well ... we were bored, pure and simple. What else could we have done? What other would any sensible being have done in our position?"

Agnes knew it would be a mistake to answer, and she kept her mouth shut. She was relieved at first that Richard did the same, but then she dared a quick sideways glance and saw that he was blushing. At a time like this! Agnes all but stamped her foot. If Richard, of all people, couldn't be relied on to keep his wits about him, then who could?

Melisaundre dangled her bauble before her lips and blew softly upon it, setting it swinging gently on the pendulum of its chain. She reached out and delicately touched it — like so! — with the tip of a tongue as pink as a cat's. "Don't you wish you could be this jewel?" she asked. "Wouldn't you like to lie between my breasts forever? Wouldn't that be the pleasantest doom imaginable?"

"Thank you, ma'am, no," Agnes said quickly, dipping the briefest of curtseys. It was essential to be polite: she realized that instinctively. And the higher the level of danger, the more polite you had to be. She knew she had to be very, very polite to the queen of the elves.

Richard stepped forward involuntarily, his eyes glowing as if lit by a flash from a hidden mirror. In a dazed voice, he said, "I think that . . ."

"Richard! No!" Agnes said.

"I mean, it kind of sounds like . . ."

"Stop! Stop! Stop!"

"Maybe, I don't know . . ."

"*Think*, Richard! Don't just —"

". . . I'd like that."

And he was gone.

The elf-queen held the pendant up, admiring its newly flawed interior. "A jewel with a soul reflects a better quality of light, don't you think?" she remarked lightly. "And as we have none of our own, we are so grateful when you volunteer yours."

Without thinking, Agnes launched herself at the elf-queen, clawing, kicking, and screaming. And found herself immediately frozen in mid-air, suspended about four feet above the floor.

"Cassis and asphalt," said the elf-queen. "Hints of anise. An elusive smoky quality. Just a trace of honey. And a flintiness under it all. We could bottle that and sell it at market." She placed her long, sharp nose in the crook of Agnes's neck and inhaled deeply. Sharp fingers pinched Agnes's arms and the inside of a leg, as if assessing her plumpness. "But with encouragement, what might you not become? Worthy, perhaps, of even a queen's palate." She raised her voice. "Store her with the others, and we'll do more with her later."

Agnes was taken away and fed — on marzipan, melon slices and sugared oranges, on candied ginger and great slabs of baklava so intensely sweet they made her teeth ache, washed down with honeyed tea. She ate until her stomach hurt. But all the while, though she was careful to hide it, she burnt with that deep inner anger of which children, in the sentimental imagination, were deemed incapable. Any casual observer of a kindergarten or a schoolyard, however, can see that the younger the child, the less capable it is of hiding any anger it may harbor. By Agnes's age, most children are able to bank their fury so that it is generally unseen by adults and, often, by the child itself. Agnes certainly could do that.

Then she was washed, in water that had been heated to body temperature, and had hibiscuses afloat in it. Needle-toothed yakshis dried her down with impossibly fluffy towels and helped her into new garments. They were of elven make and did not cover her stomach, but otherwise they seemed decent enough. Finally she was led to a large oval cushion which, though it looked suspiciously to her like the sort of thing people had for their pet dogs or cats, was nevertheless so comfortable that she fell asleep almost immediately.

When Agnes awoke, the bed was rocking gently under her. She drew aside the bed-curtain and discovered that the armies were on the march again, and that her bed was being carried by two trolls. She swung her legs over the edge so she could climb down.

"I'd advise you not to do that, Missy," one of the trolls said. He was a tusked grotesque with legs like a rhinoceros's.

"If you did," said the second, "we'll reflexively stop you in the most painful available manner."

"Which, truth be told, we'd really rather not."

"You're just another victim of elvish depravity, like we are, after all."

"So just stay with the program, okay?"

Agnes scrambled back into the center of the bed. "Okay," she said. And, "I'm sorry. I didn't want to get you in trouble."

"You can't get us in trouble, Missy."

"Even if you could, what would we care?"

"We're not self-aware."

"Just bundles of reflexive responses, is all. It's not as if we were actually conscious."

So she spent most of the day, dozing off and on, being carried along with the trooping armies of Elfland. When at last they made camp, she climbed down and fed herself from one of the many tables overflowing with food of all kinds. Then Melisaundre sent for her.

"You are a green gemstone, I believe," the elf-queen said. "So you shall be treated with jealousy."

"Ma'am? I don't understand."

"You don't need to understand. Only to obey."

Thus it was that for thrice a thousand and one nights in a row, Agnes served as the elf-queen's cup bearer. Silent and attentive, she sat on a small chair in a shadowy corner while her liege lady consulted with scholars and annotated books. Slim in green livery, she watched the elf-queen practice her archery, and brought iced tea to slake her thirst between bouts. At banquets, she poured a sip of every libation into a shallow bowl and drank it down, to test for poison. Rarely did she speak. Always did she watch. In this way, she picked up something of an education in the ways of polite society.

Even more did she learn at night, when the elf-queen retired to her bed and comported herself with whomever had caught her eye during the long day. Agnes brought flagons of wine to set the mood beforehand, vials of aphrodisiacs when the queen's lovers began to flag, and fruit-flavored ices to refresh them afterwards. She watched as the elf-queen coupled with warriors, scholars, poets, fauns, women by threes and men by the brace, with centaurs and imps as small as lapdogs and quilled apes with extra arms. It was the queen's custom that her lovers should begin by entertaining her with oration and so, night after night, they related gesta taken from the history of Elfland, or ornate tales of bawdry stemming from their own experiences. Scholars taught her alchemy and astrology and the secret workings of the crystal spheres that moved the stars and planets through their complex dance in the night. Soldiers spoke of battles they had fought and heroic deeds they had seen.

Agnes watched. And she listened.

Sometimes, when Melisaundre was bored, she brought Richard out of his gem. He hardly noticed Agnes's presence, so besotted was he with the elf-queen. Agnes, for her part, watched him steadily, but her stare was hard. Once, during the heat of passion, his eyes accidentally met hers and the elf-queen immediately plunged a hand into his chest and pulled out his living, beating heart. He arched and spasmed until she returned the organ to its proper place.

"You liked that, didn't you?" Melisaundre murmured, looking Agnes straight in the eye.

"Whatever you want me to like," he gasped, "I will."

Agnes, as always, said nothing.

After the elf-queen had ridden him like a horse, Richard rolled over onto his back, and when Agnes emerged from the shadows with the ices, he looked surprised to see her. He grinned shyly and started to say something, only to be shushed by an imperious royal finger laid across his lips. "You two are not to talk," the queen said. "Not now. Not ever."

Then she turned to Agnes. "Do you envy me, little virgin? Do you envy how many men come to pay me court, your precious friend among them, and how avidly they do so?"

"Yes, your majesty," Agnes said tonelessly.

"They'll never do any of that to you, I assure you. *He* will never so much as touch you. I'll make sure of that."

"Thank you, ma'am."

"Oh, you don't fool me. You may not want it yet, but already you know you will. And every night you'll stand and watch, yearning, always yearning ... Those whom I bring to my bed are a complaisant lot. They'd be only too happy to oblige you, especially your lovely, dimwitted Richard here. But you shall stand and watch and grow old and withered and filled with regrets, while I remain gloriously young forever. When you die, I'll have your ashes made into a godemiché, which will rest near my orgies every night, with Richard immortal and at my service. But never — not even once! — will it be used."

"As you please, ma'am."

In a fury, the elf-queen seized a goblet and flung it down on the flagstone floor. It shattered, sending fragments of crystal everywhere. "You wicked, stubborn *child!* Do you think stunting your potential will make you happy? It will not! Embrace your anger, and it will bring you vividly alive. You will be an avid, thwarted, hopelessly vengeful avatar of spite!"

"As you wish, ma'am."

Queen Melisaundre screamed in rage. Then she bade Richard mount her once more, as Agnes stood by.

But the prize of the elf-queen's collection was Frederic.

"My rough little diamond," the elf-queen called him. She dressed him in jester's motley, and brought him out to amuse her guests at banquets. They would lie in triples, twains, and tangles, on chaises about the court, while Frederic stood in the center and harangued them.

"You have no emotions of your own," Frederic said. He looked so solemn, Agnes thought, in those big round glasses of his. "That's your greatest weakness, and someday it will be your downfall."

The elves responded with gales of laughter.

"You made a terrible mistake when you destroyed almost all of my people. It made those of us who remain rare. It made us powerful. Without us, you wouldn't even know you're alive."

"And what about you, little fool?" an elf baron shouted back at him. "What would you do without us?"

"I'd just go on living. I wouldn't miss you at all."

They howled.

Another time, Frederic said, "The Earth is a sphere that revolves about a spherical Sun. The Moon is spherical too, and it revolves around the Earth." Then, as his audience convulsed, "How many years have you marched around this world without finding its boundaries? Always you search for the way back to your own world. The land you came from is as flat as a checkerboard and so ours baffles you. You stupids! You are trapped here forever by your own ignorance."

Finally, Frederic said, "You think us your prisoners, but it is you who are held captive by the topology of your thoughts. *I* am free! Unlike yourselves, I can move as I wish in all Euclidian dimensions. The only reason I share this with you is that you cannot possibly comprehend it. Should I wish, I can leave at any time by simply turning from your plane."

Abruptly he crouched down and somersaulted away, out the door and gone.

The elves continued jeering and laughing at his japes for another hour, just as if he hadn't left.

After the queen's orgies that night, Agnes lay on her pallet thinking as hard as ever she had thought before. Frederic had been speaking directly to her — she was sure of it. Was it rolling into a ball that had rendered Frederic invisible to the elves? Or was it simply his bold, spit-in-your-face self-confidence?

Agnes felt anything but bold. But the challenge had been put to her. She had to follow Frederic's example, curl into a ball, and roll outside. Either she would survive or the guards would kill her. It was as clean and simple as that.

So she rolled herself into a ball and tumbled off her pallet and out of the tent. The demon-hounds crouching by the salient did not even see her, though their eyes darted everywhere, their nostrils flared, and their ears were pricked for sounds far subtler than those she made.

Agnes somersaulted out into the moonlight.

Out on the grassy sward and down the bank she rolled, out of sight of the guards. When she came to a halt, she was not surprised to see Frederic tumbling to meet her.

"It certainly took you long enough," he said.

"Unlike you," Agnes replied tartly, "I can't simply do and say whatever I want, whenever I wish."

"And whose fault is that? The elves have no concept of reality save what they see reflected through us. I've been trying to explain that to you since forever."

"Do you know what happened to Richard? The queen —"

"What befell Richard would not have happened if he hadn't allowed it."

"She keeps him in a jewel around her neck!"

"He was the oldest. He had the choice of staying and protecting us as best he could, or a safe life of cosseted slavery, and he chose wrong. It was despicable of Melisaundre to offer such a choice to someone so weak, of course."

"You understand everyone so well," Agnes said bitterly.

"I think we have argued enough for one night," said Frederic. "Be sure to somersault your way back to your pallet. It confuses the elves when we rotate or spin, and somersaults short-circuit their brains entirely. I suspect that, like paper dolls, they're not completely suited to life in three dimensions."

He tumbled away.

Agnes stood motionless for a long time. The tents of the armies of Elfland stretched away to the horizon as numerous as blades of grass in a meadow, and the queen's tent sat at the very center of the camp. A lunar moth fluttered raggedly past, and Agnes reflected that they two — she and it — were equally free and purposeless. Yet the lunar did have a purpose: to procreate, to lay clutches of tiny eggs on the leaves of trees. She had no such destiny; in its place she was forced to watch the futile carnival of Melisaundre's endless couplings.

Now that Frederic had given her the key to freedom, she didn't know what to do with it. Where would she go? During waking hours, she could find the other children, for they were held close to the elf-queen's court, in case her whim required them. But when the revelries wound down into exhaustion, they were packed away to the fringes of the camp, to tents pitched among the ogres, dwarves, and other enslaved races.

She would not find the children tonight. And tomorrow, after the marching was done, their tents would be pitched elsewhere.

Nor could she escape into the outside world. There was nothing there but wilderness and ruins. Perhaps there were still people huddling fearfully in caves, as she once had. But what point was there in resuming that wretched and untenable existence?

Frederic, with his unique way of thinking, might be free, but Agnes was not. All the world was her prison.

Still, she had learned something tonight, and who could say it would not turn out to be useful? Clutching the knowledge tight to herself, Agnes tumbled back to her humble pallet at the foot of Queen Melisaundre's luxurious bed.

Months passed, possibly years. Agnes had no way of measuring time: marks on paper, knots in her lacings, any accounting whatsoever eased away while she slept, leaving no trace.

At last there came a day when the armies did not march. The camp swarmed with activity. Elves flew into the nearest abandoned city and plundered it of building materials. Draft-giants hauled wagonloads of stone and enormous timbers. An arena arose in what had been a meadow the night before. Bleachers surrounded the oval of grass. Tall white walls soared upward and were decorated with clusters of the severed heads of ghastly inhuman creatures that Agnes had never seen alive.

Queen Melisaundre came silently out of her tent and gazed upon the arena. Then she turned to Agnes. "So," she said. "The day has arrived at last."

Agnes did not ask, but the queen answered her anyway: "You idiot child! The day we contend in battle and one of us kills the other, of course. Whatever happens, it will be a relief to be free at last of your constant witless questioning."

Agnes knew she needed to control her response. Anger the queen would understand, and know instinctively her most effective response. Fear and defiance as well. But disregard? How could anybody dare ignore so dangerously mercurial a monarch? Agnes yawned and walked off, leaving Melisaundre speaking sharply to empty air.

She found Frederic in a brocade tent the color of dried blood, with jacquard dragons in its weave. Inside was a library whose stacks went on forever, dwindling into dusk. Bespectacled hobgoblins clambered up and down ladders, fetching and returning leather-bound manuscripts. Trolls stood by like bookstands, holding out dictionaries and volumes of encyclopediae.

Frederic sat at a small table, reading.

"What's this about me killing the queen?" Agnes asked. Somehow, she did not doubt it could be done.

Frederic shut his book. "It's time. I can read these grimoires without the queen's scholars now. So we no longer need her."

"You mean we could have been free of her before this and you did nothing?" Agnes was accustomed to holding back her emotions, but now she found herself quivering and white with rage.

"Yes, of course, long ago. You'd have noticed this yourself, if you hadn't been mooning over Richard."

Agnes slapped him as hard as she could.

One side of Frederic's face began slowly turning red. His voice remained mild, nevertheless. "I deserved that, I suppose. However, when we are married, you must not hit me again. It's not conducive to marital harmony."

"*Married!?*"

"Married." Frederic stood. He was taller than Agnes, which had never been the case before, and when he took off his glasses, as he did now, he was not entirely unhandsome. He was, Agnes realized with a shock, an adult, a man. "This has nothing to do with your personal feelings. Or mine, really. Agnes, you are the only human capable of assuming the elf-queen's role. But you have, as yet, no idea of how to wield power, and you know it. I, on the other hand, do; so we must be wed."

"It would be a loveless marriage."

"That will change," said Frederic, "if we want it to. We need each other. Our strengths are complementary; the weaknesses of one can be negated by the other." His face was as pale and expressionless as the moon. "As a basis for marriage, need is stronger than love."

Agnes thought back to all she had learned from the elf-queen's advisors and political philosophers and realized that it was true: Need was a very strong bond indeed. Those same sources, however, had also taught that once needs were met, such bonds would dissolve like fairy dew.

Agnes prepared for battle. She was given, by the elven court, an armory shed at one end of the lists and two pages to dress her. They were pubescent boys, milky-skinned, beautiful, and naked. So far as she could tell, they were identical twins.

The pages were removing her clothing when Frederic rolled in. He grabbed one by the scruff of the neck and forcibly ousted him. The second followed after.

Agnes snatched up her blouse and struggled back into it. But Frederic did not so much as glance at her. He put down a cloth-wrapped package as long as a sword and started rummaging through the armor laid out for her. "She's going to strike you three times," he said. "First, on your upper right arm. So you'll need a pauldron."

The pauldron covered her entire upper arm and was padded underneath. He strapped it on her, right over her blouse.

"The second blow will strike you directly above your left knee. You'll need a cuish."

"I feel unbalanced," Agnes said, to hide her embarrassment, as he reached between her thighs to tighten the cinches. "And just a little foolish, too."

Frederic ignored her. "Neither of those blows will be lethal: They are intended to disable and unbalance you. The third and, potentially, the killing blow will come not from the elf-queen's sword like the first two, but her spear. She'll toss the sword aside and then flip the spear up into the air and catch it back-handed behind her, so that her arm is up and ready for the strike." He held up his arm to demonstrate. "Then it will come down, and hard, right in the middle of your stomach."

"How do you know all this?"

"I've been studying. This sort of thing is all written down."

Frederic took from his kit a triple length of stiff brown leather. He wrapped it around and around Agnes's abdomen so tightly she could barely breathe. Over it he placed a chain mail stomacher. Then, atop all, he strapped on an item of shaped metal he called a tace. "There," he said at last. "She might knock the wind out of you, but she won't kill you."

"What weapon should I use?"

"None of these," Frederic said, dismissing with a glance a gleaming selection of swords, spears, and morning stars. "They're enchanted not to hurt her — you might as well try to take down a tank with a custard pie." He unwrapped the package he had brought with him. "Use this instead."

Agnes laughed involuntarily.

It was a baseball bat.

"Take it," Frederic said. "Try it out."

She swung the bat stiffly back and forth.

"Put your back into it. Swing from the shoulders." He grabbed the bat and showed her what he meant.

Agnes took back the bat and swung again, with more strength. "I could never keep my eye on the ball. It's so small and it comes at you so fast."

"It won't be a ball. It will be Queen Melisaundre's head, and it will be the size of a small melon, plenty big enough to see. Just think of how you have served her, over the years, and she you."

Agnes swung the bat with force.

"I think you're getting the feel of it."

"I wish I was a boy," Agnes said. "I hope I don't look as stupid as I feel."

To her profound surprise, Frederic grabbed her and kissed her full on the lips. Then he pushed her away and stared straight into her eyes. "You look like you're going to free us from elven tyranny forever," he said fervently. "You look like the very first human queen of all the world. I don't wish you were a boy at all."

Then the heralds blew their clarions and the doors of the shed flung themselves wide.

"Go," Frederic said. "Set us free."

Agnes did not so much stride out into the lists as stumble. Yet the throngs of elves (with here and there a human bobbing in the air; only she, it seemed, knew no magic) roared at the sight of her, as if she were an Amazon champion.

Directly across the arena, Queen Melisaundre stepped down from her throne, looking every inch the warrior-queen. Her slim, powerful figure was clad in dazzling gold plate. A scarlet cape flew out behind her, lifted by a wind that did not exist for Agnes. Her helmet was adorned with wings, as if she were a Valkyrie, and so cut that her hair flowed out becomingly behind her.

In her hand was a sword of moon-silver, harder than steel and lighter than a feather. At her back was a long spear.

Agnes hoisted her baseball bat, feeling like a clumsy human yokel. She closed her eyes in silent prayer: Make this quick, she thought. Whether I win or whether I lose, make it quick.

Somebody threw a cloth-of-gold scarf into the air. It fluttered lazily downward, drawing all eyes after it.

When it touched the ground, Queen Melisaundre screamed like an eagle and ran straight toward Agnes. Her long legs carried her quickly and effortlessly across the green lawn. She was beautiful to watch.

Agnes suddenly realized that she should be running too and began to lumber forward.

They met.

It all went as Frederic had said it would. Queen Melisaundre delivered a stinging blow to Agnes's armored and padded shoulder, and a second to her leg that would have crippled her had it not been for the cuish. Then she tossed the sword aside as if it were a plaything she had tired of. One hand deftly undid the strap holding the spear to her back. The other reached behind her and flipped the spear up into the air.

Queen Melisaundre caught the spear and froze for an instant, a goddess incarnate. Then, with her hair lashing and the battle-light blazing about her face, she drove the spear downward with every ounce of her strength.

The spearhead pierced Agnes's tace with a shriek of ripping metal. But the chain mail underneath held, and the wrapped layers of leather softened the blow.

Somewhat.

It felt like getting kicked in the stomach by a horse. All the breath flew out of Agnes and she was driven back a good three feet. But though for an instant all the world went black and there was nothing in it but pain, she did *not* fall down.

Then she could see again, and she was running forward, all in a rage, the baseball bat cocked and ready to swing. Take this, bitch, she thought. You with your perfect face and perfect legs and perfect everything else. With your courtiers and sycophants and lovers by the score. With your cruelty and power and the admiration of all the world and Richard too.

A fierce blood-lust filled her. Take this for being everything I am not.

It was that last thought that pulled Agnes out of her madness, for she recognized in it — as who would not? — the envy, jealousy, and spite that the elf-queen had so long been nurturing in her. And so recognizing it, she rejected it. She refused to let it be a part of her.

It was not a rational decision, for on purely logical grounds she understood that she had to kill the queen. It was simple revulsion that caused her to pull back before her blow reached its target. The bat swung past the elf-queen, missing her by a whisker.

Queen Melisaundre's head shattered anyway.

Frederic led Agnes away from Melisaundre's lifeless corpse toward the throne, whispering urgently in her ear. "You are the queen now. It's important that you act the part. Speak slowly and clearly. Say that your rule will be benign but absolute. A new empire shall arise from the ashes of the old — a human empire. All magical talismans, potions, et cetera, are to be presented to the royal court that they may be made subject to your power. In this way all magicks will support the State and we need never fear rebellion. Finally, if it please you, your majesty, let us be married immediately. Announce that I am to be your consort and in no sense king. I will act in a purely advisory manner, subordinate to the throne. Do you understand?"

Agnes nodded once, regally, and withdrew her arm from his. With the slightest flutter of the fingers of one hand she gestured him back into the crowd.

Frederic backed away, struggling not to grin.

She ascended to the throne.

Everyone cheered, elves as well as the humans. Looking out over them, Agnes was surprised to see that the other children were all grown now. Some of them had children of their own.

Human history has begun again, she thought. And this will be known forever as the Day of Two Queens.

Agnes raised a hand for silence. "I am your new queen and my power is absolute. Does anyone here dispute that?"

Nobody spoke.

"Well, then. My reign shall consist entirely of three edicts. The first is that Frederic shall search through the grimoires and books of spells to either discover a way to return the elves to their own world or, failing that, otherwise rid our world of their presence. That shall be his sole employment until his task is done, however many years it may take."

Frederic looked stricken.

"The second is that until that happy day when they are gone, the elves shall be set to work restoring our world to what it was before they came. We will settle here and scour the wilderness for human survivors. When such are found, those who will may join us. Those who will not shall be left in peace.

"The third and last edict is that henceforth we shall have no queens or absolute rulers of any kind. Form committees, hold elections, do whatever you like — but I will not tell you how to live your lives." Mouths fell open. Eyes widened in shock. Frederic put his head in his hands.

Agnes stepped down from the throne, a queen no more.

After her abdication, she went to see Richard.

Agnes dressed as carefully for this meeting as ever she had in her life. Her clothing was deliberately modest. Yet it did nothing to disguise her newly adult shape. Her jewelry drew no attention to itself. She wore makeup, though she doubted that Richard, used as he was to Queen Melisaundre's theatrical extravagance, would notice.

The elf-queen's tent smelled as always of incense, spices, and perfume. Yet the air felt strangely clean, for the cat-in-heat stench of the queen herself was gone. Beside her bed (sheeted in green and blue satins with foams of lace so that it was almost as vast and billowy as the sea itself) was a small obsidian box. In it rested Richard's gemstone.

When Agnes had laid out shirt and trews on the bed, she took the rock crystal gem and warmed it between her hands. It had been clear and ordinary once, but Richard's soul had deepened its color into a golden-red topaz with hints of flame at its heart. Speaking a word she had often heard from the lips of Queen Melisaundre, she summoned Richard from its depths.

He appeared, smiling sleepily, in the middle of the bed.

When Richard saw that he and Agnes were alone, he sat up and donned the russet-colored clothing — first the trousers and then the sark. They fit him well and seeing him thus clad Agnes felt a sudden flush of desire that, paradoxically, she had not felt on beholding him naked.

It was true, she thought. She genuinely had come of age, if Richard's mere presence could disorder her thinking so.

"Where is Melisaundre?" he asked.

Agnes's mouth felt dry. She could not form words with it at first. But at last she managed to croak, "There have been … I have made some changes."

Then she told him.

When Agnes emerged from the tent at last, her face was grim and a golden-red stone hung from a silver chain about her neck.

Frederic was waiting for her. "What shall we do with that?" he asked, gesturing toward the tent.

"Burn it," she said. She knew she had surrendered all authority to give such a command. But listening to her own voice, she knew too that she would be obeyed. "Burn it to the ground."

Frederic nodded and two lovely young women whom Agnes realized with dull astonishment used to be the young Lexi and Latoya raised up hands that burst into fire. Stepping forward, they stroked the silks and velvets. Soft flames rose up the sides of the tent, merged, and became an inferno. When Agnes made no motion to get away from the heat, Frederic gently took her by the arm and led her toward the cool.

Agnes could feel the flames at her back. Shadows leaped and cavorted before her.

"What of Richard?" Frederic asked.

She touched the gem. "He did not care to share our lives without Melisaundre," she said. "I gave him permission to return to his crystal, to his oblivion."

Frederic crooked a sad smile. "'He is not dead but sleeping,'" he quoted from one of Richard's favorite books. "Perhaps he will reconsider someday, when we have remade the world into a pleasant place again. I . . . I will become the junior husband then, if that is what you wish."

Agnes looked at him evenly, and realized for the first time how much Frederic desired and even, in his own peculiar way, loved her. Raising her head, she looked into the future. The humans would not rebuild the cities in her lifetime, but there would be towns. The elves would one by one fade away, into wells, into trees, into small, pathetic beings who served mankind and were rewarded with dishes of milk. She would have children, and then grandchildren. She would grow old, and fat, and revered. She would desire Richard often. But she would never see him again.

"No," said Agnes firmly. "He's gone forever. The time for fairy tales is past."

Michael Swanwick and Samuel R. Delany at the Joyce Kilmer Service Area, March 2005

OUTPUT FROM A NOSTALGIC, IF SOMEWHAT MISINFORMED,
GUYDAVENPORT STORYBOT, IN THE YEAR 2115

Transcribed by Eileen Gunn

THEIR JOURNEY TOOK PLACE in verdant March, when the sun was not yet so high in the sky as to be dangerous. The New Jersey Turnpike was redolent with the scent of magnolias, and the trees in the Joyce Kilmer Service Area were clad in exuberant green. What brought them, the nascent politician and the noted philosopher, to this place, in a vehicle that shed its rich hydrocarbons liberally into the warm, clean air?

The truth was that Michael Swanwick and Samuel R. Delany shared a taste for animal flesh, and had come to this bucolic waystation to satisfy their common need. "I'm a burger kind of guy," said the future ruler of Russia. "So am I," said the white-bearded semiotician, and they chose an imperial meat-patty palace for their repast.

As they stood in line, contemplating a panoply of burgers, fries, and blue raspberry Icee®s and basking in the cool green glow of fluorescent lights, Swanwick was struck with nostalgia for a time long past.

"I miss Howard Johnson's," he said. "Not the food, of course — I miss the orange-roofed temples, celebrated by Jean Shepard as sirens of the highway. Once upon a time, every rest area on the Jersey Turnpike had a Howard Johnson's. 'A landmark for hungry Americans.'"

Though Swanwick had spoken the words, each man, involuntarily, heard the chime of the ghastly jingle. "Funny thing," he continued quickly. "It was capitalism that killed it. Marriott bought it for the real estate."

"Red in tooth and claw," said Delany. "I miss the pistachio ice cream cones, that's all.... But *here*," he added in a soothing tone, "*here* we have trading cards with robots on them." He accepted a trading card from the cashier. It depicted Cappy, a sleekly androgynous silver-metal lover. "I want a different one," he said.

"Have it your way," said the cashier, shrugging. He handed Delany another card, this one featuring Crank, a grubby makeshift robot with rust under his gnawed fingernails.

Delany laughed, a musical sound somewhere between a snort and a giggle. "I'll keep this one," he said. He ordered a beef patty made with real beef, medium rare, topped with horseradish and béarnaise sauce, kosher dill slices on the side.

"Have it your way," said the cashier again.

"Are you a robot?" asked Swanwick, suddenly concerned. The cashier did not reply.

"I would like a big, sloppy, greasy double cheeseburger with lettuce and tomato and all the trimmings," Swanwick told the cashier. "I want ketchup, mayonnaise, mustard, and Russian dressing with beluga caviar. Hold the pickle."

"Caviar is available only at the Walt Whitman Service Area," said the cashier, frowning. "You can't *always* have *every*thing *your* way." He gave Swanwick a trading card depicting Aunt Fanny, a matronly, pink, lipstick-wearing robot with a protuberant posterior. Swanwick accepted it with bemusement, wondering whether Burger King offered the same card in the United Kingdom. "Can I have another, too?" he asked. The cashier handed him a card with a pigtailed Lolita robot on it. "Another?" The third was Madame Gasket, who was a bit scary, frankly, for a trading card. He couldn't get *anything* *his* way.

"Lucky in love, unlucky at cards," said Delany.

"They hand these things out to children?" Swanwick asked, glancing again at Madame Gasket.

They paid for their meals in the devalued currency of the late-period religio-capitalist hegemony, and took their food trays to a small table at a window overlooking the Sunoco station.

"*Bon appétit*," said Delany, gesturing with his hamburger as one would with a wineglass.

"*Priyatnovo appetita*," replied Swanwick with a similar gesture. He had recently returned from the Urals, where he had been the toast of Ekaterinburg.

At first they ate in hungry silence, gazing out at the gas station, as languid pump attendants with huge palm-frond fans hailed approaching automobiles and waved them toward available fueling bays as though they were New Jersey's famous zeppelins. Then, having taken the edge off their appetites, the two men continued the conversation they had begun in the car, the one great debate that writers and thinkers everywhere have carried on since writing and thinking first evolved: the debate about the ultimate futility of writing and thinking.

"I'm a cult writer in Russia," said Swanwick, "and I'm a cult writer in the United States. And I'm sick of it."

"Nothing so terrible about being a cult writer," said Delany. "Christianity started out as a cult, and look at it now."

"I want to make some *difference* in the world, communicate with the mass of *humanity*, have an *effect*." He gestured toward the crowded freeway. "I want to change *entire lives* for the *better*."

"Have you thought of a different career?" asked Delany gently. "Perhaps emigration to a land of greater opportunity? You speak some Russian, do you not?"

"*Nyemnoshka*," Swanwick answered, with a modest shake of his shaggy head. "A smidgeon," he translated.

"Maybe you should consider pulling up stakes, retooling for the new millennium. As a cult writer in the U.S., you're nothing. You have considerably less effect on how the world fares than a Hollywood screenwriter, which is low indeed in the social hierarchy. But as a cult writer in Russia, you'd have some clout. They are afraid of writers in Russia, and with good reason. You could leverage your celebrity into a political career, take control of that long-suffering country, and change the world. Of course, you could also get killed." He sighed. "It's a sad thing, but nobody kills writers in the U.S. They just don't matter enough."

"I will consider that," said Swanwick, and did. It would not be so difficult for him and his wife to create new lives in another land. She was a public-health scientist, although, when provoked, she sometimes described herself as a career bureaucrat. Russia had jobs in either category; like everyplace else, it needed scientists more, and paid bureaucrats better. And Michael had always enjoyed caviar and sour cream, however difficult they were to obtain on the Jersey Turnpike. It could work.

But, he thought, it was time to get back on the road. They gathered up their things, recycled the trash, slapped on their canvas hats and a heavy layer of sunblock, and hit the road.

They continued north in Swanwick's chartreuse 1959 Thunderbird, past service areas named for the heroes of New Jersey: Allen Ginsberg, Paul Robeson, William Carlos Williams, Amiri Baraka, Frank Sinatra, Bruce Springsteen, Jimmy Hoffa, Yogi Berra, and Jon Bon Jovi. Soon enough, they found themselves at the most intellectually exciting stretch of highway in the United States. Between exits 16E and 13A, the New Jersey Turnpike at that time passed over the Passaic River. The General Casimir Pulaski Skyway, a masterpiece of Depression-era engineering, soared off to one side, crossing the Passaic and Hackensack rivers in great latticework leaps. As the car approached New York City, the primeval Meadowlands swept off on the left, balancing the demands of nature and of solid-waste disposal, and the darkly crystalline rectangles of the Manhattan skyline arose to the right. Gleaming networks of railroad tracks recalled to them the glorious empire, created by commerce and forced labor, that had, until the new century and its disasters, sustained the American dream. Where the towers had been there was still, in 2005, negative space.

The car containing the two men sped across the George Washington Bridge and made its way, under Swanwick's instruction, to Delany's residence. Chip Delany, ever hospitable, invited Michael Swanwick to come upstairs and continue their conversation, but Swanwick, by now lost to American literature, made a hasty excuse in mumbled Russian, and disappeared into the grey fog of urban twilight.

Zeppelin City

Michael Swanwick and Eileen Gunn

RADIO JONES came dancing down the slidewalks. She jumped from the express to a local, then spun about and raced backwards, dumping speed so she could cut across the slower lanes two and three at a time. She hopped off at the mouth of an alley, glanced up in time to see a Zeppelin disappear behind a glass-domed skyscraper, and stepped through a metal door left open to vent the heat from the furnaces within.

The glass-blowers looked up from their work as she entered the hot shop. They greeted her cheerily:

"Hey, Radio!"

"Jonesy!"

"You invented a robot girlfriend for me yet?"

The shop foreman lumbered forward, smiling. "Got a box of off-spec tubes for you, under the bench there."

"Thanks, Mackie." Radio dug through the pockets of her patched leather greatcoat and pulled out a folded sheet of paper. "Hey, listen, I want you to do me up an estimate for these here vacuum tubes."

Mack studied the list. "Looks to be pretty straightforward. None of your usual experimental trash. How many do you need — one of each?"

"I was thinking more like a hundred."

"*What?*" Mack's shaggy black eyebrows met in a scowl. "You planning to win big betting on the Reds?"

"Not me, I'm a Whites fan all the way. Naw, I was kinda hoping you'd gimme credit. I came up with something real hot."

"You finally built that girlfriend for Rico?"

The workmen all laughed.

"No, c'mon, I'm *serious* here." She lowered her voice. "I invented a universal radio receiver. Not fixed-frequency — tunable! It'll receive any broadcast on the radio spectrum. Twist the dial, there you are. With this baby, you can listen in on every conversation in the big game, if you want."

Mack whistled. "There might be a lot of interest in a device like that."

"Funny thing, I was thinking exactly that myself." Radio grinned. "So waddaya say?"

"I say — " Mack spun around to face the glass-blowers, who were all listening intently, and bellowed, "*Get back to work!*" Then, in a normal voice, "Tell you what. Set me up a demo, and if your gizmo works the way you say it does, maybe I'll invest in it. I've got the materials to build it, and access to the retailers. Something like this could move twenty, maybe thirty units a day, during the games."

"Hey! Great! The game starts when? Noon, right? I'll bring my prototype over, and we can listen to the players talking to each other." She darted toward the door.

"Wait." Mack ponderously made his way into his office. He extracted a five-dollar bill from the lockbox and returned, holding it extended before him. "For the option. You agree not to sell any shares in this without me seeing this doohickey first."

"Oh, Mackie, you're the greatest!" She bounced up on her toes to kiss his cheek. Then, stuffing the bill into the hip pocket of her jeans, she bounded away.

Fat Edna's was only three blocks distant. She was inside and on a stool before the door jangled shut behind her. "Morning, Edna!" The neon light she'd rigged up over the bar was, she noted with satisfaction, still working. Nice and quiet, hardly any buzz to it at all. "Gimme a big plate of scrambled eggs and pastrami, with a beer on the side."

The bartender eyed her skeptically. "Let's see your money first."

With elaborate nonchalance, Radio laid the bill flat on the counter before her. Edna picked it up, held it to the light, then slowly counted out four ones and eighty-five cents change. She put a glass under the tap and called over her shoulder, "Wreck a crowd, with sliced dick!" She pulled the beer, slid the glass across the counter, and said, "Out in a minute."

"Edna, there is *nobody* in the world less satisfying to show off in front of than you. You still got that package I left here?"

Wordlessly, Edna took a canvas-wrapped object from under the bar and set it before her.

"Thanks." Radio unwrapped her prototype. It was bench-work stuff — just tubes, resistors, and capacitors in a metal frame. No housing, no circuit tracer lights, and a tuner she had to turn with a pair of needle-nose pliers. But it was going to make her rich. She set about double-checking all the connectors. "Hey, plug this in for me, willya?"

Edna folded her arms and looked at her.

Radio sighed, dug in her pockets again, and slapped a nickel on the bar. Edna took the cord and plugged it into the outlet under the neon light.

With a faint hum, the tubes came to life.

"That thing's not gonna blow up, is it?" Edna asked dubiously.

"Naw." Radio took a pair of needle-nose pliers out of her greatcoat pocket and began casting about for a strong signal. "Most it's gonna do is electrocute you, maybe set fire to the building. But it's not gonna explode. You been watching too many kinescopes."

Amelia Spindizzy came swooping down out of the sun like a suicidal angel, all rage and mirth. The rotor of her autogyro whined and snarled with the speed of her dive. Then she throttled up and the blades bit deep into the air and pulled her out, barely forty feet from the ground. Laughing, she lifted the nose of her bird to skim the top of one skywalk, banked left to dip under a second, and then right to hop-frog a third. Her machine shuddered and rattled as she bounced it off the compression effects of the air around the skyscrapers to steal that tiny morsel of extra lift, breaking every rule in the book and not giving a damn.

The red light on Radio 2 flashed angrily. One-handed, she yanked the jacks to her headset from Radio 3, the set connecting her to the referee, and plugged into her comptroller's set. "Yah?"

The flat, emotionless, and eerily artificial voice of Naked Brain xb-29 cut through the static. *"Amelia, what are you doing?"*

"Just wanted to get your attention. I'm going to cut through the elbow between Ninetieth and Ninety-First Avenues. Plot me an Eszterhazy, will you?"

"Computing." Almost as an afterthought, the Naked Brain said, *"You realize this is extremely dangerous."*

"Nothing's dangerous enough for me," Amelia muttered, too quietly for the microphone to pick up. "Not by half."

The sporting rag *Obey the Brain!* had termed her "half in love with easeful death," but it was not *easeful* death that Amelia Spindizzy sought. It was the inevitable, difficult death of an impossible skill tenaciously mastered but necessarily insufficient to the challenge — a hard-fought battle for life, lost just as the hand reached for victory and closed around empty air. A mischance that conferred deniability, like a medal of honor, on her struggle for oblivion, as she twisted and fell in gloriously tragic heroism.

So far, she hadn't achieved it.

It wasn't that she didn't love being alive (at least some of the time). She loved dominating the air currents in her great titanium whirligig. She loved especially the slow turning in an ever-widening gyre, scanning for the opposition with an exquisite patience only a sigh short of boredom, and then the thrill as she spotted him, a minuscule speck in an ocean of sky. Loved the way her body flushed with adrenalin as she drove her machine up into the sun, searching for that sweet blind spot where the prey, her machine, and that great atomic furnace were all in a line. Loved most of all the instant of stillness before she struck.

It felt like being born all over again.

For Amelia, the Game was more than a game, because necessarily there would come a time when the coordination, strength, and precision demanded by her fierce and fragile machine would prove to be more than she could provide, a day when all the sky would gather its powers to break her will and force her into the ultimate submission. It would happen. She had faith. Until then, though, she strove only to live at the outer edge of her skills, to fly and to play the Game as gloriously as any human could to the astonishment of the unfortunate earthbound classes. And of the Naked Brains who could only float, ponderously, in their glass tanks, in their Zeppelins.

"Calculations complete."

"You have my position?"

Cameras swiveled from the tops of nearby buildings, tracking her. *"Yes."*

Now she'd achieved maximum height again.

"I'm going in."

Straight for the alley-mouth she flew. Sitting upright in the thorax of her flying machine, rudder pedals at her feet, stick controls to the left and right, she let inertia push her back into the seat like a great hand. Eight-foot-long titanium blades extended in a circle, with her at the center like the heart of a flower. This was no easy machine to fly. It combined the delicacy of flight with the physical demands of operating a mechanical thresher.

"*Pull level on my count. Three ... Two ... Now.*"

It took all her strength to bully her machine properly while the g-forces tried to shove her away from the controls. She was flying straight and true toward Dempster Alley, a street that was only feet wider than the diameter of her autogyro's blades, so fine a margin of error that she'd be docked a month's pay if the Naked Brains saw what she was up to.

"*Shift angle of blades on my mark and rudder on my second mark. Three ... Two ... Mark. And ... Rudder.*"

Tilted forty-five degrees, she roared down the alley, her prop wash rattling the windows and filling them with pale, astonished faces. At the intersection, she shifted pitch and kicked rudder, flipping her gyro over so that it canted forty-five degrees the other way (the engine coughed and almost stalled, then roared back to life again) and hammered down Bernoulli Lane (a sixty-degree turn here where the streets crossed at an odd angle) and so out onto Ninety-First. A perfect Eszterhazy! Five months ago, a hypercubed committee of half the Naked Brains in the metropolis had declared that such a maneuver couldn't be done. But one brave pilot had proved otherwise in an aeroplane, and Amelia had determined she could do no less in a gyro.

"*Bank left. Stabilize. Climb for height. Remove safeties from your bombs.*"

Amelia Spindizzy obeyed and then, glancing backwards, forwards, and to both sides, saw a small cruciform mote ahead and below, flying low over the avenue. Grabbing her glasses, she scanned the wing insignia. She could barely believe her luck — it was the Big E himself! And she had a clear run at him.

The autogyro hit a patch of bumpy air, and Amelia snatched up the sticks to regain control. The motor changed pitch, the prop hummed, the rotor blades cut the air. Her machine was bucking now, veering into the scrap zone, and in danger of going out of control. She fought to get it back on an even keel, straightened it out, and swung into a tight arc.

Man, this was the life!

She wove and spun above the city streets as throngs of onlookers watched the warm-up hijinks from the tall buildings and curving skywalks. They shouted encouragement at her. "Don't let 'er drop, Amelia!" "Take the bum down, Millie!" "Spin 'im around, Spindizzy!" Bloodthirsty bastards. Her public. Screaming bloody murder and perfectly capable of chucking a beer bottle at her if they thought she wasn't performing up to par. Times like these she almost loved 'em.

She hated being called Millie, though.

Working the pedals, moving the sticks, dancing to the silent jazz of turbulence in the air around her, she was Josephine Baker, she was Cab Calloway, she was the epitome of grace and wit and intelligence in the service of entertainment. The crowd went wild as she caught a heavy gust of wind and went skidding sideways toward the city's treasured Gaudi skyscraper.

When she had brought everything under control and the autogyro was flying evenly again, Amelia looked down.

For a miracle, he was still there, still unaware of her, flying low in a warm-up run and placing flour bombs with fastidious precision, one by one.

She throttled up and focused all her attention on her foe, the greatest flyer of his generation and her own, patently at her mercy if she could first rid herself of the payload. Her engine screamed in fury, and she screamed with it. "XB! Next five intersections! Gimme the count."

"*At your height, there is a risk of hitting spectators.*"

"I'm too good for that and you know it! Gimme the count."

"*Three … two … now. Six … five …*"

Each of the intersections had been roped off and painted blue with a white circle in its center and a red star at the sweet spot. Amelia worked the bombsight, calculated the windage (Naked Brains couldn't do that; you had to be present; you had to feel the air as a physical thing), and released the bombs one after the other. Frantically, then, she yanked the jacks and slammed them into Radio 3. "How'd we do?" she yelled. She was sure she'd hit them all on the square and she had hopes of at least one star.

"*Square. Circle. Circle. Star.*" The referee — Naked Brain QW-14, though the voice was identical to her own comptroller's — said. A pause. "*Star.*"

Yes!

She was coming up on Eszterhazy himself now, high and fast. He had all the disadvantages of position. She positioned her craft so that the very tip of its shadow kissed the tail of his bright red 'plane. He was still acting as if he didn't know she was there. Which was impossible. She could see three of his team's Zeppelins high above, and if she could see them, they sure as hell could see *her*. So why was he playing stupid?

Obviously he was hoping to lure her in.

"I see your little game," Amelia muttered softly. But just what dirty little trick did Eszterhazy have up his sleeve? The red light was flashing on Radio 2. The hell with that. She didn't need XB-29's bloodless advice at a time like this. "Okay, loverboy, let's see what you've got!" She pushed the stick forward hard. Then Radio 3 flashed — and *that* she couldn't ignore.

"*Amelia Spindizzy,*" the referee said. "*Your flight authorization has been canceled. Return to Ops.*"

Reflexively, she jerked the throttle back, scuttling the dive. "What?!"

"*Repeat: Return to Ops. Await further orders.*"

Angrily, Amelia yanked the jacks from Radio 3. Almost immediately the light on Radio 1 lit up. When she jacked in, the hollow, mechanical voice of Naked Brain ZF-43, her commanding officer, filled her earphones. *"I am disappointed in you, Amelia. Wastefulness. Inefficient expenditure of resources. Pilots should not weary themselves unnecessarily. XB-29 should have exercised more control over you. He will be reprimanded."*

"It was just a pick-up game," she said. "For fun. You remember fun, don't you?"

There was a pause. *"There is nothing the matter with my memory,"* ZF-43 said at last. *"I do remember fun. Why do you ask?"*

"Maybe because I'm as crazy as an old coot, ZF," said Amelia, idly wondering if she could roll an autogyro. Nobody ever had. But if she went to maximum climb, cut the choke, and kicked the rudder hard, that ought to flip it. Then, if she could restart the engine quickly enough and slam the rudder smartly the other way.... It just might work. She could give it a shot right now.

"Return to the Zeppelin immediately. The Game starts in less than an hour."

"Aw shucks, ZF. Roger." Not for the first time, Amelia wondered if the Naked Brain could read her mind. She'd have to try the roll later.

In less than the time it took to scramble an egg and slap it on a plate, Radio Jones had warmed up her tuner and homed in on a signal. "Maybe because I'm as crazy as an old coot, ZF," somebody squawked.

"Hey! I know that voice — it's Amelia!" If Radio had a hero, it was the aviatrix.

"Return to the Zeppelin —"

"Criminy! A Naked Brain! Aw rats, static..." Radio tweaked the tuning ever so slightly with the pliers.

"—ucks, zf. Roger."

Edna set the plate of eggs and pastrami next to the receiver. "Here's your breakfast, whiz kid."

Radio flipped off the power. "Jeeze, I ain't never heard a Brain before. Creepy."

By now, she had the attention of the several denizens of Fat Edna's.

"Whazzat thing do, Radio?"

"How does it work?"

"Can you make me one, Jonesy?"

"It's a Universal Tuner. Home in on any airwave whatsoever." Radio grabbed the catsup bottle, upended it over the plate, and whacked it hard. Red stuff splashed all over. She dug into her eggs. "I'm 'nna make one for anybody who wants one," she said between mouthfuls. "Cost ya, though."

"Do they know you're listening?" It was Rudy the Red, floppy haired and unshaven, born troublemaker, interested only in politics and subversion. He was always predicting that the Fist of the Brains was just about to come down on him. As it would, eventually, everyone agreed: people like him tended to disappear. The obnoxious ones, however, lingered longer than most. "How can you be sure *they* aren't listening to *you* right now?"

"Well, all I can say, Rudy" — she wiped her mouth with her hand, as Fat Edna's bar was uncluttered with serviettes — "is that if they got something that can overthrow the laws of electromagnetism as we know 'em and turn a receiver into a transmitter, then more power to 'em. That's a good hack. Hey, the Game starts in a few minutes. Who ya bettin' on?"

"Radio, you know I don't wager human against human," Rudy said. "Our energies should be focused on our oppressors — the Naked Brains. But instead we do whatever they want because they've channeled all our aggression into a trivial distraction created to keep the masses stupefied and sedated. The

Games are the opiate of the people! You should wise up and join the struggle, Radio. This device of yours could be our secret weapon. We could use it to listen in on them plotting against us"

"Ain't much of a secret," said Radio, "if it's all over Edna's bar."

"We can tell people it doesn't work."

"What are you, some kind of no-brainer? That there's my fancy-pants college education. I'm not tellin' nobody it don't work."

Amelia Spindizzy banked her tiny craft and turned it toward the huge Operations Zep *Imperator*. The Zeppelin thrust out its landing pad and Amelia swooped deftly onto it, in a maneuver that she thought of as a penny-toss, a quick leap onto the target platform, which then retracted into the gondola of the airship.

She climbed from the cockpit. Grimy Huey tossed her a mooring line and she tied down her machine. "You're on orders to report to the Hall, fly-girl," he shouted. "What have you done now?"

"I think I reminded ZF-43 of his lost physicality, Huey." Amelia scrambled up the bamboo gangway.

"You do that for me every time I look at you."

"You watch it, Huey, or I'll come over there and teach you a lesson," Amelia said.

"Amelia, I'll study under you anytime."

She shied a wheel chuck at him, and the mechanic ducked away, cackling. Mechanics' humor, thought Amelia. You have to let them have their jokes at your expense. It can make you or break you, what they do to your 'gyro.

The Hall of the Naked Brains was amidships. High-ceilinged, bare-walled, and paneled in bamboo, it smelled of lemon oil and beeswax. The windows were shuttered, to keep the room dim; the Brains didn't need light, and the crew were happier not looking at them. Twin rows of enormous glass jars, set in dur-aluminium frames, lined the sides of the Hall. Within the jars, enormous pink Brains floated motionless in murky electrolyte soup.

In the center of the shadowy room was a semicircle of rattan chairs facing a speaker and a televideon camera. Cables looped across the floor to each of the glass jars.

Amelia plumped down in the nearest chair, unzipped her flight jacket, and said, "Well?"

There was a ratcheting noise as one of the Brains adjusted the camera. A tinny disembodied voice came from the speaker. It was ZF-43. "*Amelia. We are equipping your autogyro with an import-ant new device. It is essential that we test it today.*"

"What does it do?" she asked.

"*If it works properly, it will paralyze Lt. Eszterhazy's engine.*"

Amelia glared at the eye of the camera. "And why would I want to do that?"

"*Clearly you do not, Amelia.*" ZF's voice was as dispassionate as ever. "*It is we who want you to do it. You will oblige us in this matter.*"

"You tell me, ZF, why I would want to cheat."

"*Amelia, you do not want to cheat. However, you are in our service. We have experimental devices to test, and the rules of your game are not important to us. This may be a spiritual endeavor to yourself, it may be a rousing amusement to the multitudes, but it is a military exercise to us.*" There was a pause, as if ZF were momentarily somewhere else, and then he resumed. "*NQ-14 suggests I inform you that Lt. Eszterhazy's aeroplane can glide with a dead engine. There is little risk to the pilot.*"

Amelia glared even more fiercely at the televideon camera. "That is beside the point, ZF. I would argue that my autogyro is far less dependent on its engine than Eszterhazy's 'plane. Why not give the device to each of us, for a square match?"

"*There is only one device, Amelia, and we need to test it now. You are here, you are trusted. Eszterhazy is too independent. You will take the device."* A grinding noise, as of badly lubricated machinery. *"Or you will not be in the Game."*

"What are this bastard's specs? How does it work?"

"You will be told, Amelia. In good time."

"Where is it?"

"It's being installed in your autogyro as we speak. A red button on your joystick controls it: Press, it's on. Release, it's off."

"I'm not happy about this, ZF."

"Go to your autogyro, Amelia. Fly well." The light dimmed even more and the camera clicked again as the lens irised shut. ZF-43 had turned off the world outside his jar.

Rudy choked down a nickel's worth of beans and kielbasa and enough java to keep him running for the rest of the day. It was going to be a long one. The scheduled game would bring the people out into the streets, and that was a recruiting opportunity he couldn't pass up. He knew his targets: not the fat, good-natured guys catching a few hours of fun before hitting the night shift. Not their sharp-eyed wives, juggling the kids and grabbing the paycheck on Friday so it wouldn't be spent on drink. Oh, no. Rudy's constituency was hungry-looking young men, just past their teens, out of work, smarter than they needed to be, and not yet on the bottle. One in ten would take a pamphlet from him. Of those, one in twenty would take it home, one in fifty would read it, one in five hundred would take it to heart, and one in a thousand would seek him out and listen to more.

The only way to make it worth his while, the only way to pull together a force, was to get as many pamphlets out there as possible. It was a numbers game, like the lottery, or like selling insurance.

Rudy had sold insurance once, collecting weekly nickels and

dimes from the hopeful and the despairing alike. Until the day he was handed a pamphlet. He took it home, he read it, and he realized what a sham his life was, what a shill he had been for the corporate powers, what a fraud he had been perpetrating upon his own people, the very people that he should be helping to escape from the treadmill of their lives.

He finished his coffee and hit the street. Crowds were already building near the CityPlace — that vast open square at the heart of the city, carved out of the old shops, tenements, and speakeasies that had once thrived there — where the aerobattle would take place. He picked out a corner near some ramshackle warehouses on the plaza's grimy southern rim. That's where his people would be, his tillage, as he thought of them.

"Tillage" was a word his grandfather used back when Rudy was young. The old man used to speak lovingly of the tillage, the land he had farmed in his youth. The tillage, he said, responded to him as a woman would, bringing forth fruit as a direct result of his care and attention. Not that he, Rudy, had great amounts of time to spend on a woman — but that hadn't seemed to matter on the streets, where women were freely available, and briefly enjoyable. Sexual intercourse was overrated, in his opinion. Politics was another matter, and he made his friends among men and women who felt the same. They kept their distance from one another, so the Naked Brains couldn't pick them all off in a single raid. When they coupled, they did so quickly, and they didn't exchange names.

Moving deftly through the gathering crowd, he held out only one pamphlet at a time, and that only after catching a receptive eye. A willing offering to a willing receptor, that wasn't illegal. It wasn't pamphleteering, which was a harvestable offense. Last thing he wanted, to be harvested and, if the rumors were as he suspected true, have his grey matter pureed and fed to the Naked Brains.

But to build his cadre, to make his mark, he needed to hand out a thousand pamphlets a day, and crowds like this — in the CityPlace or on the slidewalks at rush hour — were the only way to do it.

"Take this, brother. Thank you." He said it over and over. "Salaam, brother, may I offer you this?"

He had to keep moving, couldn't linger anywhere, kept his eye out for the telltale stare of an Eye of the Brains. When he had first started this business, he had sought out only men who looked like himself. But that approach proved too slow. He'd since learned to size up a crowd with a single glance and mentally mark the receptive. That tall, black-skinned man with the blue kerchief, the skinny little freckled guy in the ragged work clothes, the grubby fellow with the wisp of a beard and red suspenders. All men, and mostly young. He let his female compatriots deal with the women. Didn't want any misunderstandings.

The guy with the kerchief first. Eye contact, querying glance, non-sexual affect, tentative offer of pamphlet. He takes it! Eye contact, brief nod, on to the little guy. Guy looks away. Abort. Don't offer pamphlet. On to the third guy —

"What's this, then?" Flatfoot! An Eye? Surely not a Fist? Best to hoof it.

Rudy feinted to one side of the copper and ran past him on the other, swivel-hipping through the crowd like Jim Thorpe in search of a touchdown. He didn't look back, but if the cop was an Eye, he'd have backup pronto. Around the big guy with the orange wig, past the scared-looking lady with the clutch of kids — yikes! — almost overturned the baby carriage. What's that on the ground? No time to think about it! Up and over, down the alleyway, and into the door that's cracked open a slot. Close it, latch it, jam the lock. SOP.

Rudy turned away from the fire door. It was almost lightless in here. He was in an old, run-down kinescope parlor, sur-rounded by benches full of kinescope devotees, their eyes glued to the tiny screens wired to the backs of the pews in front of them. On each screen the same blurry movie twitched: *Modern Times*, with the Marx Brothers.

He took a seat and put a nickel in the slot.

He was just a regular Joe at the movies now. An anonymous unit of the masses, no different from anybody else. Except that he didn't have his girlfriend with him. Or a girlfriend at all. Or any real interest in having a girlfriend. Or in anything so histor-ically blinkered as going to the kinescope parlor.

Rudy had heard about this particular kinescope in a Know the Foe session. It was supposed to be funny, but its humor originated in a profound class bias. The scene that was playing was one in which Harpo, Chico, and Zeppo were working on an assembly line while their supervisor (Groucho) flirted with the visiting efficiency inspector (Margaret Dumont). Zeppo and Chico worked methodically with wrenches, tightening bolts on the bombs that glided remorselessly into view on the conveyor belt. Harpo, equipped with a little handheld pneumatic drill, worked regularly and efficiently at first, drilling a hole in a bomb fin which Zeppo promptly unbolted and Chico replaced with a new fin. That his work was meaningless appeared to bother him not at all. But then, without noticing it, Groucho leaned against a long lever, increasing the belt's speed. As the pace increased, Harpo realized that the drill could be made to go faster and faster, just like the assembly line. He became fascinated by the drill and then obsessed with it, filling the bombs' fins with so many holes that they looked like slices of Swiss cheese.

Chico and Zeppo, meanwhile, kept working faster and faster as the line sped up. For them, this was grim business. To keep from falling behind, they had to employ two wrenches, one per hand. Sweat poured off them. They shed their hats, then their jackets, then their shirts and pants, leaving them clad only in voluminous underwear. Harpo, on the other hand, was feeling no pressure at all. He began drilling holes in his hat, then his jacket, then his shirt and pants.

Groucho urged Dumont into his office, then doffed his hat, clasped it to his chest, and tossed it aside. He chased her around the desk. Dumont projected both affronted dignity and matronly sexual curiosity. A parody of authority, Groucho backed Dumont up against the wall and, unexpectedly, plucked a rose from a nearby vase and, bowing deeply, offered it to her.

Charmed, Dumont smiled and bent down to accept it.

But then, in a single complex and weirdly graceful action, Groucho spun Dumont around, bending her over backwards in his arms, parallel to the floor. Margaret Dumont's eyes darted wildly about as she realized how perilously close she was to falling. Meanwhile, Harpo had started to drill holes from the other side of the wall, the drill bit coming through the plaster, each time missing Groucho by a whisker. His desperate gyrations as he tried to avoid the incoming drill were misunderstood by the efficiency expert, who made to slap him. Each time she tried, however, she almost fell and was forced to clutch him tighter to herself. Groucho waggled his eyebrows, obviously pleased with his romantic prowess.

Just then, however, Harpo drilled Dumont in the butt. She lurched forward, mouth an outraged O, losing balance and dignity simultaneously, and overtoppling Groucho as well. The two of them fell to the floor, struggling. It was at that instant that Chico and Zeppo, still in their underwear and with Harpo in tow, appeared in the doorway to report the problem and saw the couple on the floor thrashing about and yelling soundlessly at one another. Without hesitation, all three leaped joyously into the air on top of the pile. Behind them, the runaway assembly line was flooding the factory with bombs, which now crested into the office in a great wave. The screen went white and a single card read: BANG!

The audience was laughing uproariously. But Rudy was not amused. None of these characters had a shred of common sense. Furthermore, it was clear that appropriate measures to protect the workers' health and safety had not been implemented. Harpo should never have been given that drill in the first place. And Margaret Dumont! What was she thinking? How could she have accepted such a demeaning role?

Rudy stood up on his chair. "Comrades!" he yelled. "Why are you laughing?"

A few viewers looked up briefly, then shrugged and returned to their kinescopes. "We're laughin' because it's funny, you half-wit," muttered a surly-looking young man.

"You there, brother," Rudy addressed him directly. After all, he, of everyone there, was Rudy's constituency. "Do you think it's funny that the Brains work people beyond endurance? That they speed up assembly lines without regard for the workers' natural pace, and without increasing their compensation? Do you think it's funny that a human man and woman would take the side of the Brains against their own kind? Think about this: What if Charles Chaplin — a man who respects the worker's dignity — had made this kinescope? There would be nothing funny about it: You'd weep for the poor fellows on the Brains' assembly line. As you should weep for Chico and Zeppo, whose dream of a life of honest labor and just reward has been cruelly exploited."

"Aw, shut yer yap!" It wasn't the young man that Rudy had addressed. This was the voice of an older man, embittered by many years of disappointment and penury.

"I apologize, sir," said Rudy. "You have every right to be angry. You have earned your leisure and have paid dearly for the right to sit here in the darkness and be assaulted by the self-serving garbage of the entertainment industry. Please return to your kinescope. But, I beg of you, do not swallow the tissue of lies that it offers you. Argue with it. Fight back! Resist!"

A huge hand reached out of the darkness and grabbed Rudy's right shoulder.

"Awright there, buddy," said a firm but quiet voice. "And why don't yez come along wit' me, and we can continue this discussion down to the station house?"

Rudy twisted about in the flatfoot's grasp. A sudden head-butt to the solar plexus, a kick to take the man's feet out from under him, and Rudy was running fast, not once looking back to see if he was being pursued. Halfway to the exit, he spotted a narrow circular staircase that burrowed down into the bowels of the earth below the kinescope parlor. He plunged into the darkness, down into the steam tunnels that ran beneath all the buildings of the Old Town.

That was Phase Three of his plan: Run like hell.

Amelia had less than five minutes to the start of the Game. She sprinted to the flight deck and her autogyro. Grimy Huey was waiting, and he didn't look happy. "Why didn't you tell me you were having work done on the machine? You don't trust me no more?"

"Huey, I'm up. We can talk about it later." She swung into the cockpit. The engine was already running. Even when he was ticked off, Huey knew his stuff. "Just throw me out there. The whistle's about to blow."

Grimy Huey waved and Amelia grabbed the controls. Everything in place. She nodded, and the launch platform thrust the autogyro out of the Zep, into takeoff position.

The steam-whistle blew. The Game was in motion.

Amelia kicked, pushed, pedaled, and screamed her improbable craft into the air.

For a time, all was well. As was traditional, the flying aces appeared in goose-vee formation from opposite sides of the plaza, ignoring each other on the first pass, save for a slight wing-waggle of salute, and then curving up into the sky above. Then began the series of thrilling moves that would lead to the heart-stopping aerial ballet of sporting dogfight.

On the first fighting pass, the advantage was to the Reds. But then Blockhead O'Brien threw his autogyro into a mad sideways skid that had half their 'planes pulling up in disarray to avoid being shredded by his blades. Amelia and Hops Wynzowski hurled themselves into the opening and ran five stars, neat as a pin, before the opposition could recover.

Amelia pulled up laughing, only to discover that the Big E was directly behind her and coming up her tail fast. She crouched down over her stick, raising her hips up from the seat, taut as a wire being tested to destruction, neurons snapping and crackling like a Tesla generator. "You catch me," she murmured happily, "and I swear to God I'll never fly again for as long as I live."

Because if there was one thing she knew it was that Eszterhazy *wasn't* going to catch her. She was in her element now. In that timeless instant that lasted forever, that was all instinct and reflex, lust and glory. She was vengeance and righteous fury. She was death in all its cold and naked beauty.

Then a rocket flew up out of nowhere and exploded in her face.

Rudy pounded through the steam tunnels as if every finger in the Fist of the Brains was on his tail. Which they weren't — yet. He'd given Fearless Fosdick the slip, he was sure.

It was only a matter of time, though. Back at Fat Edna's, he knew, they had a pool going as to the date. But when the Fist came for him, he wasn't going to go meekly, with his hands in the air. Not Rudy. That was why he was running now, even though he'd given the flatfoot the slip. He was practicing for the day when it all came down and his speed negotiating the twists and turns of the tunnels would spell the difference between escape and capture, survival and death.

The light from Rudy's electric torch flashed from a rectangle of reflective tape he'd stuck to one wall at chest level. Straight ahead, that meant. Turn coming up soon. And, sure enough, up ahead were two bits of tape together, like an equal sign, on the right-hand wall. Which, counterintuitively, signaled a left turn.

He ran, twisting and turning as the flashing blips of tapes dictated. A left … two rights … a long downward decline that he didn't remember but which had to be correct because up ahead glinted another tab of reflective tape and beyond it another two, indicating a left turn. Into the new tunnel he plunged, and then, almost falling, down a rattling set of metal steps that definitely wasn't right. At the bottom the tunnel opened up into an enormous cavernous blackness. He stumbled to a halt.

A cold wind blew down on him from above.

Rudy shivered. This was wrong. He'd never been here before. And yet, straight ahead of him glowed yet another tab of the tape. He lifted his electric torch from the ground in front of his feet to examine it.

And, as he lifted it up, he cried out in horror. The light revealed a mocking gargoyle of a man: filthy, grey-skinned, dressed in rags, with running sores on his misshapen face and only three fingers on the hand that mockingly held up a flashing rectangle of reflective tape.

"It's the bolshy," the creature said to nobody in particular.

"I thought he was a menshevik," said a second voice.

"Naw, he's a tvardokhlebnik," said a third. "A pathetic nibbler at the leavings of others."

"My brothers!" Rudy cried in mingled terror and elation. His torch slid from monstrous face to monstrous face. A throng of grotesques confronted him. These were the broken hulks of men, horribly disfigured by industrial accidents, disease, and bathtub gin, creatures who had been driven into the darkness not by poverty alone but also by the reflexive stares of those who had previously been their fellows and compeers. Rudy's revulsion turned to an enormous and terrible sense of pity. "You have lured me here for some purpose, I presume. Well ... here I am. Tell me what is so important that you must play these games with me."

"Kid gets right to the point."

"He's got a good mind."

"No sense of humor, though. Heard him speak once."

Swallowing back his fear, Rudy said, "Now you are laughing at me. Comrades! These are desperate times. We should not be at each other's throats, but rather working together for the common good."

"He's got *that* right."

"Toldya he had a good mind."

One of the largest of the men seized Rudy's jacket in his malformed hand, lifting him effortlessly off his feet. "Listen, pal. Somebody got something important to tell ya." He shook Rudy for emphasis. "So you're gonna go peacefully, all right? Don't do nothing stupid. Remember who lives here and can see in the dark and who don't and can't. Got that?"

"Brother! Yes! Of course!"

"Good." The titan let Rudy drop to the floor. "Open 'er up, boys." Shadowy figures pushed an indistinct pile of boxes and empty barrels away from a steel-clad door. "In there."

Rudy went through the door.

It closed behind him. He could hear the crates and barrels being pushed back into place.

He was in a laboratory. Even though it was only sparsely lit, Rudy could see tables crowded with huge jars that were linked by glass tubes and entwined in electrical cables. Things sizzled and bubbled. The air stank of ozone and burnt sulfur.

In the center of the room, illuminated by a single incandescent bulb dangling from the ceiling, was a glass tank a good twenty feet long. In its murky interior a huge form moved listlessly, filling it almost entirely — a single enormous sturgeon. Rudy was no sentimentalist, but it seemed to him that the great fish, unable to swim or even turn about in its cramped confines — indeed, unable to do much of anything save slowly move its fins in order to keep afloat and flutter its gills to breathe — must lead a grim and terrible existence.

Cables snaked from the tank to a nearby clutter of electrical devices, but he paid them no particular notice. His attention was drawn to a woman standing before the aquarium. Her lab smock seemed to glow in the gloom.

She had clearly been waiting for him, for without preamble, she said, "I am Professor Anna Pavlova." Her face was old and drawn; her eyes blazed with passionate intensity. "You have probably never heard of me, but — "

"Of course I know of you, Professor Pavlova!" Rudy babbled. "You are one of the greatest inventors of all time! The monorail! Citywide steam heat! You made the Naked Brains possible. The masses idolize you."

"Pah!" Professor Pavlova made a dismissive chopping gesture with her right hand. "I am but a scientist, nothing more nor less. All that matters is that when I was young I worked on the Naked Brain Project. Those were brave days indeed. All the best thinkers of our generation — politicians, artists, engineers — lined up to surrender their bodies in order to put their minds at the service of the people. I would have done so myself, were I not needed to monitor and fine-tune the nutrient systems. We were Utopians then! I am sure that not a one of them was influenced by the possibility that as Naked Brains they would live forever. Not a one! We wished only to serve."

She sighed.

"Your idealism is commendable, comrade scientist," Rudy said. "Yet it is my unhappy duty to inform you that the Council of Naked Brains no longer serves the people's interests. They — "

"It is worse than you think!" Professor Pavlova snapped. "For many years I was part of the inner circle of functionaries serving the Brains. I saw ... many things. Things that made me wonder, and then doubt. Quietly, I began my own research. But the scientific journals rejected my papers. Lab books disappeared. Data were altered. There came a day when none of the Naked Brains — who had been my friends, remember! — would respond to my messages, or even, when I went to them in person, deign to speak to me.

"I am no naïve innocent. I knew what that meant: the Fist would shortly be coming for me.

"So I went underground. I befriended the people here, whose bodies are damaged but whose minds remain free and flexible, and together we smuggled in enough equipment to continue my work. I tapped into the city's electric and gas lines. I performed miracles of improvisation and bricolage. At first I was hindered by my lack of access to the objects of my study. But then my new friends helped me liberate Old Teddy" — she patted the side of the fish tank — "from a pet shop where he was kept as a curiosity. Teddy was the key. He told me everything I needed to know."

Rudy interrupted the onslaught of words. "This fish *told* you things?"

"Yes." The scientist picked up a wired metal dish from the lab bench. "Teddy is very, very old, you see. When he was first placed in that tank, he was quite small, a wild creature caught for food but spared the frying pan to be put on display." She adjusted cables that ran from the silver dish to an electrical device on the bench. "That was many years ago, of course, long before you or I were born. Sturgeon can outlive humans, and Teddy has slowly grown into what you see before you." Other cables ran from the device into the tank. Rudy saw that they had been implanted directly into the sturgeon's brain. One golden-grey eye swiveled in the creature's whiskered, impassive head to look at him. Involuntarily, he shuddered. It was just a fish, he thought. It wished him no ill.

"Have you ever wondered what thoughts pass through a fish's brain?" With a grim smile that was almost a leer, the scientist thrust the silver dish at Rudy. "Place this cap on your head — and you will know."

More than almost anything, Rudy wanted *not* to put on the cap. Yet more than anything at all, he wanted to do his duty to his fellow beings, both human and fish. This woman might well be mad: she certainly did not act like any woman he had ever met. The device might well kill him or damage his brain. Yet to refuse it would be to give up on the adventure entirely, to admit that he was not the man for the job.

Rudy reached out and took the silver cap.

He placed it upon his head.

Savage homicidal rage filled him. Rudy hated everything that lived, without degree or distinction. All the universe was odious to him. If he could, he would murder everyone outside his tank, devour their eggs, and destroy their nests. Like a fire, this hatred engulfed him, burning all to nothing, leaving only a dark cinder of self at his core.

With a cry of rage, Rudy snatched the silver cap from his head and flung it away. Professor Pavlova caught it, as if she had been expecting his reaction. Horrified, he turned on her. "They hate us! The very fish hate us!" He could feel the sturgeon's deadly anger burning into his back, and this filled him with shame and self-loathing, even though he knew he did not personally deserve it. All humans deserved it, though, he thought.

All humans supported the idea of putting fish in tanks. Those who did not were branded eccentrics and their viewpoint dismissed without a hearing.

"This is a terrible invention! It does not reveal the universal brotherhood natural among disparate species entwined in the Great Web of Life — quite the opposite, in fact!" He despaired of putting his feelings into words. "What it reveals may be the truth, but is it a truth that we really we need to know?"

Professor Pavlova smiled mirthlessly. "You understand so well the inequalities in human intercourse and the effect they have on the human psyche. And now! Now, for the first time, you understand some measure of what a fish feels and thinks. Provided it has been kept immobile and without stimulation for so many years it is no longer sane." She glanced over at Old Teddy with pity. "A fish longs only for cold water, for food, for distances to swim, and for a place to lay its eggs or spread its milt. We humans have kept Teddy in a tank for over a century."

Then she looked at Rudy with almost the same expression. "Imagine how much worse it would be for a human being, used to sunshine on his face, the feel of a lover's hand, the soft sounds an infant makes when it is happy, to find himself — even if of his own volition — nothing more than a Naked Brain afloat in amniotic fluid. Sans touch, sans taste, sans smell, sans sound, sans sight, sans everything. You have felt the fish's hatred. Imagine how much stronger must be the man's." Her eyes glittered with a cold fire. "I have suspected this for years, and now that I have experienced Teddy's mind — now *I know*." She sliced her hand outward, as if with a knife, to emphasize the depth of her knowledge, and its force. "The Naked Brains are all mad. They hate us and they will work tirelessly for our destruction."

"This is what I have been saying all along," Rudy gasped. "I have been trying to engage — "

Pavlova interrupted him. "The time for theorizing and yammering and pamphleteering is over. You were brought here because I have a message and I need a messenger. The time has come for action. Tell your superiors. Tell the world. The Naked Brains must be destroyed."

A sense of determination flooded Rudy's being. This was what all his life had been leading up to. This was his moment of destiny.

Which made it particularly ironic that it was at that very moment that the Fist smashed in the door of the laboratory.

Radio Jones had punched a hole in the center of a sheet of paper and taped it to the casing of her all-frequencies receiver with the tuner knob at the center, so she could mark the location of each transceiver set she found. The tuner had a range of two hundred ten degrees, which covered the entire spectrum of the communications band. So she eyeballed it into quarters and then tenths, to give a rough idea how things were laid out. It would be better to rank them by electromagnetic frequency, but she didn't have the time to work all that out, and anyway, though she would never admit this out loud, she was just a little weak on the theoretics. Radio was more a vacuum-tube-and-solder-gun kind of girl.

Right now the paper was heavily marked right in the center of the dial, from ninety to one-sixty degrees. There were dozens of flier-Brain pairs, and she'd put a mark by each one, and identified a good quarter of them. Including, she was particularly pleased to see, all the big guys — Eszterhazy, Spindizzy, Blockhead O'Brien, Stackerlee Brown. When there wasn't any room for more names, Radio went exploring into the rest of the spectrum, moving out from the center by incremental degrees.

So, because she wasn't listening to the players, Radio missed the beginning of the massacre. It was only when she realized that everybody in Edna's had rushed out into the street that she looked up from her chore and saw the aeroplanes falling and autogyros spinning out of control. She went to the window just in time to hear a universal gasp as a Zeppelin exploded in the sky overhead. Reflected flames glowed red on the uplifted faces.

"Holy cow!" Radio ran back to her set and twisted her dial back toward the center.

"...*Warinowski,*" a Naked Brain was saying dispassionately. "*Juric-Kocik. Bai. Gevers...*"

A human voice impatiently broke in on the recitation. "What about Spindizzy? She's worth more than the rest of them put together. Did she set off her bomb?"

"*No.*" A long pause. "*Maybe she disarmed it.*"

"If that's the case, she'll be gunning for me." The human voice was horribly, horribly familiar. "Plot her vectors, tell me where she is, and I'll take care of her."

"Oh, no," Radio said. "It can't be."

"*What is your current situation?*"

"My rockets are primed and ready, and I've got a clear line of sight straight down Archer Road, from Franklin all the way to the bend."

"*Stay your course. We will direct Amelia Spindizzy onto Archer Road, headed south, away from you. When you see her clear the Frank Lloyd Wright Tower, count three and fire.*"

"Roger," the rocket-assassin said. Now there was no doubt at all in Radio's mind. She knew that voice. She knew the killer.

And she knew what she had to do.

Amelia Spindizzy's ears rang from the force of the blast, and she could feel in the joystick an arrhythmic throb. Where had the missile come from that had caused the explosion? What had happened to Eszterhazy? She was sure she had not accidentally pressed the red button on the joystick, so he should be fine, if he had evaded the blast. Hyperalert, Amelia detected an almost invisible scratch in the air, tracing the trajectory of a second rocket, and braced herself for another shock.

When it came, she was ready for it. This time she rode, with her whole body, the great twisting thrusts that came from the rotor, much as she would ride a stallion or, she imagined, a man. The blades sliced the air and the autogyro shook, but she forced her will on the powerful machine, which had until this instant been her partner, not her opponent, and overmastered it.

It might be true that you never see the missile that kills you. But that didn't mean you couldn't be killed by a missile you could see. Amelia needed to get out of the line of fire — a third missile might err on the side of accuracy. She banked sharply down into Archer Road, past the speakeasy and the storefront church, and pulled a brisk half-Eszterhazy into an alley next to a skeleton of iron girders with a banner reading FUTURE HOME OF BLACK STAR LINE SHIPPING & NAVIGATION. All that raw iron would block her comptroller's radio signal, but that hardly mattered now. At third-floor level, slowing to the speed of a running man, she crept, as it were, back to where she would see what was happening over the Great Square.

Eszterhazy was nowhere in evidence, but neither was there a column of smoke where she had seen him last. Perhaps, like herself, he'd held his craft together and gone to cover. Missiles were still arcing through the air and exploding. There were no flying machines in the sky and the great Zeppelins were sinking down like foundering ships. It wasn't clear what the missiles were aimed at — perhaps their purpose at this point was simply to keep any surviving 'planes and autogyros out of the sky.

Or perhaps they were being shot off by fools. In Amelia's experience, you could never write off the fool option.

Radio 2 was blinking and squawking like a battery-operated chicken. Amelia ignored it. Until she knew who was shooting at her, she wasn't talking to anybody: any radio contact would reveal her location.

As, treading air, she rounded the skeleton of the would-be shipping line, Amelia noticed something odd. It looked like a lump of rags hanging from a rope tied to a girder — possibly a support strut for a planned crosswalk — that stuck out from the metal framework. What on earth could that be? Then it moved, wriggling downward, and she saw that it was a boy!

And he was sliding rapidly down toward the end of his rope.

Almost without thinking, Amelia brought her autogyro in. There had to be a way of saving the kid. The rotor blades were a problem, and their wash. She couldn't slow down much more than she already had — autogyros didn't hover. But if she took both the forward speed and the wash into account, made them work together…

It would be trying to snag a baseball in a hurricane. But she didn't see any alternative.

She came in, the wash from her props blowing the lump of rags and the rope it hung from almost parallel to the ground. She could see the kid clearly now, a little boy in a motley coat, his body hanging just above Amelia. He had a metal box hanging from a belt around his neck that in another instant was going to tear him off the rope for sure.

There was one hellishly giddy moment when her rotors went above the out-stuck girder and her fuselage with its stubby wings went below. She reached out with the mail hook, grabbed the kid, and pulled him into the cockpit as the 'gyro moved relentlessly forward.

The tip of the rope whipped up and away and was shredded into dust by the whirling blades. The boy fell heavily between Amelia and her rudder, so that she couldn't see a damned thing.

She shoved him up and over her, unceremoniously dumping the brat headfirst into the passenger seat. Then she grabbed the controls, easing her bird back into the center of the alley.

From behind her, the kid shouted, "Jeepers, Amelia. Get outta here, f'cripesake! He's coming for you!"

"What?" Amelia yelled. Then the words registered. "Who's shooting? Why?" The brat knew something. "Where are they? How do you know?" Then, sternly, "That was an insanely dangerous thing for you to do."

"Don't get yer wig in a frizzle," said the kid. "I done this a million times."

"You have?" said Amelia in surprise.

"In my dreams, anyway," said the kid. "Hold the questions. Right now we gotta lam outta here, before somebody notices us what shouldn't. I'll listen in on what's happening." He twisted around and tore open the seat back, revealing the dry batteries, and yanked the cords from them. The radio went dead.

"Hey!" Amelia cried.

"Not to worry. I'm just splicing my Universal Receiver to your power supply. Your radios are obsolete now, but you couldn't know that...." Now the little gremlin had removed a floor panel and was crawling in among the autogyro's workings. "Lemme just ground this and... Say! Why have you got a bomb in here?"

"Huh? You mean... Oh, that's just some electronic doohickey the Naked Brains asked me to test for them."

"Tell it to the Marines, lady. I didn't fall off no turnip truck. The onliest electronics you got here is two wires coming off a detonator cap and leading to one of your radios. If I didn't know better, I'd tag this sucker as a remote-controlled self-destruct device." The imp stuck its head out of the workings again, and said, "Oh yeah. The name's Radio Jones."

With an abrupt rush of conceptual vertigo, Amelia realized that this gamin was a *girl*. "How do you do," she said dazedly. "I'm..."

"I know who you are," Radio said. "I got your picture on

the wall." Then, seeing that they were coming up on the bend in Archer Road, "Hey! Nix! Not that way! There's a guy with a coupla rockets up there just waiting for you to show your face. Pull a double curl and loop back down Vanzetti. There's a vacant lot this side of the Shamrock Tavern that's just wide enough for the 'gyro. Martin Dooley's the barkeep there, and he's got a shed large enough to hide this thing. Let's vamoose!"

A rocket exploded behind her.

Good advice was good advice. No matter how unlikely its source.

Amelia Spindizzy vamoosed.

But as she did, she could not help casting a wistful glance back over her shoulder, hoping against hope for a glimpse of a bright red aeroplane. "I don't suppose you've heard anything about Eszterhazy surviving this?" she heard herself asking her odd young passenger. Whatever was happening, with his superb skills, surely he must have survived.

"Uh, about that ..." Radio Jones said. "I kinda got some bad news for you."

Rudy awoke to find himself in Hell.

Hell was touchless, tasteless, scentless, and black as pitch. It consisted entirely of a bedlam of voices: "Lemme outta here — wasn't doing nothing — Mabel! Where are you, Mabel? — I'm serious, I got bad claustrophobia — goddamn flicks! — there's gotta be — minding my own business — Mabel! — gonna puke — all the things I coulda been — I don't like it here — can't even hear myself think — Oh, Freddy, if only I'da toldja I loved you when I coulda — got to be a way out — why won't anybody tell me what's happening? — if the resta youse don't shut —"

He knew where he was now. He understood their situation. Gathering himself together, Rudy funneled all the energy he had into a mental shout:

"Silence!"

His thought was so forceful and purposive that it shocked all the other voices into silence.

"Comrades!" he began. "It is clear enough what has happened here. We have all been harvested by the police lackeys of the Naked Brains. By the total lack of somatic sensations, I deduce that we have ourselves been made into Naked Brains." Somebody sent out a stab of raw emotion. Before his or her (not that gender mattered anymore, under the circumstances) hysteria could spread, Rudy rushed onward in a torrent of words. "But there is no need for despair. We are not without hope. So long as we have our thoughts, our inner strength, and our powers of reason, we hold within ourselves the tools of liberation."

"Liberation?" somebody scoffed. "It's my body's been liberated, and from *me*. It's them is doing the liberatin', not us."

"I understand your anger, brother," Rudy said. "But the opportunity is to him who keeps his head." Belatedly, Rudy realized that this was probably not the smartest thing to say. The anonymous voices responded with jeers. "Peace, brothers and sisters. We may well be lost, and we must face up to that." More jeers. "And yet, we all have family and friends who we left behind." Everyone, that is, save for himself — a thought that Rudy quickly suppressed. "Think of the world that is coming for them — one of midnight terror, an absolutist government, the constant fear of denouncement and punishment without trial. Of imprisonment without hope of commutation, of citizens randomly plucked from the streets for harvesting..." He paused to let that sink in. "I firmly believe that we can yet free ourselves. But even if we could not, would it not be worth our uttermost efforts to fight the tyranny of the Brains? For the sake of those we left behind?"

There was a general muttering of agreement. Rudy had created a community among his listeners. Now, quickly, to take advantage of it! "Who here knows anything about telecommunications technology?"

"I'm an electrical engineer," somebody said.

"That Dutch?" said another voice. "You're a damn good engineer. Or you were."

"Excellent. Dutch, you are now the head of our Ad Hoc Committee for Communications and Intelligence. Your task is first to work out the ways that we are connected to each other and to the machinery of the outer world, and second, to determine how we may take over the communications system, control it for our own ends, and when we are ready, deprive the government of its use. Are you up to the challenge, Comrade — ?"

"Schwartz. Dutch Schwartz, at your service. Yes, I am."

"Then choose people to work with you. Report back when you have solid findings. Now. Who here is a doctor?"

"I am," a mental voice said dryly. "Professor and Doctor Anna Pavlova at your service."

"Forgive me, Comrade Professor. Of course you are here. And we are honored — honored! — to have you with us. One of the greatest — "

"Stop the nattering and put me to work."

"Yes, of course. Your committee will look into the technical possibilities of restoring our brains to the bodies we left behind."

"Well," said the professor, "this is not something we ever considered when we created the Brains. But our knowledge of microsurgery has grown enormously with the decades of Brain maintenance. I would not rule it out."

"You believe our bodies have not been destroyed?" somebody asked in astonishment.

"A resource like that? Of course not," Rudy said. "Think! Any despotic government must have the reliable support of toadies and traitors. With a supply of bodies, many of them young, to

offer, the government can effectively give their lackeys immortality — not the immortality of the Brains, but the immortality
of body after body, in plentiful supply." He paused to let that
sink in. "However. If we act fast to organize the proletariat, perhaps that can be prevented. To do this, we will need the help
of those in the Underground who have not been captured and
disembodied. Who here is — ?"

"And you," somebody else said. "What is your role in this?
Are you to be our leader?"

"Me?" Rudy asked in astonishment. "Nothing of the sort! I
am a community organizer."

He got back to work organizing.

The last dirigible was moored to the tip of the Gaudi Building.
The *Imperator* was a visible symbol of tyranny which cast its
metaphoric shadow over the entire city. So far as anybody knew,
there wasn't an aeroplane, autogyro, or Zeppelin left in the city
to challenge its domination of the air. So it was there that the
new Tyrant would be. It was there that the destinies of everyone
in the city would play out.

It was there that Amelia Spindizzy and Radio Jones went,
after concealing the autogyro in a shed behind Dooley's tavern.

Even from a distance, it was clear that there were gun ports
to every side of the *Imperator*, and doubtless there were other
defenses on the upper floors of the skyscraper. So they took the
most direct route — through the lobby of the Gaudi building
and up the elevator. Amelia and Radio stepped inside, the doors
closed behind them, and up they rose, toward the Zeppelin.

"In my youth, of course, I was an avid balloonsman," somebody said from above.

Radio yelped and Amelia stared sharply upward.

Wedged into an upper corner of the elevator was a radio.
From it came a marvelous voice, at once both deep and reedy,

and immediately recognizable as well. "... and covered the city by air. Once, when I was a mere child, ballooning alone as was my wont, I caught a line on a gargoyle that stuck out into my airspace from the tower of the Church of Our Lady of the Assumption — what is now the Sepulchre of the Bodies of the Brains — and, thus entangled, I was in some danger of the gondola — which was little more than a basket, really — tipping me out into a long and fatal fall to earth. Fortunately, one of the brown-robed monks, engaged in his Matins, was cloistered in the tower and noticed my predicament. He was able to reach out and free the line." The voice dropped, a hint of humor creeping in. "In my childish piety, of course, I considered this evidence of the beneficent intercession of some remote deity, whom I thanked nightly in my prayers." One could almost hear him shaking his head at his youthful credulousness. "But considering how fortunate we are now — are we not? — to be at last freed from the inhuman tyranny of the Naked Brains, one has to wonder whether it wasn't in some sense the hand of Destiny that reached out from that tower, to save the instrument by which our liberation would one day be achieved."

"It's him!" Radio cried. "Just like I told you."

"It ... sounds like him. But he can't be the one who gave the orders you overheard. Can you be absolutely sure?" Amelia asked her unlikely sidekick for the umpteenth time. "Are you really and truly *certain*?"

Radio rolled her eyes. "Lady, I heard him with my own two ears. You don't think I know the voice of the single greatest pilot ..." Her voice trailed off under Amelia's glare. "Well, don't hit the messenger! I read *Obey the Brain!* every week. His stats are just plain better'n yours."

"They have been," Amelia said grimly. "But that's about to change." She unsnapped the holster of her pistol.

Then the bell pinged. They'd reached the top floor.

The elevator doors opened.

Rudy was conferring with progressive elements in the city police force about the possibility of a counter-coup (they argued persuasively that, since it was impossible to determine their fellow officers' loyalties without embroiling the force in internecine conflict, any strike would have to be small and fast) when his liaison with the Working Committee for Human Resources popped up in his consciousness and said, "We've located the bodies, boss. As you predicted, they were all carefully preserved and are being maintained in the best of health."

"That is good news, Comrade Mariozzi. Congratulations. But none of that 'boss' business, do you understand? It could easily go from careless language to a common assumption."

Meanwhile, they'd hooked into televideon cameras throughout the city, and though the views were grim, it heartened everybody to no longer be blind. It was a visible — there was no way around the word — sign that they were making progress.

Red Rudy had just wrapped up the meeting with the loyalist police officers when Comrade Mariozzi popped into his consciousness again. "Hey, boss!" he said excitedly. "You gotta see this!"

The guards were waiting at the top of the elevator with guns drawn. To Radio Jones's shock and amazement, Amelia Spindizzy handed over her pistol without a murmur of protest. Which was more than could be said for Radio herself when one of the goons wrested the Universal Receiver out of her hands. Amelia had to seize her by the shoulders and haul her back before she could attack the nearest of their captors.

They were taken onto the *Imperator* and through the Hall of the Naked Brains. The great glass jars were empty and the giant floating Brains were gone who-knows-where. Radio hoped they'd been flung in an alley somewhere to be eaten by dogs. But hundreds of new, smaller jars containing brains of merely human proportions had been brought in and jury-rigged to oxygen feeds and electrical input-output units. Radio noticed that they all had cut-out switches. If one of the New Brains acted up it could be instantly put into solitary confinement. But there was nobody monitoring them, which seemed to defeat the purpose.

"'Keep close to the earth!'" a voice boomed. Radio jumped. Amelia, she noticed, did not. Then she saw that there were radios set in brackets to either end of the room. "Such was the advice of the preeminent international airman, Alberto Santos-Dumont, and they were good enough words for their time." The familiar voice chuckled and half-snorted, and the radio crackled loudly as his breath struck the sensitive electroacoustic transducer that had captured his voice. "But his time is not my time." He paused briefly; one could almost hear him shrug his shoulders. "One is never truly tested close to the earth. It is in the huge arching parabola of an aëroplane finding its height and seeking a swift descent from it that a man's courage is found. It is there, in acts outside of the quotidian, that his mettle is tested."

A televideon camera ratcheted about, tracking their progress. Were the New Brains watching them, Radio wondered? The thought gave her the creeps.

Then they were put in an elevator (only two guards could fit in with them, and Radio thought that for sure Amelia would make her play now; but the aviatrix stared expressionlessly forward and did nothing) and taken down to the flight deck. There the exterior walls had been removed, as would be done under wartime conditions when the 'planes and wargyros had to be gotten into the air as soon as possible. Cold winds buffeted and blustered about the vast and empty space.

"A young man dreams of war and glory," the voice said from a dozen radios. "He toughens his spirit and hardens his body with physical activity and discomfort. In time, he's ready to join the civil militia, where he is trained in the arts of killing and destruction. At last, his ground training done, he is given an aeroplane and catapulted into the sky, where he discovers ..." The voice caught and then, when it resumed, was filled with wonder, "... not hatred, not destruction, not war, but peace."

To the far side of the flight deck, unconcerned by his precarious location, a tall figure in a flyer's uniform bent over a body in greasy coveralls, which he had dragged right to the edge. Then he flipped it over. It was Grimy Huey, and he was dead.

The tall man stood and turned. "Leave," he told the guards.

They clicked their heels and obeyed.

"He almost got me, you know," the man remarked conversationally. "He came at me from behind with a wrench. Who would have thought that a mere mechanic had that much gumption in him?"

For a long moment, Amelia Spindizzy stood ramrod-straight and unmoving. Radio Jones sank to the deck, crouching by her side. She couldn't help herself. The cold and windy openness of the flight deck scared her spitless. She couldn't even stand. But, terrified though she was, she didn't look away. Someday all this would be in the history books; whatever happened, she knew, was going to determine her view of the world and its powers for the rest of her natural life, however short a time that might be.

Then Amelia strolled forward toward Eszterhazy and said, "Let me help you with that." She stooped and took the mechanic's legs. Eszterhazy took the arms. They straightened, swung the body — one! two! three! — and flung it over the side.

Slapping her hands together, Amelia said, "Why'd you do it?"

Eszterhazy shrugged in a self-deprecating way. "It had to be done. So I stepped up to the plate and took a swing at the ball. That's all." Then he grinned boyishly. "It's good to know that you're on my team."

"That's you on the radios," Amelia said. They were still booming away, even though the buffeting winds drowned out half the words that came from them.

"Wire recording." Eszterhazy strode to a support strut and slapped a switch. The radios all died. "A little talk I prepared, being broadcast to the masses. Radio has been scandalously underutilized as a tool of governance."

Amelia's response was casual — even, Radio thought, a bit dunderheaded technologically. "But radio's everywhere," she said. "There are dozens of public sets scattered through the city. Why, people can hear news bulletins before the newspapers can even set type and roll the presses!"

Eszterhazy smiled a thin, tight, condescending smile. "But they only tell people what's happened, and not what to *think* about it. That's going to change. My people are distributing sets to every bar, school, church, and library in the city. In the future, my future, everyone will have a bank of radios in their home — the government radio, of course, but also one for musical events, another for free lectures, and perhaps even one for business news."

Radio felt the urge to speak up and say that fixed-frequency radios were a thing of the past. But she suppressed it. She sure wasn't about to hand over her invention to a bum the likes of which Eszterhazy was turning out to be. But what the heck was the matter with Amelia?

Amelia Spindizzy put her hands behind her, and turned her back on her longtime archrival. Head down, deep in thought, she trod the edge of the abyss. "Hah." The word might have meant anything. "You've clearly put a lot of thought into this ... this ... new world order of yours."

"I've been planning this all my life," Eszterhazy said with absolute seriousness. "New and more efficient forms of government, a society that not only promotes the best of its own but actively weeds out the criminals and the morally sick. Were you aware that before Lycurgus became king, the Spartans were a licentious and ungovernable people? He made them the fiercest warriors the world has ever known in the space of a single lifetime." He stopped, and then with a twinkle in his eye said, "There I go again, talking about the Greeks! As I started to say, I thought I would not be ready to make my move for many years. But then I got wind of certain experiments performed by Anna Pavlova which proved that not only were the Naked Brains functionally mad, but that I had it in my power to offer them the one thing for which they would give me their unquestioning cooperation — death.

"In their corruption were the seeds of our salvation. And thus fell our oppressors."

"I worked with them, and I saw no oppressors." Amelia rounded her course strolling back toward Eszterhazy, brow furrowed with thought. "Only nets of neurological fiber who, as it turned out, were overcome by the existential terror of their condition."

"Their condition is called 'life,' Millie. And, yes, life makes us all insane." Eszterhazy could have been talking over the radio, his voice was so reassuring and convincing. "Some of us respond to that terror with useless heroics. Others seek death." He cocked a knowing smile at Amelia. "Others respond by attacking the absurdity at its source. Ruled by Naked Brains, humanity could not reach its full potential. Now, once again, we will rule ourselves."

"It does all make sense. It all fits." Amelia Spindizzy came to a full stop and stood shaking her head in puzzlement. "If only I could understand — "

"What is there to understand?" An impatient edge came into Eszterhazy's voice. "What have I left unexplained? We can perfect our society in our lifetimes! You're so damnably cold and analytic, Millie. Don't you see that the future lies right at your feet? All you have to do is let go of your doubts and analyses and intellectual hesitations and take that leap of faith into a better world."

Radio trembled with impotent alarm. She knew that, small and ignored as she was, it might be possible for her to be the wild card, the unexpected element, the unforeseeable distraction that saves the day. That it was, in fact, her duty to do so. She'd seen enough Saturday afternoon kinescope serials to understand *that*.

If only she could bring herself to stand up. Though it almost made her throw up to do so, Radio brought herself to her feet. The wind whipped the deck, and Eszterhazy quickly looked over at her. As though noticing her for the first time. And then, as Radio fought to overcome her paralyzing fear, Amelia acted.

She smiled that big, easy Amelia grin that had captured the hearts of proles and aristos alike. It was a heartfelt smile and a wickedly hoydenish leer at one and the same time, and it bespoke aggression and an inner shyness in equal parts. A disarming grin, many people called it.

Smiling her disarming grin, Amelia looked Eszterhazy right in the eye. She looked as if she had just found a brilliant solution to a particularly knotty problem. Despite the reflexive decisiveness for which he was known, Eszterhazy stood transfixed.

"You know," she said, "I had always figured that, when all the stats were totted up and the final games were flown, you and I would find a shared understanding in our common enthusiasm for human-controlled — "

All in an instant, she pushed forward, wrapped her arms around her opponent, and let their shared momentum carry them over the edge.

Radio instantly fell to the deck again and found herself scrambling across it to the edge on all fours. Gripping the rim of the flight decking with spasmodic strength, she forced herself to look over. Far below, two conjoined specks tumbled in a final flight to the earth.

She heard a distant scream — no, she heard laughter.

Radio managed to hold herself together through the endless ceremonies of a military funeral. To tell the truth, the pomp and ceremony of it — the horse-drawn hearse, the autogyro fly-by, the lines of dignitaries and endlessly droning eulogies in the Cathedral — simply bored her to distraction. There were a couple of times when Mack had to nudge her because she was falling asleep. Also, she had to wear a dress and, sure as shooting, any of her friends who saw her in it were going to give her a royal ribbing about it when next they met.

But then came the burial. As soon as the first shovel of dirt rattled down on the coffin, Radio began blubbering like a punk. Fat Edna passed her a lace hanky — who'd even known she *had* such a thing? — and she mopped at her eyes and wailed.

When the last of the earth had been tamped down on the grave, and the priest turned away, and the mourners began to break up, Radio felt a hand on her shoulder. It was, of all people, Rudy the Red. He looked none the worse for his weeklong vacation from the flesh.

"Rudy," she said, "is that a *suit* you're wearing?"

"It is not the uniform of the oppressor anymore. A new age has begun, Radio, an age not of hierarchic rule by an oligarchy of detached, unfeeling intellects, but of horizontally structured human cooperation. No longer will workers and managers be kept apart and treated differently from one another. Thanks to the selfless sacrifice of — "

"Yeah, I heard the speech you gave in the Cathedral."

"You did?" Rudy looked strangely pleased.

"Well, mostly. I mighta slept through some of it. Listen, Rudy, I don't want to rain on your parade, but people are still gonna be people, you know. You're all wound up to create this Big Rock Candy Mountain of a society, and good for you. Only — you gotta be prepared for the possibility that it won't work. I mean, ask any engineer, that's just the way things are. They don't always work the way they're supposed to."

"Then I guess we'll just have to wing it, huh?" Rudy flashed a wry grin. Then, abruptly, his expression turned serious, and he said the very last thing in the world she would have expected to come out of his mouth: "How are you doing?"

"Not so good. I feel like a ton of bricks was dropped on me." She felt around for Edna's hanky, but she'd lost it somewhere. So she wiped her eyes on her sleeve. "You want to know what's the real kicker? I hardly knew Amelia. So I don't even know why I should feel so bad."

Rudy took her arm. "Come with me a minute. Let me show you something."

He led her to a gravestone that was laid down to one side of the grave, to be erected when everyone was gone. It took a second for Radio to read the inscription. "Hey! It's just a quotation. Amelia's name ain't even on it. That's crazy."

"She left instructions for what it would say quite some time ago. I gather that's not uncommon for flyers. But I can't help feeling it's a message."

Radio stared at the words on the stone for very long time. Then she said, "Yeah, I see what you mean. But, ya know, I think it's a different message than what she thought it would be."

The rain, which had been drizzling off and on during the burial, began in earnest. Rudy shook out his umbrella and opened it over them both. They joined the other mourners, who were scurrying away in streams and rivulets, pouring from the cemetery exits and into the slidewalk stations and the vacuum trains, going back home to their lives and families, to boiled cabbage and schooners of pilsner, to their jobs, and their hopes, and their heartbreaks, to the vast, unknowable, and perfectly ordinary continent of the future.

> *It followed that the victory would belong to him who was calmest, who shot best, and who had the cleverest brain in a moment of danger.*
> —*Baron Manfred von Richthofen (1892–1918)*

Phantom Pain

HE WAS IN THE LIBRARY. It was quiet. No guns. No mud. He could crawl in peace, as long as he didn't make any noise. Mrs. Dientz, the librarian, wouldn't allow noise.

Ed was worried that he would get dirt in his wound, and it would get infected. The library is full of fungus, like a locker room: you can get athlete's foot in places you would never put your feet. Wet, too. It was raining, a hot tropical rain, but he was cold and it didn't warm him. In the library, there was a bamboo umbrella stand that always had a couple of umbrellas in it, no matter what the weather, and a mahogany rack with a pair of rubbers. Maybe he could borrow them. He'd return them. He needed them right now, that was all. The jungle was always so wet. He had forgotten his rubbers, and he needed to get home.

The rain stopped, and steam rose from the dirt. He kept crawling. The mud, thick as peanut butter, smelled like chocolate and skunk cabbage. Large, leathery leaves brushed wet against his head and shoulders as he pushed through them.

His leg was broken, he knew it, and it was chewed all to hell. Bullets from their own gun, captured by the Japs, in one leg, shrapnel from somebody's mortar — Jap? Yank? Who knew whose? — in the other. His fatigues were torn up and soaked with blood, and there were little ants crawling on them. The jungle wouldn't even wait for him to die.

———

The library was cool and quiet, and Ed was talking to Katie. He was whispering, because they were in the library, but he was all muddy because they were in the jungle. He was asking her a question. Had she ever wondered what it would be like to have all the money she could imagine? Just squander it, spend it wildly on everything she wanted? He used to wonder about money, before he joined the Marines, before he shipped out. How did you ever get enough, and what did you do when you got it? Katie was looking at him very seriously, and she nodded her head a little, not like she had ever wondered such a thing, but like she was encouraging him to keep talking. "Well, darling," he said to her, "this leave I have is our fortune. Let's spend it like we've never spent thirty days before, and just as though we'll never have thirty days to spend again."

Did he make that up himself, or did he hear it in a movie? It didn't sound like a movie with a happy ending. In movies, the soldiers who said things like that always got shot. He hadn't even said that to Katie, but he got shot anyway. If he ever got another leave, he would be spending it in Australia or New Zealand with a bunch of other leathernecks, not in the South Weymouth public library with his girl.

He sure wanted to see Katie again. He wanted to see his dad and his sister and his librarian. He wanted to tell Katie the things he had never told her except in letters from halfway around the world. He hadn't even told her that he loved her. It's the kind of thing you want to say in person.

Ed wouldn't have gotten shot, except that he was in the wrong place at the wrong time. It wasn't his job to carry ammunition to the guns, but sometimes there's things that have to be done, and you do them. The day before, the company had cleared an area of underbrush, leaving the tall trees as cover against air attack, and dug themselves in for their first night on the island.

It was raining, of course. It rained and rained in this place. Ed dug himself a hole, shared rations with the guys in the holes on either side of him, hunched under his poncho, and managed to get some shut-eye before his watch.

The next morning, the captain and Ed and Johnny Dahn had left the camp to check the position of the left flank of the Third Battalion: the company was due to tie in with them later in the morning. They found the Third, checked their position, made arrangements for later. Then they started back, taking an inspection tour of the lines.

They were just finishing the first platoon when a volley of enemy fire broke loose. They hit the ground fast — it sounded like it was aimed right at them. Marines in the line behind them answered with M1s and machine guns.

The call and response of gunfire was like the responses at Mass: first the priest, "*Introibo ad altare Dei*," then the altar boys, "*Ad Deum qui laetificat juventutem meam*." You could count on it, and you knew all the voices: the heavy, adult voice of a water-cooled gun, then the chatter of light machine guns; quick, sharp automatic-rifle bursts, followed by flat rapid fire from the Japanese guns, all of it against a staccato drone of grenades and mortar.

When the volley was over, the jungle went as quiet as death. The rain had stopped. In front of the platoon, there was a green wall of trees and brush. Nothing moved there. In the foxholes, marines held themselves immobile, guns in hand, watching the jungle for the slightest movement. Occasionally the sound of a ricochet rang through the trees.

The three marines waited in the silence. Maybe it was five minutes, but it seemed like an hour. Then, dripping wet, like the jungle itself, they made their way back in the rain to the Command Post. They moved cautiously: they didn't want to startle anyone.

When they got to the CP, however, all hell was breaking loose. The radio was on the fritz, and the men were quickly organizing a circular defense in case of a breakthrough in the lines. While they were busy with that, a wounded kid crawled in on his hands and knees. Ed and Johnny helped him turn over and lie down. He'd been shot three times, once in each thigh and once in the pelvis just below the beltline. No blood, just little round holes, blue at the edges. He was very pale and breathing shallowly: in shock, probably bleeding internally. None of the medical corpsmen were at the CP: the kid needed to be at the battalion aid station, four hundred yards away. Ed and Johnny laid him on a canvas stretcher, and, following the telephone wire, carried him through the heavy warm rain, struggling to keep their feet in the mud.

They'd only gone a short way when they met a party of marines bringing ammunition to the CP. "That was where we got ourselves outfoxed," Johnny would say later, retelling the tale, "when we met those guys bringing in boxes of ammo. Quickest shuffle I've ever seen. All of a sudden, they were carrying the stretcher away from the lines, and we were headed back to the front, carrying the ammo."

When they got back to the CP, the captain didn't even say anything. He just grabbed a couple of boxes and started to the lines. "They were pretty heavy," Johnny would say. "It seemed like the right thing to just grab a couple myself and follow him." Ed never talked about it.

Carrying the boxes, they moved up into a haze of gunsmoke and a stench of sulfur. There was an opening in the trees, and they could see one of the guns.

Katie was Irish, of course. Katie Kelly, what else would she be? Not Boston Irish: she was from Pennsylvania and California and New York. Katie liked the Boston Bruins, though. She liked to drive cars, and she liked to drive them fast. She was a fashion-design student, tall and glamorous, with a mass of dark brown hair. Her letters came in Kelly-green envelopes, so he always knew right at the beginning of mail call whether he had gotten anything from her. Sometimes she would send packages, brownies or chocolate-chip cookies, direct to the jungle from Dorchester, Massachusetts.

His mother, rest her soul, had never met Katie, but his father liked her, his brother liked her, his little sister liked her. If he didn't make it out of the library, maybe he would get to see his mother: he had been to Mass last Sunday, every Sunday, even in the jungle. He had to get to Mass again. Just needed to keep crawling.

You can know only your own pain. This ought to be obvious. You know what's hurting you, and you try to keep quiet about it — or maybe not. Maybe you wince, maybe you yell — maybe you make a big fuss about nothing. But it's your own pain, it starts inside you, it is part of you. Only you know what it really means, what it says to you when nobody else is around. You know it like a friend, like a member of your family, like a fraternal twin.

Somebody else's pain, you'd think you'd have enough sense to know that you don't know it. But almost everyone has an idea of the appropriate display of someone else's pain. You say, "You're being very brave." Or, "You're making an awful fuss about nothing." You say, "That doesn't hurt so much, now does it?"

For no reason Ed could figure out, he was lying in bed, an ordinary bed in a nice house. No jungle, no rain, no library. He smelled ether. A blonde woman was rubbing ether on his left foot. It was icy cold where it hit the skin, and the heavy, sweet smell of it cut into his head. It hurt like hell, or maybe it was his leg in the jungle that hurt like hell. That's Katie! he thought, looking at the woman. That's Katie, but she's blonde. A thin little boy and a round-faced girl were watching silently. He was not in his proper body: he had only one leg. Why is Katie rubbing ether on it, he wondered. What happened to the other one?

Ether is an antiseptic. Maybe Katie was cleaning some wound he didn't have yet. Ed was pleased at the thought that there were wounds he didn't have.

The medic was dead, killed by the same shrapnel that had shredded his leg, and Katie had taken the medic's place. If he died here, he would just sink into the mattress and feed the trees and the bugs. Mud thou art, to bugs thou shalt return. Ed was muddy, but he would not return to bugs, at least not as long as he could crawl.

When you're shot, you might feel the pain or you might not. If you need to move quickly, to jump out of a burning plane, for instance, you might not even notice that you are injured until you are, fortunately, safe. Maybe you are so busy trying to survive that you are pain-free until you're dead. Or maybe not.

If you survive, the cause of your pain will migrate as your condition changes. Before your leg is amputated, your pain is caused by trauma or disease in the part that will be cut off. Afterward, your pain, at first anyway, is caused by the new damage to your flesh and bone that is the amputation. Your body quickly gets to work to repair itself. It knows what to do: local pain first, then a widespread area of pain and tenderness, to keep you still while you heal. Barring infection or gangrene, the inflammation recedes, the wound and stitches heal, the stump forms properly, and the rest of your body gets on with its life. But the major nerves that served your leg have been cut, and they don't heal in the same way as muscle and skin.

When you have a leg amputated, you may sometimes feel that your missing limb is still there. At first, the sensation may not be painful. It may tingle or tickle or itch. Then it may start to hurt. Your missing toes may be twisted or cramped, and you can't uncramp them. Your brain is looking for sensation from your foot, and it turns up the volume in search of it. It picks up noise and tries to make sense out of it.

At first, this doesn't hurt, but as time goes by, the cut nerves in your stump try to grow back down into your leg. They send out tiny fibers, and these fibers have nowhere to go. They get all tangled up. They send impulses to your brain: an itch here, a tingle there. For the rest of your life, your nerves will try to grow into your leg, and will be unable to, because it's gone. You may interpret these commendable efforts as pain.

The jungle ahead looked as though something heavy had been dragged through it. There was a gunner, Ed remembered. The guy had been covering Ed, running right alongside of him. He had been hit first, before Ed, and that must be him, dragging himself through the jungle, crushing leaves into the mud. Ed was following his path. Where are we headed, he wondered.

The funniest thing about the jungle was that it was made up of giant houseplants. Ed's mom had worried over her philodendrons, pinching them, watering them, feeding them, and here they were all over the trees. The damn philodendrons had trunks, for Pete's sake. They were holding him back as he tried to crawl forward. Houseplants holding him back. You had to laugh, really.

You also had to keep your head down. Keep moving. It had been so hard to start crawling, mustn't stop. Get rid of anything that keeps you from crawling. Ed unhooked his cartridge belt and pushed it to one side. Pack long since gone. He had had it that morning, hadn't he? He had dug himself a foxhole last night, and he was still covered with mud from that, and mud from crawling, and mud from mud.

He still had his canvas wallet, with his pocket sketchbook and a colored photo of Katie. Yesterday he had lost the silver Sacred Heart medal that Katie sent him. He and his buddy Dick were washing at the beach: a salt-water bath, but better than none. He noticed right away that the medal had slipped off, and he and Dick dived for it for an hour. No luck. It was just a piece of silver, it held no protection in itself. But he had felt awful about losing it, and here he was, shot. He could feel the wallet still buttoned into his pocket. He was not going to lose that picture. He was not going to lose his sketches. He was going to crawl out of there.

Ed wasn't crawling now, though. He was sitting at a table in a big, warm kitchen, eating dinner, and his leg, the one he didn't have, was acting up. It seemed to have a life of its own, but it wasn't even there. When he needed the leg — to run, to jump, to dance, to play football — it wasn't there, but when it hurt and gave him trouble, it was all there, hot as molten metal, and it wouldn't hold still. It jumped, it ran, it danced by itself. He grabbed it and tried to hold it quiet. The table shook.

None of the other people at the table looked at him, as he shook and held onto the stump of his leg. Was he even there? Katie was sitting at the table. She was blonde: maybe she was coloring her hair. She kept getting older. She must have been nearly forty. Still beautiful, he thought, but she looked … weathered. There were children, four of them now: the two older ones that he'd seen before, plus a little girl with a dutchboy bob and a baby in a high chair. Mrs. Kelly, Katie's mother, was there, too. They were aware of him, he knew, but they looked elsewhere — at the baby, at the dog, at their plates. One of the kids had her nose buried in a magazine. At the dinner table. Times change: his dad would never have allowed that.

Ed pulled himself through the pain on his own. On the table in front of him was a cold glass of Pepsi. Ice all the way up to the top, and then the Pepsi poured over it, that was the way to do it. Let the foam settle, and then fill the glass right to the rim, a tiny fountain of carbon-dioxide bubbles dancing briefly in the center. The Pepsi was really cold, and condensation ran down the side of the glass. It sat there untouched. He couldn't drink it now, because the pain made him nauseous. He would drink it when his leg stopped shaking. He would get an ice-cold drink, he promised himself, when he stopped crawling.

Pain is not the same as damage to your body — just as you can be injured and feel no pain, you can also feel pain even though you have no detectable injury. Pain is just one small part of what's happening to you. You'd be so much wiser if you could see the whole picture.

Take a look at your healed stump. Pain is useless to it. The time for action is past: it's too late to avoid or reverse the damage. The muscles have been cut, the nerves have been severed, the bone has been sawn, above the knee in your case, and a flap of skin has been folded and stitched. When they were cut, the nerves first sent out a message of massive injury and then, after a time, they began to put out new fibers. The endings of the nerve sprouts tangle and loop, and they find themselves in a very different area, chemically, than where they used to end. The inflammation is gone. The wound has healed — indeed, it's been healed a long time. But to the nerve endings, there is still something seriously amiss. They fire repeatedly, sometimes massively. They overreact to ordinary signals. A gentle touch to an unmarked area of skin may stab or burn or throb. Different people will respond differently, but every stump, not just yours, will have areas of exquisite sensitivity.

Look at this map of your brain. See these parts here and here that are working so hard? That one is the sensory cortex and this one is the motor cortex: their nerve cells are especially busy when you're feeling pain. Now look over here, and you'll see more action going on, in other cortical areas of the frontal lobes, in the midbrain, in the anterior cingulate, in the hypothalamus, and in the cerebellum. Someone reading a map of your brain might think that you were planning to jump out of the way of something, because of all the activity here in the motor cortex, the basal ganglia, and the cerebellum. But no, you're just sitting there, suffering the usual steady throb in that damaged nerve.

Memory is not so different. Bits of your life and thought are stored all over your brain and chemically connected to one another. You experience a memory, say the thwack of a football hitting your hand as you scrimmage with your brother in the street on a fall afternoon, and suddenly you can smell the flowers at his funeral, ten years later. The funerals all are linked together — your brother, your mother, your child. Memory gives an innocent stimulus in an unmarked area a chemistry you can neither understand nor erase.

Ed was sitting in a chair, looking at a cartoon in a little movie-box that looked like an upright radio. In the cartoon, a kangaroo sat at a table with a checkered tablecloth. A waitress came up to take his order. The kangaroo said he wanted a Narragansett lager beer. This was bizarre but familiar. He'd seen kangaroos in Adelaide, at the zoo: they really looked like that. Half human, half animal, the ideal subject for a cartoon. Ed was going to be a cartoonist when he finished art school. The cartoon waitress brought the kangaroo his beer and set it down in front of him. There was more dialog, but Ed wasn't really listening: he was dissecting the cartoonist's style. Great brushwork, great command of line. This was really good stuff. Then the waitress snapped her gum and said, "Say! How do I know you're not just a guy in a kangaroo suit?" Ed leaned forward to catch the rest. The kangaroo looked up at the waitress, raised one eyebrow, and said, "You don't. How do I know you're not a kangaroo in a girl suit?" Then the Narragansett logo appeared. It was a beer commercial.

Ed wanted a cold beer. A Narragansett would be fine.

His right leg was broken, that was for sure. It just dragged. He could use his left leg, though it was full of shrapnel, as a prod to help push himself forward. He moved like a worm in the mud, inching along in the faint path of the guy in front, the guy who had been wounded in the neck. That guy was getting way ahead of him. Must be easier to crawl if you're wounded in the neck.

There was no shooting here now, no mortar. The fighting was somewhere else: he could hear it move off. Maybe the mortar fire that hit him had wiped out the guys that were shooting at him. Whose mortar had it been, Japanese or American? The Japanese had captured the gun and turned it on Ed and his buddies as they brought ammunition, and then the mortar started. Maybe the Japanese had been wiped out by their own mortar, mistaken for Yanks because they were shooting a Yankee gun. Or maybe they had run out of ammunition and been taken out by the Yanks, and the shrapnel in his leg was government issue. They should have waited until I delivered the ammo, he thought, before opening fire. The joke was on them.

The joke was on him, too. As he had approached the gun, he had heard it firing, and he yelled, "I'm a marine! Don't shoot!" The Japs had turned the gun right on him. Maybe they didn't speak English.

Ed raised his head to see where he was going. Watch your head, he thought. There was a marine nearby, prone in the grass. So still, so quiet, he hadn't even known the guy was there. Only the guy's eyes were moving, sweeping from left to right. His gun was pointed in front of him. Snipers? The guy tensed and fired right past him. The shooter didn't speak or even move as

Ed crawled past, following the almost-invisible trail.

He could use a beer, he thought again. Brown long-neck bottle. Cold, just pulled from a tub of ice. There probably wasn't a tub of ice for 1500 miles. There were drops of water on the outside of the bottle, and it was starting to get cloudy from the humidity. His fingers left prints on the glass. He flipped the cap with his pocket knife. The bottle was so cold. He was about to take a gulp, but he needed to crawl just a little bit forward.

Ed was leaning on wooden crutches that supported him under his armpits. He was standing in a small, bright bedroom. Twin beds, yellow walls, white trim. A girl's room. Sunlight streamed through the windows. There was a child lying in one of the beds, covered with a cheerful yellow blanket. He'd seen her before — she was about ten or eleven now, with her straight brown hair still in a dutch-boy cut. Her face was puffy, and she was breathing in intermittent gasps. Her skin was almost transparent, and he could see the veins blue beneath it. Katie was sitting on the bed next to her, holding her hand. The child's gasps came more slowly. Katie's face — it was Katie, really, he knew — was desolate. There was nothing he could do. There was no way to pull himself past this, or make Katie feel any better, or help the dying child. There was no cold drink that could reward him if he made it through, and there would be no cold drink to reward the little girl.

He was so confused. How had he ended up so far away from the jungle? Could he please get back to the jungle?

When you are injured suddenly, you may not immediately feel pain. You may have higher priorities than caring for your wound. You may need to get yourself out of the jungle, away from the people who are shooting.

This is not an unusual reaction. It is not even necessarily a human reaction. Dogs do it, horses do it, deer do it. You will have plenty of time to feel the pain later, when you're having dinner with your family, perhaps, or working alone at the drawing board, late at night.

To feel pain, you need to pay attention to it. Pain can capture your attention, and once it's captured, you may not be able to release it. It can hold you prisoner in this way, and force you to invent increasingly clever ways of escaping it.

You hear about people having a high threshold for pain or a low one, as if pain leaked into your body over some kind of baffle. But in fact, every healthy human being has about the same pain threshold, the point at which you notice a mildly unpleasant sensation — pressure, heat, prickling, whatever — that would be intolerable if it were stronger. What varies wildly from one person to the next is the point at which you would describe the sensation as actually painful, and the point at which the pain becomes intolerable.

Chronic pain doesn't take you by surprise. You can plan for it, as you would a deadline, or a business trip. Will you accept the pain this time, or push it away? You can contain the pain, isolate it: this body has nothing to do with you. You can defer the pain, but it will seek you out later, and will not be denied.

What about the other pain, equally chronic? Will it keep that pain at bay if you never talk of your mother, dead of a stroke before she was forty, or your brother, shot down over the Pacific, or your daughter, stricken by a virulent infection? If you collect all their pictures and put them away, will that make the pain recede, or will pain take the place of pictures and become a way of keeping your memories alive?

He couldn't tell if he was going uphill or down. There had been a ridge, that's where the machine gun was, so he must be going downhill. He blacked out, it was like falling and falling, but when he came to, he was in the same place. He had thought his leg hurt before, but he was wrong. Now it really hurt. He pushed the pain aside. It had crept up on him, but he could squeeze it down to a pellet, a seed, and store it away. He inched forward on the trail.

Ed was in the kitchen of a house he had never been in, talking to a dark-haired, middle-aged woman dressed like a G.I., in dungarees and an undershirt. She wasn't Katie, but she looked vaguely familiar, like an aunt he had never met. He looked at his hands — they were baggy and wrinkled and freckled with age. His body was, well, it wasn't *his* body. He asked the woman, maybe she knew: "How did I get so *old?*"

The woman shook her head and smiled wryly. "I don't know, Dad. I ask myself the same question."

He didn't really need an explanation: he was getting the hang of this. He was old, and he was getting older.

Getting old was not the real question, though. The real question was why the pain didn't recede with time. Why didn't it fade, just as his dexterity and strength were slowly fading? Why did a glance at Katie's desk, at the misshapen kid-made ashtray with the naïve sketch of a horse's head, yield a stab of pain? Why did she keep it there, when the wound re-opened every time he looked at it? Why didn't she put it away, as he had put away the photographs?

"Your mother was a beautiful young woman," he said. "So lovely. So lovely. She let herself get old."

Ed raised his head and peered through the leaves. There was a motionless marine lying on the ground ahead of him. The guy was wearing a combat pack, and he was soaked and dirty, and had been moving away from the front. He was facedown, his arms and legs too still. Dead, for sure. Between them ran a line of disturbed vegetation, bisected at an angle by the path that had been their goal.

Suddenly he didn't feel as though he could go any further

either. He could see the dark ahead, like a pit. It would be so easy to fall in.

When you're injured, your body uses pain to keep you from moving the injured part. Parts of you that aren't actually injured may hurt. What is going on here? The chemistry of those un-injured parts changes. The pain circuits in your spinal cord re-adjust to produce a widespread area of pain. It makes you want to hold still, doesn't it? It feels better if you hold still, and it's better for you, too. Damaged tissue — muscles, joints, and liga-ments — needs time to recover, even after a minor injury. If you don't hold still and let them heal, the membranes that cover the surfaces of these tissues become chronically inflamed, and death-dealing bacteria eagerly find their way to the very marrow of your bones. Pain protects you from this. Pain keeps you still and safe. Pain works.

Lung cancer starts out small, a few cells with a reproductive imperative. At that stage, it doesn't hurt. Your body doesn't even recognize that it is being colonized — these are your own cells — so it doesn't fight back, it doesn't warn you. You have no idea that the tumor is there, but as it grows, it will block small air passages. Your body will try to remove the dysfunctional parts of your lung via inflammation. Macrophages come to your aid, the diseased tissue swells and pushes against nerve endings, and that hurts. Much of your pain, when you have cancer, comes not from the cancer itself, but from your body's reluctance to give your cancer the room it needs to grow.

Like the pain of childbirth, the pain you feel from cancer does not function as a warning. It comes too late.

Ed was sitting in a wheelchair, in an alien body that wouldn't do what he wanted. It took so long to die. The doctor looked at him and said, "Goodbye, old friend. We've come to the end of the road." Then the doctor looked beyond him, and continued the conversation with somebody that Ed couldn't see. "I can prescribe some palliative measures, and I think you should make arrangements with Hospice. My nurse will give you a phone number."

Ed understood that the doctor wasn't an old friend, but he didn't say anything. He was having trouble thinking. He had always been careful about taking painkillers when his leg bothered him, but now the doctors kept telling him he didn't need to be careful. He didn't want the drugs: he wanted his head to be clear. He wanted to be able to move, get in and out of bed, pull himself up onto the board and slide across it to the wheelchair. If the drugs were strong enough to deaden the pain, he couldn't do that.

And if it weren't for the pain, he wouldn't know where the world started and the imagination left off. If he hurt, he must be alive. If the priests were right, they were all waiting for him there: his parents, his brother, his uncle, his daughter. If that was true, what was all the pain about? If he really believed in heaven, shouldn't he just give up and die? How was pain protecting him here?

Like crawling through the jungle, or getting out of bed, dying was work. It wasn't a matter of giving up. It was a matter of pulling himself forward, inch by inch. He wasn't alone. He could hear familiar voices, and there was always someone sitting there next to the bed. But they couldn't help with the actual dying part. Katie was there, but the spirit had gone out of her, and she couldn't help either.

He heard his sister's voice nearby, talking to somebody. "He's still holding on. Tell him that it's okay to let go. Let him know it's all right."

Someone sat down next to him and took his hand. She said quietly, "It's okay, Dad. You can go now. It's okay. You can go."

Part of dying, if you had any time to think about it at all, was letting go — not an easy thing to do, after holding on for so long, after making it through all the mud. At the very center of dying was wanting to let go, and eventually the wanting comes to you, whether you invite it or not. Easy and hard are not a part of wanting.

Right now he didn't want to let go. He heard footsteps approaching, the sound of sucking mud. Marines. He recognized the boots. They stopped in front of the other soldier.

"He's dead."

I could have told them that, Ed thought, if they had had the courtesy to ask. That marine was definitely dead.

Then there was someone standing over him. "This one's dead, too." It was Dugan from his patrol, redheaded Irish guy from Rhode Island .

That was the crowning ignominy, after all that work. He pushed himself up on his elbows and said, "The hell I'm dead." He was sure that he was not dead. "I'm Irish," he added, by way of explanation. It didn't seem that he could be both.

"Hey!" said Dugan. "That's Eddie McMurray under all that mud." He put a hand on Ed's shoulder. "We'll send a corpsman up here, Eddie." He patted Ed on the shoulder again, and then the two marines, rifles ready, walked quickly back down the trail.

Ed twisted his head to watch them go.

Dugan was glad to see me, he thought. That's nice.

ACKNOWLEDGMENTS

THESE STORIES were not written by someone working alone in a basement, much as it felt that way at the time.

I thank my collaborators on several of the stories, Michael Swanwick and Rudy Rucker. I thank participants in the Sycamore Hill, Rio Hondo, and Turkey City writers' workshops and the San Francisco workshop that doesn't have a name. I thank everyone who offered feedback on specific stories, especially Martha Bayless, Ted Chiang, L. Timmel Duchamp, Andy Duncan, Carol Emshwiller, Karen Joy Fowler, Molly Gloss, Leslie What and Gary Glasser, Ursula K. Le Guin, Kelly Link, Karen Meisner, Pat Murphy, Nick Nussbaum, Peter H. Salus, Ann Sandomire, Nisi Shawl, JT Stewart, and Avon Swofford.

I thank all the people who allowed me to use their names. They are not responsible for anything I made up about them. None of it is true.

For instance, all opinions and hamburger preferences attributed to Michael Swanwick and Samuel R. Delany in the story named for them were invented by me. All trading cards described therein were actually offered by Burger King in March 2005, though not necessarily to Messrs. Swanwick and Delany. Mr. Swanwick does not, to my knowledge, own a chartreuse 1959 Thunderbird.

Protagonists in the Steampunk Quartet — Carmen Machado, Ellis McKenzie Creel, Santosh Philip, and David Gardner and his son Ridley — are real people who bravely volunteered and donated a few biographical details. I thank the authors of the original steampunk stories, who are also real people, for their forbearance.

For "Speak, Geek," Susan Gossman lent not only her name but her spiffy blue suit, and Mary Kay and Jordin Kare proffered their macho cat Dominic.

I thank all the historical people I mentioned, all the famous people, all the notorious people (you know who you are).

Most of all, I thank everyone who helped make this book a book: Gavin J. Grant, Kelly Link, Paul Witcover, and John D. Berry.

It takes a village to raise a book. None of the parts you don't like is their fault in any way.

If I've forgotten anyone, I plead insanity.

— EILEEN GUNN

ABOUT THE AUTHOR

EILEEN GUNN is a writer and editor. Her fiction has received the Nebula Award in the United States and the Sense of Gender Award in Japan, and has been nominated for the Hugo, Philip K. Dick, and World Fantasy awards, and short-listed for the James Tiptree, Jr. award. She was the editor/publisher of the edgy and influential Infinite Matrix webzine (2001–2008), and on dark nights can hear it stomping about in the attic. She also edited, with L. Timmel Duchamp, *The WisCon Chronicles 2: Provocative essays on feminism, race, revolution, and the future.*

Originally from the Boston area, she has lived in Los Angeles, New York, and San Francisco, and now makes her home in Seattle, with her husband, typographer and book designer John D. Berry. She has an extensive background in technology advertising, and was Director of Advertising and Sales Promotion at Microsoft in the mid-1980s; her stories sometimes draw on her understanding of the Byzantine dynamics of the corporate workplace. Gunn retired in 2010 from the board of directors of the Clarion West Writers Workshop after twenty-two years of service, and is presently at work on a novel.